VAMPIRE'S SIN

MAFIA MONSTERS SERIES BOOK TWO

ATLAS ROSE

I was their payment on a debt...and they were my salvation.
My Vampires dragged me from the river and brought me back
to life, and in turn I saved the one man who gave his life for
me...my bodyguard, Russell.
Only to save him will be to turn him into the monster he despises.
With Unseelie Fae blood in his veins he locks himself away until
danger comes for me once more.
I vowed revenge on those who tried to destroy us.
I'll make them pay with five *merciless* Immortals at my side.
Because to them, I'm not a possession...to them I am *forever.*
I'm starting to think they're my forever too...

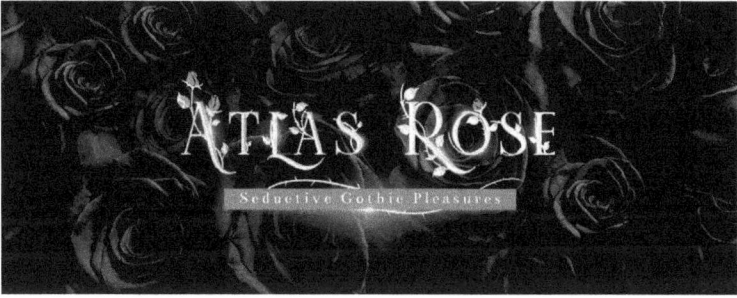

BE THE FIRST TO KNOW OF A NEW RELEASE!
Click here to signup for my newsletter.
Like my Facebook Page
Join my Facebook Group

RUTH

"**R**uth, *breathe!*"

I coughed and rolled to my side, digging my fingers onto the hard asphalt.

Cold water sloshed in my belly. Fire burned through my lungs.

I took in great gulps of air, but they didn't quell that burn in my chest, or the churning of my stomach. My throat was fisted tight, unable to open, unable to release. I was on the edge of consciousness...half swallowed by the dark...part of me was still in the water...*still drowning*.

"That's it. Just breathe, *come on.*"

Someone rubbed my back with long, careful strokes. The same someone murmured in my ear. Somehow, I was sure the deep, guttural snarl was meant to be soothing, but inside, I was *terrified.*

"I'm going to kill them, whoever did this to you...*I'm going to tear them a-fucking-part!*" Another male roared, his movement a blur in the corner of my eye as he paced.

The soothing motion on my back stopped. "Justice," the male behind me growled.

It was just one word. He never yelled…never swore. But the way he spoke made the strongest part of me want to cower.

I closed my eyes for a second and tried to gather the threads of my memory, tried to remember who they were and why I was here. But the harder I pushed, the more panic seemed to rise. My belly clenched, driving bitter water up my throat and onto the ground.

Not just water…river water.

I coughed and gagged, then lifted my head, strands of hair sticking to my face.

The river?

My body shuddered. Soaking clothes stuck against my skin underneath a pile of expensive jackets. Two cars sat in the distance, one small and blue, the driver's door still open, the interior light on. The other was hulking and wide, its black paintwork gleaming against the weak yellow light in the middle of the parking lot. It was *that* vehicle that called me. That vehicle I knew.

It was a Chrysler…

Someone's Chrysler…

A shadowed outline was slumped against the car. Dark and hazy, the blur spilled onto the ground beside the driver's door. I tried to blink, tried to focus on that darkened form, until the male in front of me shifted, and blocked my view.

That blur…something about it. Something desperate. Something I needed to understand.

I cough and wretched and more water shot from my mouth.

*It's okay, Ruthy…*dad's voice pushed through my mind. *It's okay to remember.*

Dad?

Stars exploded behind my eyes. Screams and gunshots followed, making me flinch and whimper…*making me fear.*

"It's okay," the guy beside me murmured, doing his best to make me feel safe. *But* still, the loss of my father pushed into my mind, the pain so vivid it was a punch to my chest. The image of a casket lowering into the ground made me sway before another memory swept the agony away.

Desire, so crystal clear it cut like glass.

Desire hidden in the steely gaze of four of them.

The nightclub...the sex...Jesus, the sex...

"Elithien." His name a whisper.

"I'm right here," he murmured at my side, his hand gentle on my back.

I blinked into a trickle of water from my sodden hair as I lifted my head. Silver shone in the perfection of his eyes, catching me off guard. I froze, my breath burning. *Vampire.* The word surfaced.

My Vampires.

I was going to take you with me. But when I saw what they did to you, I knew that was no longer part of my plan. Alexander's voice spoke in my head.

Alexander?

His hate.

His rage.

All simmering under the surface.

No, Alexander, no! My own scream rang in my ears, making me flinch. Those gray, Immortal eyes hardened as the Vampire pulled away. Fear and rejection colliding in his eyes. But it wasn't him I was afraid of...it wasn't him at all.

Terror moved in. My family. My business...my *life.* Gunshots rang out in my mind. Gunshots here. The end rose up. The phone ringing in the car. I flinched with each one. But there was no more shattering of glass...no more cries from the impact. The bullets were all spent, burrowed in the body of the man who tried to save my life.

I lifted my head, and that shadow beside the black car sharpened. I knew what it was now...I knew *who* it was. "Russell. *Russell!*"

"Easy." Elithien grabbed me. *"Ruth!"*

I froze with his panic.

"He's gone," Elithien whispered in my ear as he pressed me close against his body. *"Ruth, listen to me...your bodyguard is gone."*

"No...*no...no...no...*" Grief swallowed me.

I could still hear his deep, rumbling chuckle, still see the sparkle in his eyes when he smiled, still feel the warmth of his respect and friendship...

Ruth...RUN!

Still hear those desperate pleas to save me.

I swayed with the impact of the memories and turned to Elithien. Sodden strands of his hair dripped down his face, and the wet clothes stuck against his skin. "Alexander...Alexander did this. It was all him...*all of this was him.*"

"Fucking sonofabitch," Hurrow hissed, and bared long white fangs.

"The lawyer's dead." The quiet voice was so controlled, but the words were strangled. Justice stood beside me, his clothes dripping an enormous conduit of menace. "They're *all* dead. Every one of them, Ruth. I swear it on my life."

"Justice..." Elithien called.

But torment sparkled in Justice's eyes as water trickled down the bridge of my nose. Fangs punched out from between his lips. "I have to kill him...*I have to...*"

"Justice, no." Elithien rose from behind me.

But he was too late, as the towering Immortal stepped backwards.

He curled his hands into fists and wrenched his gaze from mine. His movement was a blur speeding through the parking area before a thunderous *crack* shattered the silence. The weak yellow light from the power pole brightened for an instant before it flickered out.

Flashes sparked before I saw the destruction. The thick timber was snapped like a toothpick. Live wires sparked blinding white as the pole fell and hit the ground with a loud *thud.*

A scream followed from my protector, bloodcurdling and horrific, filled with anguish and need, and in the sparks of faint light, all I saw was savage love.

"I'm going after him," Hurrow snarled. "Right now...*right fucking now, Elithien.*"

"No," Elithien commanded, and lifted his gaze to Hurrow. "*Ruth* is our priority right now. She's the *only* thing that matters. Do you hear me? There are *other* times, Hurrow. I promise you. There *are* other times."

Something shifted in Hurrow's gaze as he found mine. There was a flinch, followed by a deep breath. He licked his lips and gave a nod. "You're right...*of course you're right.*"

"*Save* Russell," I whispered and turned my head, my focus fixed on the blur beside the black car.

My Vampires looked at me...with murder in their eyes.

"Ruth." Elithien shook his head. "He's gone."

I closed my eyes and shook my head as the last moments of my bodyguard's life rushed back to me. *Don't...Don't hurt her. We can talk about this. We can...*

"I don't care," cold, unflinching words slipped from my lips as I opened my eyes and met my Vampire's stare. "Whatever it takes, Elithien."

Suddenly, those gray eyes hardened to steel. "You don't understand what you're asking."

"I *do*." The words burned. I shoved upwards on trembling arms and reached for him, clutching hold of the sodden shirt sticking to him. "He tried to save my life, doesn't that count for something?"

Rule stepped backwards and followed my stare across the parking lot to the black blur against the side of the car. He hurried now, stepping around live wires that lashed the ground to kneel beside my bodyguard's shadowed form. His fingers fumbled at Russell's neck.

Please, God...please...

"There's a flicker of life," he called. "It's faint, but it's there."

My heart hammered...waiting. I met Elithien's gaze. He was both monster and man. Both lethal and love, and he was all mine. *"Please."*

Hurrow turned his head, and Rule's focus followed. Moments later, the faint sound of sirens echoed in the distance.

"You really want this?" Elithien searched my gaze. "Even if he doesn't..."

"I want to give him a chance." I sucked in hard breaths. "I *need* to. I owe him that much, at least."

There was a twitch in the corner of his eye. A battle raged inside his mind.

"His last words were *'don't hurt her.'*" I clenched my fists around my Vampire's shirt. "He died saving me."

"Elithien," Rule cut in. "We have to leave."

Silence swallowed us. Silence while I searched his eyes.

Silence while I waited for him to answer.

He's not going to do it...he's not going to—

"Take him," Elithien commanded. "But you're coming with us, Ruth...*for good this time.*"

"*That* was never in doubt." Hurrow stepped close and bent, picking me up from the ground.

The sudden movement made the water in my belly slosh and rise once more. The world spun, cold and dark, threatening to take me under. I whimpered as Hurrow pulled me close.

"I've got you," he murmured. "Hold onto me, Ruth. *Hold on.*"

"Rule," Elithien commanded. "We were never here."

"Got it," the Vampire answered, and stepped away, then stopped, staring at the destruction. "But I think I'm going to need some help."

But we were already moving, striding toward a flare of

headlights as a black four-wheel drive pulled through the gates. I gripped Hurrow's shoulder.

"Keep your eyes down," he commanded. "The Fae don't like to be seen."

His grip tightened, arms curling, pulling me harder against him. "Don't ever do that to us again, Ruth." Blazing eyes found mine, and there was a dangerous edge to his tone. "I'd kill the entire fucking city just to keep you safe."

I shivered as our ride pulled up hard. Shadows spilled around us. Doors opened before we climbed in. But there was no interior light to see where we were going, only the faint green glow of dashboard lights.

Doors closed and then opened.

"Phone." Elithien thrust his hand through the passenger-side window.

Shadows shifted as the blur behind the wheel reached over, opened the glove compartment, and handed the Vampire a cell. Movement came from outside as the glove compartment closed. A second later, Elithien slipped into the passenger's seat, closed the door behind him, and looked over his shoulder at me.

"Home," he instructed, and the soft clunk of shifting gears filled the space.

I closed my eyes and lowered my head, finding comfort against Hurrow's chest.

"He *will* pay," Hurrow whispered. The words vibrated through his lifeless chest as the car moved. "Believe me...he... will...pay."

I gripped his arms and held on, my teeth chattering as shudders set in.

"She needs heat," Elithien commanded.

The shadow shifted behind the wheel. Seconds later, a warm blast of air hit me. I coughed, and retched...my eyes fluttered closed as the burn settled deep.

"Ruth?" Hurrow called.

I tried to open my eyes, but they were weighted down, like chains around my ankles, like my father's last goodbye.

"Ruth?" Hurrow barked.

"I'm o-okay," I murmured before fire raged through my chest.

"She needs a doctor." The deep unknown rumble came from the front. "A human doctor."

Tires howled, and the engine raced as we flew through the city streets.

I didn't care anymore. Not about the sparkling lights of my home, or about the heavy *thuds* as we flew across the bridge between one side of the city and the other.

I didn't care about the fight.

Not anymore.

Shudders racked my body. I curled stinging fingers against his arm. I couldn't control anything, not the darkness.

Not the pain...

Not the rage...

I saw you...last night with them in the alley. I watched you.

A whimper tore free with the memory. Alex raged to the surface, his eyes wide, teeth bared...*so much hate...for me.*

I'd like to say we had some good times, Ruth. But you ruined it... you ruined it all.

When did he change? When did he—

"Jesus fucking *Christ!*" The roar filled my head.

My eyelids fluttered open. Movements jolted my body. My arm fell, finding nothing but air as I was wrenched from the warmth of the car.

"The doctor? How far away?"

Muffled words, an answer I couldn't catch. My eyes opened again for a moment, finding the glowing moon in the night sky.

"Ruth, stay with us. Ruth, you hear me?" Hurrow's desperate plea pulled me back into the burn.

I fought to move my lips, to force the words past the fire in my chest. "H-Hurrow."

"I'm right here." He gripped me harder, holding me across his chest. "Ruth, I'm right here."

The front door of their home was open. The panicked face of the young kid filled my view before we raced through the doorway and into the Vampires' den.

Footsteps echoed. Orders were barked. A glass smashed.

Rage filled the air all around me, cold, bitter rage.

He saw me...

"What did you say?" Elithien murmured.

Sobs tore free, and it felt like my heart went with them. "He saw me with you."

Movement stopped...for a heartbeat, before I opened my eyes, and Hurrow lowered me to the bed. I'd never seen brutal, unending fury before, like the cutting edge of a blade.

Like the murderous stare of a Vampire.

But I saw it now.

"He saw me with you." I met Hurrow's gaze. "That's why he tried to kill me."

There was a flinch, a shattering of a thousand lifetimes of pain.

"But he didn't win." Elithien lowered his body to the side of the bed. "He didn't win at all. You're alive...and you're going to stay that way."

"Sire," a murmur from the doorway. "The doctor is fifteen minutes away."

"The doctor's coming, Ruth. He's the best in the city." Elithien brushed wet hair from my face.

"You sound like my dad when you say that," I croaked.

The corners of his lips twitched. The steel found his spine as he swallowed hard. "You're going to be fine, Ruth. We're going to take care of you."

Elithien rose from the bed and turned to Hurrow.

"I'm staying," my Immortal guard growled. "Don't ask me to leave."

"Russell," I whispered as my eyes closed. "Please."

"We're trying," Elithien answered. "But he has...extensive injuries. The Fae...*the Fae...*"

I lost track of the words then, falling under as darkness swept across my mind like a storm. Footsteps echoed, fading away, only to return again to what felt like a heartbeat later.

"Ruth, this is Samuel Horne. Ruth, *can you hear me?*"

Cool hands pressed against my neck, then opened my eyes. I surfaced fast, shivering and whimpering, my voice burning as I croaked, "Sam?"

"It's me," he reassured as I blinked and focused.

Gone were the business suits, gone was the clean-shaven appearance, as the Chief Executive of Crown City's Memorial Hospital leaned over the bed and peered at me.

My Vampires did indeed obtain the best human doctor they could find and, by the looks of his pajama shirt tucked into a pair of sweats, it looked like they'd ripped him from his bed.

"I'm sorry," I whispered, and winced at the burn.

"You have nothing to be sorry for." He seated his stethoscope in his ears and pressed it to my chest. "But I see you've made some new friends."

The growl of warning came from Rule.

"Very *enthusiastic* new friends," Samuel muttered, his focus slipping to my chin as he moved the cold steel of the stethoscope over my chest. "Can you roll onto your side for me?"

Hurrow was there in a heartbeat, racing around to the other side of the bed, holding me gently as he eased my back from the mattress. I tried to fight the shudders, tried to swallow the cough, but the sickening taste of river water welled in the back of my throat.

"I've got you," Rule whispered.

10

I retched, holding onto Hurrow's hand as the cold spilled from my lips and into the towel Rule held. They never once flinched, never gagged. He never looked away in disgust.

"First thing we need is to get these clothes off her and get her dry," Samuel ordered.

The heaves died away, leaving my stomach clenched tight and aching.

"I can help you—" Samuel started.

"No." Hurrow rose from the bed. "That's *our* job now."

Tension filled the air.

"Ruth, are you okay with this?" Samuel leaned close.

I saw the question in his eyes...*are you okay with these monsters touching you?*

I sucked in a deep breath and nodded. "Yes."

Yes, I was okay with them...I needed them in that moment, and it had nothing to do with lust.

It was survival, cold, *savage survival.*

Pride flared in Hurrow's savage gaze. The tide had indeed turned in my life. Gone were the ties I'd had to my normal life, my family...my friends...my company.

I'll burn it all, Hurrow's stare promised. *Burn it until there's not a shred of your past left...only your future...with us.*

"Okay, I'll be back to see you before I leave, Ruth," Samuel said.

The slow hiss of a door sounded. Cooler air rushed in as footsteps echoed. I knew where I was now. The bed I'd made love in hours ago was the same one I shivered in now as they rolled me onto my back.

"You heard the good doctor," Hurrow murmured, and reached for my shirt.

"I'll grab some of my sweats." Rule pressed a clean towel into my hands and hurried from the room, leaving us alone.

Hurrow kneeled on the bed and stared down at me. It was

just the two of us, ...*alone...vulnerable.* Warmth slid down my cheeks. "I thought..." my throat clenched tight. "I thought..."

"No," he answered. *"Never.* Not while any of us are alive."

My lips trembled as I reached for his hand. I was shattered in that moment, broken into pieces I couldn't understand.

"We can heal you." Hurrow's fingers were slow, lifting the bottom of my shirt and baring my stomach. He leaned down slowly and pressed his lips to my bare skin, kissing just above my navel. "Let us heal you...and when you're ready, we'll avenge you, as well. We'll leave no one standing, Ruth...*no one at all.*"

I closed my eyes at the feel of his love and let it sweep me away.

"Here—" Rule started, and then silence.

There was a shift on the mattress. Rule's touch followed, sliding my shirt from the other side before he eased it over my head and pulled it free. Lips pressed to mine, so gentle and careful. He kissed my lower lip, then my top, working his way to the edges of my mouth.

The straps of my bra were slid down my shoulders. I trembled from the cold, nipples hardening as Hurrow slid his hand under my back to the clasp.

They worked in silence and I gave into them. Letting them slide my bra from my body. Their cool hands felt almost warm against my skin. A warm towel brushed over my arms and across my stomach.

One kissed the valley of my breasts, then pressed his lips over my heart. I opened my eyes as one lifted me enough to slide a sweatshirt under me, then they fed my hands through the sleeves and zipped it.

My pants were next, the wet slacks sticking to the skin as they were gently worked free. "I don't want to see those clothes ever again," I whispered.

"Done," Hurrow answered as he slid his fingers under the

sides of my panties. Rule gently lifted my hips and Hurrow slid the lacy fabric down my legs.

Shudders tore through my body as Hurrow tossed my panties aside. Rule dried my skin, rubbing the towel along the insides of my thighs. I parted my knees, letting him take care of me. He kissed my thighs and ran his hand over my mound, his finger sliding along my slit before he reached and lifted one foot. Warm sweats slid up my legs, closing over the lower half of my body.

"We have the heat on high and more blankets on the way," Hurrow assured me.

"The bed," Rule commanded as he tugged my shirt down low.

The fabric smelled of him, musky and dark, savagely seductive. Hurrow slid one arm under my knees and one under my shoulders as he lifted.

I was warm in his hold, soft cotton pressing against my skin. I never thought I'd feel like this again, never thought I'd feel their love—or their vengeance.

Or my own.

The bed was stripped and remade in the blink of an eye before I was lowered to the soft mattress once more. Blankets and pillows were piled high, pressed against my side, the heated air soothing on my face.

*Russell...*his name filled me.

I knew deep down it was over…it had never had a chance to begin. Tears were brushed away by my Vampire's gentle touch. I tried to stay with them, tried to fight the terror that waited for me in the dark.

But it rose swiftly, swallowing me like the river…*and took me down.*

2

ELITHIEN

"**S**tay with her." I cast a glance at the doctor. "Do not leave her side. You understand?"

"Are you leaving?" Horne's eyes flared with surprise.

Betrayal bled into his tone, stopping me cold. "I need to take care of...*things.*"

"She's in a bad way..." he started with a shake of his head. "I don't think..."

My lips curled. Fangs sliced the inside of my lip. *"You think I don't know that?"*

The sour scent of fear bloomed in the air as he shuffled backwards.

I didn't want him afraid of me...I couldn't afford for him to be thinking about anything other than her. Only her...

"Justice and Rule will be here," I said carefully. "If there's the slightest change in her condition, I want to know *immediately.*"

One glance at the entrance of her wing and I left, making my way to the front door of the house and stepping out into the night.

Her wing.

Her house.

Her damn city if she wanted it. All she had to do was say the words.

I was already turning my life upside down for this mortal. Already shoving aside everything I'd become to be what she needed. I was a different monster now. A different killer... hiding the worst of my nature from her. But that didn't change what I was on the inside...or what I'd do to keep her safe.

For her, I'd tear the world apart...

The doors on the Explorer unlocked. Hurrow appeared at my side in an instant, matching my stride as he headed for the driver's side. I climbed in as my second-in-command slipped behind the wheel and started the car. We existed in silence, both consumed by deep-seated rage and hopelessness.

Headlights carved through the fog as I pulled away from the house, heading for the warehouse.

Save Russell...Whatever it takes, Elithien.

Her words surfaced as the four-wheel drive surged forward.

The damn bodyguard.

I inhaled hard as we carved through the darkness, heading for the glittering lights this side of the harbor. I was lost in the darkness, tilted off my axis...and I wasn't alone in that feeling. I didn't need to shift my gaze to know Hurrow felt it too.

"I want blood, Elithien. I want *so much fucking blood I can't stand it.*"

"You'll have it. We'll all have it." My voice was as cold as ice, for that was all I felt.

Cold. Empty. *Undead.*

The Explorer's engine raced, and the white lines on the road blurred. Lights sparkled far off in the distance. Bridge lights, the same bridge we'd hurtled across hours ago on our way to claim her.

It was supposed to be the first night of forever, the night she closed the door on her lonely existence and claimed ours instead. Only it didn't end like that.

She'd died tonight...

She'd died.

And even though we'd brought her back to the living, she was barely holding on.

"We can't let her..." Hurrow murmured. "If she goes, then one of us needs to be the one to turn her."

And have her hate us forever? It was better that than not have her at all.

"I'll do it."

"Your blood's the strongest. We need her to survive."

Not live. We never lived. Only survived.

We tore past the Hunting Ground. Lights were on inside, and cars lined the street. As hard as I tried to stop it, the throb of a beat surfaced, but it wasn't the nightclub beat. No, this music was smoother, seductive and *private.*

Memories surfaced, the way lights had kissed her bare skin as she danced for us in our home, her long legs trembling as she bent at the waist, revealing the perfection of her body.

She was real for me...more real than I'd touched in forever.

And he'd tried to take her from me...

We turned at the end of the road, and followed the new one to the industrial part of my town.

And it was *my town...*

My streets.

My monsters.

That walking-dead-man's face returned to me. But I didn't shove it away...I didn't even flinch from the memory. Alexander's face was one I wanted to know in intricate detail. One that'd be etched into my memory forever.

Just like her cousins, Judah and Blane. And every other piece of shit that hurt her.

I'd find them, no matter which rock they'd crawled under. I'd find them...and I'd tear them apart.

Glaring security lights from a high-end automotive repair

shop made me wince before they were gone, then the Explorer slowed at the ten-foot razor-wire fence enclosing a compound.

Red lights blinked from CCTV cameras high up on the warehouse. A warehouse that currently held close to twenty-five million dollars...*and counting.*

The black Explorer pulled up at the gate. There was a second before it rolled backwards, then we were through, pulling up to the huge outer garage doors. With a tremble, the massive armor-plated doors rose, allowing the bright lights from inside to spill outward.

"I could've handled the drop-off," Hurrow declared as he eased the Explorer through the door. "I would've said you were unavailable. Fuck them if they didn't understand."

We pulled up at the end of the enormous warehouse, leaving more than enough room for the truck to arrive. I reached for the door handle, then turned. "I appreciate that. You're a good friend, Hurrow, the best kind."

But Tribus and the Inner Circle waited for no one, especially not me.

Money would flow...just like it always did.

Money from drugs, power...and sex.

A late shipment wouldn't just bring me a reprimand. It'd bring them...and that was one thing I couldn't afford, not now. I stepped out of the Explorer and scanned the locked steel doors of the vaults, then lifted my gaze, finding the second floor.

All twenty-four vaults.

Giving us a total of six million dollars.

Six million, all heading to the ones who ruled us all...

Vampire. Wolf. Fae.

"Can't seem to stay away from her, can you?" The growl came from the darkened corner where the flaring inside lights never seemed to reach.

The male languidly uncrossed his arms and pushed himself from the wall, keeping those dark, inhuman eyes trained on my second as one dark brow arched high. "One more favor, Vampire, and we're going to have to reassess the terms of our agreement."

"Suck it, Kapre," Hurrow growled. "Goddamn Unseelie."

The creature just smiled and strode past us, heading for the open garage doors. But the darkness followed him, flaring out like a cloak, swallowing the wall and lashing the twenty-foot-high roof, giving us a hint of how truly formidable this beast was.

A banshee shriek tore through the air from somewhere outside, making even Hurrow wince.

"Goddamn hounds are late." Hurrow checked his watch. "I want this over with…"

He tried to pretend the Unseelie didn't make his skin crawl, but I knew the truth. Owing an Unseelie, especially someone like Kapre, was Russian roulette for a mortal.

Only, the mortal the shadowed beast was here for had already lost the game.

I lifted my gaze to the blacked-out windows high above. This place wasn't just a vault for money, it was an outpost…a safe harbor, only it didn't feel safe right now. It felt *fragile*.

I closed my eyes and sent my senses prowling through the compound, and in an instant, I heard it.

Thud…thud…thud…

A mortal heartbeat. Alive. Faint…but alive.

The *screech* of the gate tore through the early morning air. I dragged in the fetid scent of fur and turned as the Wolves drove in and parked their silver Escalades next to us. They were out in an instant, all quick glances and thundering pulses. Church was first, casting a glare through the warehouse to Hurrow, then shifting that glare to me.

I gave a nod, watching as Phantom climbed out of the rear seat and straightened his jacket. The guy looked tight, with a crisp navy suit and an open collar of his shirt. As Wolves go, he was a good-looking guy, only I'd never seen him with a woman, not like the others, at least.

Like Arran, the handsy sonofabitch.

"E," Phantom murmured as he stepped around the front of the Escalade and headed toward me.

"They're late."

"They'll be here, brother." The Wolf gave a nod to Hurrow and turned to stare at the open door. "How is she?"

"Alive."

Another nod, nice and calm, like she was barely more than a passing interest.

"Tell the Wolf I appreciate the heads-up."

"I will. Arran will be glad to know she's okay."

I hated owing a debt, especially to a Wolf. He'd been the one to scent her, the one who called Phantom in a panic...and in turn, Phantom called me.

It was almost too late. One more minute...one more damn *minute*, and there'd be no talking...no turning. No anything. Just the whisper of a promise before she was snatched away.

"If there's anything I can do..."

I met those steely blue eyes and nodded. Headlights carved into the dark and poured through the open warehouse doors as the first truck pulled in.

"Looks like we're on." Phantom looked at the others.

Church and Vitold stepped into the blinding lights as the second truck pulled in behind the other, and the roller doors descended. In an instant, the warehouse was filled with men... and one woman.

Two Wolves and one female Fae special ops soldiers climbed out of the cabs of the trucks and got to work.

"You ready?" Hurrow asked, waiting for my command.

I looked at Phantom, who gave a nod. Church and Vitold took their time, searching the trucks inside and out. I waited for a moment, then gave the order. "Go ahead."

Hurrow strode to the first vault, pressed the combination, and unlocked the door. One by one he worked, opening the doors of every vault, until he climbed the stairs and disappeared. It was these times we were at risk, these times when the vaults were emptied and the money had turned from 'ours' to 'theirs'.

"All that green," Phantom sighed, and turned away. He lifted a hand to the two others. "Help them out, boys, and let's get out of here."

It was hard seeing every dollar you'd worked for loaded into the back of two trucks and driven away. But this was the way of the Circle. This was what kept us safe and unseen...and unseen was the best you could hope for with the Inner Circle. I only wish Alliard had listened when I'd told him that.

The trucks were loaded, each vault was cleaned out, and the doors were locked once more. Tomorrow, we'd change the code to the doors and start over again, filling the vaults from the shipments of drugs, arms, and all the other crime we took care of...and that was just the Vamps.

Phantom gave a nod and lifted his hand. "Let's go, get these trucks out of here!"

The special ops soldiers climbed into the cab and started the trucks once more. We never spoke to them, never asked which depot they were headed to. Once the trucks left the compound, the money was out of our control. It all belonged to the Circle... and it was theirs to defend.

Air brakes hissed, and the trucks began to roll.

My gut clenched as the doors clanked upwards and the Wolves stepped out to scan the night. Before I knew it, the trucks were leaving and taking our money with them.

That was the way of the Circle, the way of beasts like me. We took...and took, and took, until there was nothing left but solid, stony emptiness. I lifted my hand and checked my watch. Fifty minutes. *Too long.*

Headlights from the two trucks blinded me for a second before they swung, and the money was gone. I waited for a moment before lifting my gaze to Hurrow. The Vampire was ready, waiting on the nod of my head before a look of relief crossed his face. But the look didn't last long.

"Phantom," I called.

The Wolf turned, one brow rising as he shifted his gaze from me to my second. "Go on, we can close this up."

I gave the other Immortal a nod of respect and turned to that darkened hallway where Kapre had stood almost an hour ago. An hour was an hour too long. Heavy footsteps followed mine as I strode through the dark.

An hour of damn agony, waiting for all this to be over.

Power swept over me as I neared the doorway and stopped at the lock. Dark power, *bestial power*. I punched in the one combination that never changed in this place. The one combination no one but us would dare enter. The door unlocked with a *click* before I bore down on the handle and pushed in.

And in an instant, I was swallowed by an animalistic throb of power.

The kind of power that reached through the doorway with primal hunger. For a second, I fought the flare of panic, that moment where I wanted to rethink the deal with the dark ones, until a grating sound found me. "Vampire."

I stepped inside, glancing at the dull glow from the screens mounted against the wall. "Mojin."

"Everything went well."

An ache swelled in the middle of my gut. "It did?"

In my head, I saw Ruth smiling, turning her head to unleash that look of love and desire on the bodyguard.

"The money." Darkness gathered substance as the creature stepped from the corner of the room. "There were no problems."

"Yes," I forced the word. "No problems."

The dark ones weren't just shadows, they were *empty.* Devoid of light, just as they were devoid of happiness. I stared as that outline hardened and the creature lifted his hand and the screen on the wall slowly brightened.

Images of the warehouse appeared in each corner of the screen. There were more screens, rows of them stretching into the endless dark of this place.

"The bodyguard," Hurrow urged.

"He has a pulse."

My breath caught.

"That is what you wanted, wasn't it?"

"Yes," I answered, even as a tremble of fear took hold. *Save him Elithien...whatever it takes, save him.*

Her words haunted me as the Unseelie's eyes came to life, brightening until they shone with an eerie glow that was neither darkness nor light. "You'll want to see him?"

"Yes." *No.*

The screen glowed, brightening into a near-blinding glow until it dulled as the Wolves backed their Escalades out of the warehouse and through the opening gates. We were alone here now, alone with the dark ones and the damn thorn in my side.

The heavy thud of boots shattered the thought as Hurrow followed the dark one, leaving me behind. I turned from the dimming screen as the front gate of the compound rolled to a close and followed them to the entrance of a hallway.

Energy slithered around the corners and crawled along the walls of this place. This compound was for protection, for the outer reaches of the Fae stronghold. And it was a stronghold. Their dark magic was the lifeblood of our Immortal existence, feeding, *corrupting,* growing roots into this mortal world until we sucked the life from every living thing...leaving Immortals to rule.

My steps grew heavy as a door opened at the end of the

hallway and a soft green light spilled out. I could hate us, hate our very fucking existence and our predatory nature. But I'd rather change it, even if changing it came with a price, and Alliard had paid that price with his life.

There was a hiss from the corner of the room. Shadows snarled, flicking out along the walls and the ceiling like a midnight fire before they drew away, sucking downwards from the walls to gather into the outline of a male on a stretcher.

I swallowed hard and stepped closer, wincing at the ghastly gray tone of his skin and open, unblinking eyes. "You said he was alive."

"You see the chest rise?" Mojin gave one slow nod toward the *thing* on the table. "Then he's alive…which is a lot more than we had when he was brought here."

Hurrow cut me a look of concern. But it was too late to back out now.

Ruth's desperate words pushed into my mind.

Far too fucking late.

"You said Kapre's power would be strong enough to bring him back." Anger rose inside me.

"Bring him back…yes. But there's no undoing this." Mojin stepped close and lifted the edge of the sheet, revealing the bodyguard's mess of a fucking body.

"Fuck me." Hurrow looked away. "Did you have to do that?"

Still the edge of the sheet hovered in the air. I couldn't look away, not from the bullet-riddled mess, or the hard muscle left behind. She liked the guard…maybe even felt a flicker of desire for the mortal. But what would she think about him now? Would she be horrified? Would she hate me for what he'd become?

One nod, and Mojin lowered the sheet, letting it suck back down against the slick, bloody mess. "Is he going to become…"

"Like Kapre? Partially. Even a taste will be enough to break his mortal coil. You wanted alive. So he's alive. How alive he becomes is up to him. But make no mistake, Vampire. As far as mortals go, this...male is going to be terrifying."

Hurrow clenched his jaw and met my gaze as the answer came to the only question that mattered.

Even if the bodyguard survived all of this, there was no way we'd trust him.

No way we'd let him anywhere near her.

And no way in hell we'd ever tell her the truth of what the mortal was now.

"I appreciate all you've done," I murmured, and met that piercing Unseelie stare. "Call me if anything changes."

Stop fighting, the words flew as I glanced at the bodyguard and strode to the door. *It'd be better for her if you died.*

3

RUTH

*A*lexander, NO!

"Ruth...*Ruth, I'm right here.*"

Chains around my ankles, pulling me down into the dark...*holding me under.*

Fire raged in my chest and ripped from my throat.

I yanked my feet high and kicked, fighting... *fighting...FIGHTING.*

Screams filled my ears, sounding hoarse, broken...*raw.*

"Ruth, you're safe." Strong arms wrapped around me, pressing me against a mammoth chest.

I coughed and heaved, clenched fists pummeling a muscled back as I opened my eyes and sucked in lungfuls of air, but still the fire burned.

"I won't let anything happen to you."

Long hair tickled my cheek. I tried to crawl back into my skin, tried to remember where I was as someone stroked my hair, comforting me.

"It's Justice," the Vampire murmured in my ear. "It's just me."

"Justice?" His name was a hoarse burn that tore through my chest.

"It's me, Ruth. You're safe, baby, you're safe."

But the chains were cinched tight around my ankles, and the metallic tang of blood welled in my mouth. "My ankles...there's something around my ankles."

Callused fingers skimmed my knee and brushed the side of my foot. "There's nothing there," he reassured me. "See? Not around your ankles or your wrists...or your neck."

I flinched as he skimmed his fingers along my chest and over the base of my throat. But still, desperation clung to my bones. It filled my heart and raced through my veins. It welled in jumping muscles and nerves wound tight.

It hid in the darkness of my mind...in the sleep that waited. "I don't want to go back there." His face blurred as I met his gaze. "I can't go back there."

"You won't have to," Justice promised.

The leather patch over his eye shone in the soft bedroom light. "How long have I been asleep?"

"Three hours." He brushed the hair from my face. "And this is the second nightmare you've had. You're so tired, you just need to rest, so just relax and let yourself rest."

I lowered my head to his shoulder and took comfort in his touch. He cradled me, running his hand down one side of my spine and back up again.

"The doctor...Samuel."

"Yes, the good doctor's checked on you. He's going to stay here for as long as you need."

There was something he wasn't saying. Something he was hiding under the rhythmic motion of his hand as he lulled me back to sleep. But the darkness waited down there, the cold like I'd never felt before. "I don't want to sleep...ever again."

His silver eye glinted in the soft bathroom light as he held my gaze. Had someone like him ever known fear? Real fear, the kind that slipped into your heart and found a home? I lifted my hand, fingers trembling as I skimmed the thick bones of his wrist.

Corded forearms tightened under my touch as I opened my hand wide and circled the bulging muscle of his arm. "Have you ever been terrified? The kind where you feel totally out of control...'cause right now I feel out of control."

"Yes." He inhaled hard, his chest pressing into mine. "I felt *very* out of control last night..."

My hand froze at the top of his shoulder as I met that steely stare.

Why?

The word raged.

Why care about me? After all...I was only mortal.

I'd known these Vampires mere months, and yet...it felt like I'd known them my entire lifetime. They should hate me...at the very least distrust me. After all, it was my family who'd led to the Immortal Vampire, Prince Alliard Xuemel, being brutally murdered.

And the killer hadn't been caught.

So, why me? Why any of this?

*If you have to ask that question, then you really don't know us at all...*Elithien's voice slipped into my mind. *Look into his eyes... press your hand against his chest. There's your answer, Ruth.*

I swallowed hard and let my hand slide. The Vampire's lips parted with the sudden breath as I rested my hand over the hard muscle of Justice's chest.

Thud...thud...thud...

I wrenched my hand away, my eyes widening.

"You make us feel alive," Justice murmured, his panicked gaze searching mine. "And we haven't felt like this in over five hundred years."

"Five hundred years?" I gasped.

Five hundred years, Elithien repeated. "And we've not known you for just a few short months," my Vampire said as he stepped

27

through the open stainless steel door and into his bedroom chamber. "I listened to every story your father ever told me about his lioness of a daughter. I've read every article, and watched every company takeover you've ever led. I've shared your father's pride over more than a few bottles of Scotch and late-night talks. The more I listened, the more I was certain our paths were destined to cross...and then there was that night in the alley. The night I cannot get out of my head."

My breath caught, and in an instant, I was taken back there, my spine pressed against the wall, his leather-clad fingers drifting down over my breast.

"I want you to know I've sent out word for that...*fucking coward.*" Elithien growled. "It's only a matter of time until he's found."

He stepped closer and reached out, his fingers skimming my cheek. It was the first time he'd touched me since he pulled me from the water, and even though his fingers felt like Justice's, he was so very cold. So stony, so...deadly. A cough tore from my chest. I closed my eyes and whimpered with the burn.

"You need to go back to sleep." Elithien dropped his hand. "You're not out of the woods yet, Ruth, but we're going to take care of you. Sleep well, knowing that one of us will be here with you all the time."

I nodded as exhaustion wrapped its arms around me. I didn't fight this time when Justice lowered me down until my head hit the pillow. Sweat beaded along my temple and prickled in my hair. "So hot."

A hand was pressed to my forehead before Justice growled, "She's burning up."

"I'll get the doctor."

I clenched my eyes tight as a shudder raced through my body. My teeth clacked as an ache moved through my bones. Something was very wrong, something deep inside me. This was no broken bone to mend or busted lip to heal.

"I'm right here," Justice whispered and swept the back of his hand across my brow.

Panicked footsteps entered the room. I opened my eyes and reached out my hand. My trembling fingers found a hold as I clenched Justice's wrist.

"Hey, Ruth," Samuel gave me a smile before he met Justice's deadly stare. The curl of his lips faltered before he cleared his throat and turned back to me "Let's have a look at you."

Steel glinted as he pulled his stethoscope forward and reached for the bottom of my shirt.

A guttural sound filled the room, a warning that rattled in my ears, stopping the doctor cold.

"Justice," Elithien warned. "Let the doctor help her."

My lips trembled as sweat gathered along my hairline. I clenched my hold and met the gaze of my protector. "Justice." His name was seared into the back of my throat.

The Vampire gave a nod, his gaze watching every movement as Samuel slipped the cold steel drum higher and pressed it to my chest.

"Breathe deep for me, Ruth."

I tried, but flames licked higher, rattling something deep inside with the effort. He tried again, moving the warming steel over my chest twice more until he commanded, "I need to listen to her lungs, can you help her sit up?"

He didn't need to say more as my giant Immortal moved forward and slid his arms under mine.

"You ready?" he asked as his gray eye met mine.

I gave a slow nod. He was so gentle, so kind, searching my eyes for a hint of pain as Samuel pressed the stethoscope to my back once more. That rattle in my chest only became louder, shuddering my bones as that searing blade of agony moved deeper.

"She's drowning," Samuel muttered, and eased back.

Justice wrenched that hateful stare the doctor's way. *"What… did…you…say?"*

"You wanted it straight up." Samuel's gaze softened as it met mine. "You're very sick, Ruth. I'm concerned about the fluid in your lungs, bacterial pneumonia is a very real threat right now. I think your best chance of survival is hospitalization."

"And leave her vulnerable to anyone with a grudge?" Justice snarled. "This is what happened the last time she was vulnerable. No…"

"Justice," Elithien warned.

"He. Treats. Her. Here." Justice insisted as he lay me back against the pillows.

"I wasn't…on my own." I forced the words through the fire in my throat.

"You weren't with us…so you're always going to be vulnerable, Ruth." Justice brushed some hair back from my eyes. "I can't take that chance, not again."

Fear made his fingers tremble against my cheek. He looked away, unable to meet my eyes. I licked arid lips and whispered, "So it looks like you're treating me here, Samuel."

The doctor exhaled a long, slow sigh. "Then I'm going to need supplies."

"Whatever you need," Elithien declared. "Spare no expense."

"Oh, I won't be," Samuel assured. "And I'll take a nice fat check for the new maternity wing while you're at it. God knows you have the finances."

One simple nod was all it took. Elithien didn't care, he barely seemed to notice. I was the center of his attention…and suddenly, that unflinching focus was all I cared about. I lifted my trembling hand to him.

Two long strides and he was beside me, taking my hand. "You tell me what you want to do and it's done, Ruth. But I agree with Justice. We can't take the risk now it's…"

"Morning," I answered for him. I lifted my head and met his gaze. "It's morning. No wonder you're pissy."

There was a small, sad smile. "You don't have to worry about us right now."

Samuel cleared his throat. "I can stay with her today," he muttered, glancing away from the show of affection. "While you…umm, rest."

"Thank you, doctor," Elithien said, never breaking my gaze, curling his fingers to clasp my hand tight. "That would be very much appreciated. I want you to know you're completely safe here. The entire place is surrounded, no one is getting in or out without my say-so."

A tremor raced through me at the thought of being without them. I glanced at Justice.

"I'll be here," my protector announced. "I'll sleep on the damn floor if I have to."

"No." I shook my head as that burn tore along my throat once more. I coughed, and wretched.

Rule was there, holding out a towel once more. But I could tell they were heading into the danger zone. Dark circles rimmed their eyes. They moved more slowly, smothering agony with each movement. They needed sleep…they needed the night. "Go. I'll be okay. I need to sleep, too."

"You sure?" Justice brushed his fingers along my leg.

All I could do was nod, biting down on the insides of my mouth, trying to quell the nearly uncontrollable desire to hack and heave. The bedroom darkened, shadows bleeding into the edges before the doctor moved in, taking over. "Okay, that's enough. Out, *all* of you. Let me do what you dragged me out of my damn bed to do."

But there was no chuckle of amusement, just the shuffling of footsteps, until all four of my powerful Vampires lingered at the door.

Samuel eased my head against the pillow and turned,

yanking open a duffel bag filled with medical equipment. *"Out,"* he commanded.

Shadows shifted in the doorway, then they were gone.

"They're a little protective, aren't they?" Samuel muttered as he fixed the blood pressure cuff to my arm, and hooked up a sensor to my finger.

I closed my eyes, biting hard on the soft flesh inside my cheek, and whimpered.

"A little sting."

I barely noticed, trying to hold on. Movement rustled at my side.

"Just something to help you rest. Let your body work."

There was a flare of panic, one that rushed to the surface as the drug roared through my system...*my ankle...there was something—*

Darkness moved in, swallowing me in a rush. But unlike the river, there was no burn in my throat, no tearing in my chest. There was nothing but the rich smell of moss in my nose and the feel of cold bricks at my back.

You know where you are? The growl came from the shadow at my right as the dream took hold.

She should know. Another voice at my left.

She knows. Movement from the shadows in front of me as the weak light from the building washed into the middle of the alley.

He stepped out of the darkness, a black leather patch covering one eye. *You're right where you're supposed to be, aren't you, my Ruthless.*

Justice. My heart hammered with his name. He smiled as he took a slow step toward me, the tips of white fangs flashing under his perfect lips.

You're with us, Ruth. Rule stepped out beside him.

Right where you're supposed to be. Hurrow moved out of the darkness at my left.

This time, you're never going to leave. My heart skipped as I turned my gaze to my right.

He was there, just like I knew he'd be, reaching up to drag a gloved finger down my cheek, with a look of insatiable hunger as he whispered...*my lioness.*

4

ELITHIEN

We stayed with her, tied by the fantasy we wove through her mind. A fantasy *we* could control. A fantasy where we *could* protect her, even if physically we were weak.

There was no rush of the river here.

No screams that rocked her mind.

I took them all away...

The steel doors of our chamber were locked. The fireproof, bombproof, steel-reinforced vault housing that we were in was as safe as you could get as the sun rose in the sky and night remained out of reach.

I sank into that fantasy, stepping out of the alley's shadows, and lifted my hand to her. "My lioness."

We were in back of the Jewel on that same night we'd first met, and yet we weren't. Everything looked faintly familiar. Moss grew from the cracks between the bricks. Rubbish bins overflowed further back toward the street, and the faint sound of a can rolling drifted on the wind. The heady smell overpowered my senses, but to her it was just the same.

The same alley, same city...

That's how I wanted it.

Familiar.

Her breath caught and her eyes widened as she lowered her gaze to the shine of leather over my hand. She liked the gloves… liked them very much. Leather shone against her pale skin, and the hint of a blush rose in her cheeks.

Elithien, she whispered.

Jesus. My name on her lips made that hollow pit inside me tremble. I lifted my hand to the curve of her neck. "God, you're beautiful."

There was a flicker of panic across her face as my touch drifted lower and, for a second I didn't understand her fear, until I touched her mind.

Water…in my throat. I can't breathe…I can't breathe! I CAN'T BREATHE!

I jerked away from the terror, and let my power wash through her mind…through *all* our minds. "I remember this top," I whispered, letting my gaze skim the perfect swell of her breasts, bringing her back to *this* moment.

Still, the haunting touch of her panic stayed with me.

I clutched that pain and drank it deep, pushing it down into the endless wrath inside where I could keep it from her. Her body was fighting, racked with tremors. One touch of her mind and I tasted the drugs that the doctor was pushing through her veins.

Drugs that could help her.

Drugs that would save her.

My jaw ached. My fangs punched out, driven by that savage need inside me. But I kept my face a mask of calm and curled my finger, dragging my knuckle over the swell of her breast. "I remember it very well, indeed."

The shine of panic faded from her eyes. Hurrow braced one arm against the brick wall above her head, his gaze taking in every inch of her bare skin. "I don't think I've had the pleasure."

"I like her better without it," Justice declared, stepping closer.

"As do I," Rule added.

We blocked her in. There was no escape, not that she wanted to. A smile curled the corners of her lips as she glanced at Hurrow. "I assume that means you want me to take it off?"

"Not if you don't want to," Hurrow disagreed, and leaned down.

He kissed behind her ear, giving her freedom to move.

"Tell me where you want to be," I commanded, my finger cresting the peak of her breast. Her nipple puckered with a tremble. "Do you want to dance for us?"

I made the alley fade and give way to a shadowed outline of a bed. Long leather seats took the place of the brick walls and, in an instant, we were transported into our home once more.

A glint of glass caught the faded light. A bottle of Scotch was sitting on the floor in the middle of the room. I lowered my hand and stepped backwards. Hurrow, Justice, and Rule followed, leaving her standing on the other side of the room.

Her eyes widened as I sat on a leather seat along the wall and crossed my legs. She didn't know...didn't remember, only the things I wanted her to remember. The things that occupied her mind...and us, if I was honest.

"Music?" Hurrow inquired, and on command, sound filled the room.

Her eyes sparkled at the familiar beat and she closed her eyes.

She liked that...*James...Arthur.* Liked the angst in his words and the huskiness of his voice. She liked plunging down into the depths of her soul. That's where she came alive. In this moment, she was very much alive.

I smiled at her and recrossed my legs, *because that's what she needed me to do.* I played the part, the one her mind clung to, and she relaxed, those gorgeous lips curling as she closed her eyes.

Just like the real version of this night, that salacious hunger came alive inside me, driving the tips of my aching fangs along the soft flesh of my mouth. Hurrow grew still with the rapture of watching her body.

"Jesus fucking *Christ*," Rule whispered, but she never heard him speak.

Instead, she dragged her hands over her hips as she turned, giving us her back.

We all knew what was coming…still, it barreled toward us like a runaway train. Tendons stretched and muscles flexed as that gorgeous round ass filled our view. My cock twitched and punched against the zipper of my pants as she bent at the waist.

Fuck, I wanted her…more than I'd wanted anything in my life.

Hurrow swallowed hard and gripped the cushion beside him. The leather punctured from the strength of his grip, foam stuffing poking through. I'd never seen him react like that, not in the five hundred years I'd known the soldier.

But here the sonofabitch was…just as consumed as the rest of us pathetic creatures.

His chest rose in one driving swell, then stopped dead. I turned back to her, my gaze drifting to the perfect slit of her pussy and the riveting dusty-pink puckered hole. *Fuck.*

Now *I* swallowed hard as she stroked those elegant hands down the outsides of her thighs, all the way to her ankles.

I knew the moment she touched the delicate bones of her ankles…knew the moment her terror broke through the fantasy and rose inside her. "Hurrow," I commanded, but he was already rising from the ripped cushions, his cock tenting his damn pants.

He crossed the room like the hunter he was, silent and deadly, and reached out, sliding his hand along the sweet curve of her ass. A faint flicker of jealousy flared, driving my fangs between my lips.

I swallowed the savage growl of warning, and watched her rise at his touch.

"Seems like such a waste," he hummed, his other hand

drifting over the small of her back and along her spine. With a gentle push, he urged her to bend again, exposing her as his thumb slid down the swell of her buttock to her crease.

Blood-red hair shimmered as it fell from one shoulder to fan her face. Her eyes sparkled, hungry with desire, as Hurrow slid his thumb between his jutting fangs and sucked. Saliva glistened when he pulled it free and questioned, "Why only look when I can touch?"

"Oh," the word was whispered on a shudder.

That perfect fucking hole puckered as Hurrow's finger lingered at the top of her ass. I swallowed, watching her spine curl and her belly tremble in anticipation. It was just a dream... no more than a fantasy. This, right here, was off script...

My script.

My carnal control.

And she was center fucking stage.

Hurrow's desire, Justice's need...Rule's hunger, swirled around in my head like a damn whirlwind. They drove it all, every depraved yearning, every unexplored obsession. Then she moaned, drawing my focus back to her. I drank in her tremors, swallowed down her moans. God, I wanted it all.

*Take her...*I was rocked by desire.

Hurrow cupped his hand, sank his forefinger into her pussy, and circled that tight rim of muscle with his thumb. Her long legs trembled, calves tensed, already shaking.

"Fuck. Me." Justice almost whimpered.

Still, my second-in-command barely moved, sliding his finger deep inside only to draw it back out. Ruth lowered her hands to the leather cushions. Her legs were splayed wide, the tips of those perfect breasts trembling with each breath.

"You like this?" Hurrow growled, his thumb pulsing against that muscle, pushing a little deeper with each thrust.

Her answer was a whimper and a jerking nod of her head.

Desire glistened on the Vampire's finger.

It wasn't the first time I'd watched the male fuck a mortal. But they all blurred in my mind, fading away under the blinding light of our *Ruthless.*

She was the one…the last one.

The only one…

My cock was fucking rock-hard, the head twitching, desperate to take the place of his finger, or his damn thumb, and slide in deep.

"Come for me," he growled as she rocked backwards, hungry for more. "That's it."

"Get on your damn knees, Hurrow," Justice demanded. "'Cause if you don't, brother…*then I will.*"

A warning vibrated in the back of Hurrow's throat. Silver eyes glinted with a smug smile as my second dropped to his knees. Ruth made that primal side of us rise to the surface. For her, we'd fight…for her, we'd kill…for her, we'd damn well tear each other apart just to taste her.

He skimmed one hand along her leg and eased his head closer, but his other hand never stopped moving, two fingers delving into her pussy as his thumb slid in deep into her ass.

He ducked his head between her legs and twisted until he rested the back of his head against the seat, his gaze consumed by her sweet slice of heaven. I had never seen him this…*fucking ready,* his cock thick and bulging in his pants as he pulled her against his mouth.

She obeyed, working her hands onto the backrest, and lifted one perfect fucking knee.

I stared at the pointed heel of her black stiletto as she straddled his mouth, hovering just out of reach so he teased and licked. The glint of large white fangs pressed against delicate, dusty-pink flesh. She dropped her head backwards, leaving long red hair to flow along her spine. The sight of that was so goddamn perfect. Her…*him…*us.

I eased away from the fantasy, unweaving my senses, even

though I was desperate to stay and see her through to the end. Instead, I wove my power through the fantasy, linking each mind until they were all connected to her. She would come for him...*she'd come for them all* for as long as the fantasy lasted.

Right now, that was all that mattered.

I let my mind drift higher, the slow, aching feel of my body was gone, and I felt rested. One probe of the house, and I felt the brush of impending twilight.

Night was coming, almost as fast as Ruth. I opened my eyes and stared at the darkened ceiling. The vault was quiet, the others staying behind in the fantasy. I took a breath and pushed up from the bed.

My damn cock was hard, and my balls were aching and heavy, falling to hit my thighs as I rose naked from the bed. I hurried, pulling on a shirt, boxers, and slacks, and went to the automatic locks.

The sensor came alive with my movement. Every inch of this system was state of the art, wired, welded, buried into the brickwork, and protected by steel housing. No one and nothing was getting into this place...not unless I allowed it to.

Green sensor light blinded me for a second before the locks released with a *thud*. I glanced over my shoulder at the others, then stepped through the steel automatic doors and sank into the darkness.

Shutters were still down on the windows, providing protection from bullets just as much as they did from the sun. I waited for the hiss of the door closing behind me before I stepped out into the hallway.

Her energy called me, even in the throes of fever as her body raged. I felt her, more than I'd ever felt anyone. I strode along the hallway and headed for the west wing.

"Elithien."

Movement came from the kitchen. Kern stepped out,

gripping a half-filled bottle of water. He took one look at the hallway behind me and met my gaze. "Everything okay?"

"How is she?" I searched his gaze, taking in the fresh ink above one brow.

The kid was just that…nothing more than a kid. A *punk,* Ruth had called him. He might've been that once, but not anymore.

He'd come to me, broken, beaten, and begged me to end his miserable life. But I saw past the burden of his mortality, to the potential he kept inside, and instead of finding death in my home, he found purpose. Now he was cleaned, saved from a life on the streets, and given a chance at redemption.

"She's fighting." He stepped closer, holding my gaze. "I promise you, she *is* fighting."

Those were the words I needed. The *only* words I'd allow.

I exhaled hard, letting the tremor wash through me, and braced myself on the edge of the counter. "That's good." I stared at the floor and closed my eyes for a second. "That's really good."

"I gotta say, she's one tough lady," Kern muttered. "And the doc hasn't moved from her side. I just forced him to eat a sandwich. I can make you one, if you want?"

I shook my head as my stomach clenched tight at the thought. The foul taste of gasoline still coated my stomach from the gutfuls of oil and river water.

"The others?" he inquired.

"They'll be up soon enough." I glanced over my shoulder to the east end hallway. "You find anything new?"

"The trail is dead," he grumbled. "We can't find a damn thing. We've gone over every inch of the place, met with everyone the Prince came into contact with over the last six months of his life, and they all check out, Elithien. It's like the guy just…*died.*"

I closed my eyes as the stab of pain cut deep. "That *guy* was the Prince of Vampires, and *my* oldest friend."

"Sorry," the kid apologized. "But Red and the others are just at a loss. We need a new direction...we need something concrete."

A new direction? I knew what he wanted.

He wanted a name. He *needed* a fucking name.

But it was a name I wasn't yet ready to give, and neither were the Alpha's. Months after Prince Alliard Xuemel was murdered there, was still no evidence that led back to the ones responsible.

I needed proof, *undeniable proof.* Proof that was found on its own, without any hint of tampering from us. If I was going to war, I needed to know it was a war I could damn well prove *why*, but so far, this young...*band of brothers had* found nothing.

"So you're giving up?" I met his gaze. "Just like that?"

"Giving up?" The freshly tattooed brow rose. "Hell, no. You gave us a mission, one we plan to see through to the very fucking end. We'll find out who murdered the prince, or I'll die trying."

It was an interesting choice of words, seeing how he was the only mortal in a gang with two young Wolves and two young Immortals. Kern wanted a purpose, and being our eyes and ears in a gang of young Immortals was the perfect answer.

"Good," I muttered and straightened. "Bring me something concrete, something I can use. Find the new direction you need, Kern."

The young mortal squared his shoulders. Those dark eyes glinted with purpose. "I won't let you down."

I strode toward the hallway and answered, "I know you won't."

Hurrow said I was naive to send a boy to do a man's job. But what he failed to see *was* the man behind the boy.

Kern wasn't just a kid, or just a mortal, not now he lived with us and spent his days hanging around with Wolves and the Dark Fae. Now he had a single-mindedness, an almost suicidal need to honor and obey—one I'd given him. One I'd earned. My bare feet made no sound as I moved past the foyer and the front door.

Steel shutters glinted, still secured in place. They'd rise soon…and so would the others. I turned at the end of the foyer and made my way along the east wing, to my bedroom.

The bedroom was expansive and neat, the bed still made, the bathroom unused. I hated the faint smell of stale sex that clung to the air. I hated the memories more, faceless women, empty hearts, centuries of searching for something more than the sins of the flesh. I'd longed for more, always more.

Now that I had found her, I wasn't letting her go.

A steel door sat on the far wall, a red light on the keypad blinking as it waited. I stepped close and entered the code. The red light turned green and the locks disengaged, allowing me to step into the dark and leave the rest of the house behind.

I closed the door behind me as the faint lights lit up the space. One more door, one more sensor, so I stepped close and pressed my face to the camera.

The second door unlocked with a *thunk* and I was inside, listening to the throaty snores of the doctor. A flare of anger cut through me, until I found her on the bed, her eyes closed, her breaths deep, and this time there was no faint crackle in her lungs. This time, she was soundless and still.

"Russell…*no*," she mumbled.

Snores ended as the doctor surfaced.

"Russell! RUSSELL, NO!" she screamed.

The doctor wrenched awake in an instant, lunging forward, hands fluttering against her arms. "Ruth, you're okay. Ruth, it's okay, honey. You're okay…"

Sweat shone on her skin. Her breaths were brutal and consuming as her eyes fluttered open, instinctually finding me in the dark. That hunger was still there as her gaze bored into mine.

"Is he…?" she whimpered. "Is he dead?"

Samuel Horne stiffened and turned, his eyes widening as I stepped closer. "Jesus Christ, you scared the life out of me."

"Elithien," she commanded.

She was the only one who *could* command me…in *five hundred fucking years*.

"No. He's not dead."

She cared about the bodyguard, cared enough that her first waking fucking thought was of him. I fought the dangerous need to kill the bastard myself and watched as her breaths deepened and the deep creases along her forehead smoothed.

"Don't let him die, Elithien." Her words were a mumble, but I knew what she said even as she sank back into fevered slumber once more. "Don't let him die…"

"Is she still having nightmares?" I asked.

"No, strangely enough. She's been quiet, a little too quiet." The doctor pressed the stethoscope to her chest, then moved her gently to listen to her back. "Scared me a few times, to be honest."

If I wasn't so pissed off about the guard, I'd have cause to smile.

"Her lungs are clearer, temperature's dropped. She's a long way from healthy, but at least she's not…"

His words trailed off. I took in every contour of her perfect lips as the others stepped out of the west wing chamber. "Thank you, Doctor." I gave a slow nod. "You have my utmost appreciation for your efforts."

He just nodded, turning back to her as I swung and strode from the room.

Anxiety rolled off them in waves. I pressed my face to the sensor, and then my thumb. The steel doors locked as the sound of steel shutters rising rung throughout the house.

Elithien? Hurrow's questioning voice filled my mind.

I opened myself to him, letting him see what I had seen…

watching as he flinched with her desperate plea...*don't let Russell die...*

"Goddamn bodyguard's going to be a pain in our ass."

I lifted my gaze, meeting his as he turned the corner and came into view.

"Yes," I answered. "Yes, he is."

Hurrow cut a savage glare toward the bedroom and let his words roll through my head...*do I take him out of the equation?*

I thought about that for a second...*a long damn second,* and finally shook my head. "No, not yet. But I want to know the moment he wakes up. I want him debriefed to the last fucking inch of his pathetic existence, Hurrow. Leave no stone unturned, you understand me?"

"Perfectly," he answered, his stony gaze darkening.

I followed his gaze to the locked bedroom door. "If he had anything to do with this, even in the slightest, his life *will* be forfeit...*I'll end the bastard myself.*"

I *felt* the twitch in my second, knew immediately there would be no stopping the Immortal once he found those responsible.

"*Now* is the time, Hurrow," I commanded. "I want the lawyer's life ripped apart. I want him...*fucking obliterated.* I want him hunted down like the animal he is, then I want you to bring him to me. *That* is a command."

Silence filled the space. But this was no reprieve, no calm before the storm.

This was *the fucking storm.*

The chill in the air cut like a blade...like a thousand of them actually. Tiny nicks of a razor's edge sliced away at his resolve.

Five hundred years I'd fought alongside Hurrow. In two hundred years, we'd forged an understanding. I knew the Immortal better than I knew myself. I knew how hard it'd be for him to follow some of my orders—*especially that order.* But I'd take no more risks, not with her. "I have to know this stops with him. I *have* to know there isn't someone else waiting in the shadows to hurt her. *None* of us will be able to rest…I'll shatter his mind to find out."

"If he's in the city, I'll find him."

"And us?" Rule met my gaze. The hallway was filled with the thud of the giant's heart behind him.

"Justice, you're with me. Rule…"

"Find her belongings, and watch her damn family, especially Bevis and Butthead," Hurrow commanded.

"On it." Rule gave a nod and glanced toward the doorway behind me.

Justice's steely gaze hadn't moved from the panelling behind me. All three Immortals were strung tight…just like I had been before I saw her.

"Just…*try* not to scare the doctor," I sighed, and stepped out of their way.

5

HURROW

I closed the car door with a *thud* and stared at the nondescript brownstone and the five others just like it.

"You sure this is the place?"

Justice stepped up to the sidewalk as a female jogger ran past. "Guess we're about to find out."

Mortals walked past us. An older woman clutched a fluff-ball in her arms, watching me nervously as she scurried. A young couple, hand in hand, headed our way from the opposite direction. A busty blonde in a skintight pink dress chattered away, oblivious to our presence.

But her date wasn't.

The beefy dude sized up Justice in an instant, then shifted a critical gaze my way. That's where he stopped, eyeballing me as the bitter stench of his fear bloomed in the air. Tension rose inside me, wound tight by the roar inside my head. *Boom... boom...boom.* Slow, thready...*fucking arrhythmic* pulses made my fangs ache. I swallowed hard, and focused all my rage onto the fucking lawyer. "Fuck, I hate this side of the river."

"Me, too, brother," Justice snarled, and cut across the sidewalk. "Me, too."

We climbed the narrow stairs with the skinny iron railing and tried the door. A *crunch* and a *snap,* then the door gave way and we were inside, stepping into an empty fucking room.

Justice pushed ahead, striding past a rolled up Egyptian rug. Heavy thuds reverberated as he climbed the stairs and disappeared from view. I scanned the room and headed for the closed door. The handle resisted, locks firmly in place. I forced the steel, bearing down until the thick rod inside the mechanism snapped.

Like I wanted to snap...*keep it together.* I inhaled hard and shoved the door open. Steel bolts fell as the lock disintegrated. But I was already moving inside, into the darkened mess of a study...or what was left, anyway.

The desk was a mess of papers, scattered around one space in the center—*where a computer used to be.* Glass glinted under the spread of court documents. Court documents and scribbled notes. Floorboards creaked overhead as Justice moved around upstairs, checking bedroom after bedroom before he came back down. "He's gone."

Gone. I moved closer to the desk, dragging in the stale air of the place. "There's something missing."

Justice looked around the room and waited.

"Fear." I explained, and slid the top abandoned page closer. "There's no fear, no panic. You'd think this place would be filled with the stench after what he did. You'd think he'd leave behind fucking terror."

But there was none of that, just stale air...and a writ dated six months ago.

Six months?

"Tell me, what do you smell?"

"Fucking dust," the mountain growled. "Makes my damn skin itch just standing here."

"Exactly," I agreed. "The bastard didn't disappear last night. He hasn't been here in months."

Justice jerked his gaze toward me, and the leather patch shone in the light. "So where the fuck has he been?"

"That's a good question," I replied, scanning the rest of the papers. "A *very* good question indeed."

Rage rolled off me in waves. I closed my eyes and tried to hold on.

Easy...easy now.

The faint sound of chains rattled inside my head. I plunged down into the darkness where the old me still lingered. In the silence, the beast lifted his head and bared his fangs. No one wanted that part of me to rise...*especially* me.

But the damn mortal woman was making me come undone, like a faded doll, overstuffed and frayed, splitting at the seams. Hate spilled out, and this time I couldn't stop it. The desk rattled and metal howled, the sound tearing through my head like a gunshot. I snapped my eyes open, sucked in an all-consuming breath, and drove my fucking fist through the plate glass desktop.

Shards splintered and flew before they fell, crunching under my boots as I picked up the steel fame and hurled it across the room. *"I'm going to fucking KILL YOU!"*

Inside my head, I still saw her, drenched, pale...*lifeless.*

He did that to her. The sickening *beast* inside me yowled. *The fucking lawyer did that to her...Let me out. I'll take care of the piece of shit...*

"Hurrow?" Justice called, snapping me out of the darkness.

I stared at the steel frame half embedded in the wall and tried to get a hold of myself. "Yeah?"

"You see this?"

I turned my head and stared at a real estate flyer in his hand. "The bastard was looking at properties." The edges of the paper crumpled under the Vampire's grip. "He was looking at fucking *properties.*"

His eye glinted, and cold, bitter rage plunged the temperature in the room to almost zero. "What is that?"

"What?" I followed his gaze.

A small wire stuck out from the wall. a speck of black plastic sheath against pale cream. I strode toward the cable and bent. It was half embedded, and mostly painted over, as though someone wanted it hidden.

Hidden enough to paint it...and conceal it behind a cabinet. I touched scratches on the wooden floor, deep gouges where someone had dragged the end of the cupboard aside...not once...*but countless times.*

Someone in a hurry...

"That wall's wrong." Justice raised a massive hand against the surface and knocked.

Hollow, and empty. I rose from the ground and searched for the seams.

"Wait." He pressed against the corner, and a *click* sounded.

In an instant, the wall swung open. Tiny lights flickered red and green in the darkness. I stepped inside, my gaze lingering on the steel rack and the server tucked away.

As Justice wiggled a mouse, a screen came to life on a tiny desk mounted on the wall. The image was still, and shrouded, frozen on some kind of room before he clicked play.

Sound came from a speaker, fabric shifting, something smooth...like silk sheets.

"*Hurrow...*" I froze at the whisper through the speaker. Ruth? *She called my name.* "*Oh God, yes...*"

"What the fuck..." Justice growled.

In an instant, I knew what we were watching. Ruth shifted under the sheets. Her eyes were closed, lips parted, a perfect mask of ecstasy. Her hand was under the covers, between her legs, rubbing, sliding the leather glove between her thighs.

"*Elithien...*" she cried out.

"He *fucking watched her?*" Justice couldn't tear his gaze from the screen. "That piece of *fucking filth watched her?*"

"I want...I want..." she whimpered, her hand moving faster now, bringing her to the point of no return. *"I want all of you."*

In a blur, Justice lunged, grabbed the screen, and with a guttural roar, ripped it free. Plastic shattered, bits of cable whipped the wall before it fell. I stepped aside as he hurled the monitor across the room for it to smash into the wall. "You *fucking watched her?* WHAT KIND OF SICKO DOES THAT!?"

He gripped the server and tore it free from the shelving. All I could see was her...her perfection, her love...her desire.

"Wait!" I roared, lifting my hand. "There could be something on that. Something we can use to find him."

Heavy breaths sawed through his chest as he lifted his gaze to mine.

I'd seen destruction.

I'd seen blind rage.

But Justice was terrifying. He stared at the hardware in his hand, then turned and strode from the room, carrying the server. I followed, glancing at the scattered images of real estate properties before I left the room.

The lawyer was dead...he was so fucking dead he didn't even understand the level of death he'd become. But he'd find out soon enough.

I shoved open the broken front door and crossed the sidewalk before I climbed into the car. We sat in silence, both shaken by our own rage.

"We have to find him, Hurrow."

"I know."

"We have to."

6

_____

RUTH

F ire burned in my chest. Flames rose to lash the back of my
throat with every shuddered breath.

I fought the fire, fought the ache…and fought the water
when it came for me.

That black, unfathomable water that didn't seem to quench
the burn. Instead, it made it worse.

Panic swelled inside me as the cold hands of terror wrapped
around my ankles. It was the same dream, the same
darkness…*the same fate.*

Pain ripped through my lungs with the scream. But there
was no sound…only silence, *endless silence.* I kicked, driving my
body to the surface…*desperate to escape.*

And still the fire raged.

I'm right here, Justice whispered in the dark. *Easy now, I'm
right here.*

His voice echoed all around me. I stopped kicking…stopped
fighting, and focused on that voice.

That's it…that's it, nice and slow now…nice and slow.

My breaths evened as the water slipped away. I sank back
into the loneliness, where the *crack* of gunshots and the sounds

of shattering glass waited. It was always the same. The water. The gunshots…*the screams.*

Until slowly, that burn in my chest eased. One draw of a breath, and it didn't hurt now, not as much as it had before. Guttural draws of air echoed beside me, the sounds savage and consuming, followed by a grunt. Something heavy landed across my belly and spread out. But instead of suffocating, the weight trapped me with ease.

Breath by breath, I beat back the flames, until the burn eased and the pain grew light. So light, I opened my eyes. Carefully taking deep breaths, I waited for the gloom to move, but the shadows still clung, not to the room…*but to me.*

"Welcome back."

Someone shifted at the end of the bed. There was the soft scrape of a chair, then a muttered curse as the male slowly rose. A heavy snore turned into a growl beside my ear. That heavy weight on my belly shifted, rising higher until fingers curled over the swell of my breast. I felt him…the *Vampire* beside me. *Justice.* I knew him instantly…but not the outline of the male who stumbled around the foot of the bed toward me.

Fear rose, trapping a scream in the back of my throat.

"*Easy,*" the faintly familiar groan echoed. "It's just me, Samuel."

"Samuel?" The burn took hold, and I winced with the pain. "*Horne?*"

"Yeah, it's me." He sank to sit on the side of the bed and grabbed the stethoscope from around his neck. "Welcome back to the land of the living. You had me worried there for a while."

I blinked and tried to focus, seeing bloodshot eyes and greasy, unkept hair, not to mention the five o'clock shadow that had been gone. This wasn't the doctor I remembered.

"He hasn't left your side," Samuel stated, glancing at the towering male that sank on half of the bed beside me, and breathed on the end of the 'scope. "That male makes dedicated look fucking useless."

I caught my breath. He was careful, moving it over my shirt. "Breathe in."

Razor blades carved through my insides. My stomach clenched, a cough raging like wildfire through my chest. I swallowed the burn, until my eyes watered and a whimper tore free.

"You're doing okay, under the circumstances." Samuel commented as he pulled back.

"How long?" The words were a hiss as the need to hack and heave eased.

He glanced at the Vampire before answering. "Three days."

Three days? I tried to sit up.

"Easy..." Panic flared in Samuel's eyes as he glanced at Justice.

Three days? I couldn't sleep for three days...I couldn't even sleep for three minutes. I had the company...*the company*...memories pressed in, shrouded memories. Gunshots cracked through my mind, making me flinch as the past roared back to me.

My company. My friends. Jesus, Russell. Russell was dead...

And Alex.

Alex waited for me in that emptiness. His cruel sneer and quick hand had bruised more than my face. I felt myself slipping, sinking to a place I'd never been before.

Guilt...

Betrayal...

Depression.

"Ruth?" The deep growl followed the slide of his hand.

Justice leaned on one elbow beside me on the mattress, piercing me with the stare of his one eye. But tears shimmered, blurring him before they slid down my cheeks. The pain was wicked, cutting me deeper than I'd ever felt before.

My lips trembled and my body shook as thick, heaving sobs

tore free. The Vampire engulfed me in an instant, grabbing my arms and pulling me back down to the bed and against his chest.

"It's okay," he murmured. "Let it all out. It's okay."

Terror took over, swallowing me in a sudden rush. I couldn't save myself, couldn't hold on, even as my Vampire held onto me.

"I'll leave you." Samuel stepped away, then left the room.

I didn't even hear him retreat. Didn't hear anything other than the muffled sounds of my own grief. I never cried…not even when my father had died…not even when I…*when I had died.*

That empty pit of despair swallowed me whole.

I stayed there, wrapped tight in his heavy arms, when the *whoosh* came from the doors and my Vampires filled the room.

"Ruth?" Elithien called.

I couldn't even answer.

Finally, he continued, his voice low and somber. "Take care of her, brother. We'll be out here."

The shuffle of boots and the snarls of concern were all they left behind.

I wept until my body shuddered and trembled and there were no more tears to shed. Still, the Vampire beside me rubbed my shoulders with long, tender strokes, until he murmured, "Maybe a nice, hot shower will make you feel better?"

The thought of water filled me with dread. But I was frozen on the inside, and the smell of sweat clung to my skin. I must disgust him.

"Never." Justice captured my chin and lifted. "Don't think that again, you understand?"

I just held his gaze while my eyes burned and my belly howled. Until he dropped his hand and muttered. "A hot shower and soup. You need to eat."

Three days…

It haunted me as Justice slid from underneath me and strode

to the bathroom. Bright lights blinked on. I winced at the glare as the huge male stepped confidently into the pristine white. The hiss of the shower water followed seconds later, then he returned, striding to the edge of the bed.

"We're going to do all this slowly, okay?" He gripped my hand and gently pulled until I sat on the side of the bed. "I want to know the minute it hurts."

I don't why he asked me. If he read my mind, he'd know it all hurt.

My heart. My soul.

Everything was breaking, shattering into a million pieces and each edge was razor-sharp. But I lifted my hands when he guided me, until even that made me shake.

I wasn't this *broken thing!* I *wasn't* weak. I was the daughter of the most dangerous man Crown City had ever seen. I was bred from a nest of vipers with a knife pressed to my back.

I was the sole director of Costello Corporation...

And I was alive.

I was alive.

Those words claimed me, but they gave me no comfort...not like they should. My shirt was eased free, the clasp of my bra undone. I shivered in the cool air for a second, until Justice strode to the row of controls. The hum of a motor in the ceiling grew louder.

"It'll warm soon," he said, turning to kneel at my feet. He ran his hands along my arms, then dropped them to my waist. "You ready to do this?"

He waited, his hands lingering on my waist and I realized he was unsure how to touch me...how to care for me...how to heal my pain. "It's okay." I met that steely gaze. "It's going to be okay." I repeated his own words back to him.

He was the most terrifying creature I'd ever met, towing in stature, with massive arms and powerful hands, and fangs that were long and sharp. I'd seen grown men tremble when Justice entered the room. I'd seen men weep...and I'd also seen them bleed, and die.

And yet here he was, trembling at the thought of touching me.

He swallowed hard and drew in a breath. "Okay. Hold onto me. You're going to be a little weak."

His touch was so gentle as he helped me. My legs trembled, but my knees locked and held as he slid Rule's baggy sweats down, leaving me naked. "Can you walk?" he asked as he met my gaze.

I gave a nod, forcing my feet to move as he rose to loom above me.

"Hold on to me."

I did, clutching hold of his hand, and together we slowly made it to the piercing glare of the bathroom. Steam billowed from the large open shower stall. I grasped the edge of the counter as Justice adjusted the temperature of the spray and turned toward me. "Ready?"

My hands trembled and my eyes fought the need to rise and find my own reflection. Purple hovered at the edge of my view.

"Not yet...just not yet."

I swallowed and slowly shuffled toward him. My pain was echoed in the silver shine of his eye. The kind of pain that made itself at home, or had it already? Maybe this was an echo of his past...one I couldn't hope to fathom. He lifted his hands to me. "Let me wash your body and soap your hair. I'll even use Elithien's good stuff."

The corners of my lips rose in a halfhearted smile as he held my hands and stepped backwards into the spray.

Water slammed against him, soaking the white cotton t-shirt against his skin in an instant. But he never even noticed, just drew me closer and slowly turned.

Warmth beat against me with the needle-fine spray. It stung at first, until the warmth bled away the pain to leave me floating, anchored by the feel of his hands. I stepped into him and wrapped my arms around his waist. "Who am I?" I dropped my forehead to his chest and whispered. "Who the hell am I?"

"You're Ruth Costello...*and you're a goddamn survivor.* That's who *you* are."

The deep growl reverberated through his massive chest. His fingers were gentle as they stroked my hair and ran down my spine. His words lingered, but they never pierced my mind. I wanted to cling to them, to feel the vibration through my soul.

I knew who I was...knew where I was born, and where I was raised. But I didn't feel it, not that strength of my resolve, or the power I'd once commanded. I felt empty, broken and afraid. More than that...*I felt responsible.*

Memories surfaced as Justice reached down and picked up the shampoo. The feel of his hands lathering my hair was unable to stop the sound of gunshots as they rang inside my head.

The shadow beside the Chrysler still haunted me, splayed out, dark shirt soaking with blood. Russell's pale face returned to my mind, his eyes wide with terror...*pleading.* But it wasn't for his life—it was for *mine.*

Ruth, RUN! His desperate plea punched through to the surface. "It's all my fault. Everything...if I hadn't pushed Alex, if I hadn't turned him down."

"Hey!" The soothing voice turned savage as Justice captured my chin and lifted my head. Water sluiced down the sides of his strong jaw and cascaded off the point of his chin. I stared into his gaze, fixated by the piercing shine. "There is *nothing* you could've done to stop this. No amount of pleading, no amount of *placating* pathetic excuses to men like him. This was going to happen...*because he deemed it so.*"

His fingers were all I felt. Strong fingers...pressing skin against bone as he tried to make me see reason. But the longer he stared at me, the more the guilt took hold. I wanted to tear away from him. I wanted to scream and shout and *rage.*

Inside me, there was a part of me that did just that. Who howled her injustice and raked claws against her own pain. A part that was the old me, the one before the gunshots and death. But that part of me was down in the darkness now, sinking under the weight of my despair.

That old me wasn't me anymore.

I was changing. I was feeling. I was hating and hurting.

I was *numb*.

Justice washed me, taking care with my hair, until the bathroom was filled with perfumed steam, and when my skin had pruned and my bones had stopped shaking, I heaved a deep sigh.

"Okay, I think you're done," he muttered, his hand trembling over the curve of my ass. "Maybe just your feet first."

My hand fell away as the mountain of a Vampire slowly sank to his knees. His breath blew against my breasts and my nipples hardened under his stare as he hit the floor. His hands ran over the swell of my hips to cup my ass as he lowered his head to press against my stomach.

There was a tremble in my Vampire.

And then a quake.

His splayed fingers gripped my ass tightly. "I thought I'd lost you." His voice quivered as he turned his head and pressed his cheek to my stomach. "For the first time, I knew fear...it fucking terrified me, Ruth. It. Fucking. Terrified. Me."

I closed my eyes to the brush of his lips against my abdomen and lowered my hand to the back of his head. He kissed my stomach and pulled my body against him...like he couldn't get enough of me, couldn't feel enough. He couldn't kiss enough, and in that moment, I was consumed by his desire.

"Don't...don't ever leave me," he pleaded. "Not like that, not ever again. I'm not a man when I'm not around you...*I'm a monster.*"

My fingers sank into his soaked hair, finding the contours of his skull. He was so hard, fangs and bone, and yet underneath all that death and destruction there lay a trembling heart—one that throbbed for me.

His hard breaths slowly eased, along with the vise-like grip on my ass. He didn't want sex from me, not this time. This was about breathing, this was about life. This was about gathering strength for what was to come. *For him.*

He ran his hand down my calf and gently cupped the back of my foot, lifting it from the floor. He washed my feet, his long fingers sliding between my toes as he cared for me until both feet were soaped and clean. Then he rose, his powerful shoulders rounding as he came to his full height, towering over me once more.

Agony raged in his gaze. His white fangs had descended, the points pressing against his perfect lips, and still his body was racked with tremors.

My wrist was so pathetically small, purple veins under pale skin. Still, he needed me, needed more than the press of his lips against my body. "It's okay," I whispered. "Drink."

He stiffened in an instant, dark brows furrowed as he stared at my trembling hand. "You think...*you think I'd drink from you?*"

His words were a slap to my face. I flinched and lowered my hand. He moved faster than I could track, one second, he was careful, then the next, he was a damn lion, lunging to grasp my hand and yank it to his lips. "You think I'd take one fucking drop from you?"

Pain ripped through my chest, tearing me open and laying my heart bare. "I'm not diseased, Justice."

"Let me be perfectly clear here. There is *not a fucking thing wrong with your blood.* But if you think for a second that I'd take one damn drop when your body is fighting to survive, then I feel sorry for you, Ruth, because you've known some pathetic men in your life. *I am not* one of them."

Heat rushed to my cheeks as I tried to pull my hand away.

But his grip was a vise, welded closed and encased in concrete, unmovable.

"You mean more to me than my own fucking hunger, Ruth. You are more than my own lust, more than my own desires. This isn't about me...it's *never* going to be about me...*or any of us.*" His grip eased, leaving my fingers to throb as he lifted his hand and tucked strands of hair behind my ear. "It's only ever going to be about *you*, female. The sooner you get that, the sooner you can start to heal."

With those words, he reached around me and hit the lever, ending the spray.

Cold plunged through me, even though my skin was warm. He turned and stepped out of the shower, his gaze aimed at the floor, his words dropping like gravel. "There's towels there. Will you manage to dry and dress on your own?"

"Yes."

I'd hurt him somehow, unleashed a blow I never saw, and drew blood in ways I hadn't imagined. I saw it in his face, in that flinch of betrayal in his eye and the hard clench of his jaw.

"What have I done?" The word sounded so damn needy, but fuck, that's exactly what I felt...*needy.*

"Don't ever apologize for what you need, Ruth. Don't ever bow down to another, not even to us. Be unapologetically brutal in your own survival. Be who you were meant to be. Be...*ruthless.*"

One sad smile and he left, striding from the bathroom to disappear into the darkened room beyond. Leaving me alone. Fuck, I felt so alone. Alone in a house filled with Vampires. But it didn't matter who was here. I could be standing at a podium under the blinding glare of floodlights and still, I'd feel alone, *empty.*

Worthless.

I gripped the edge of the glass shower wall and stepped out, lifting my gaze as I neared the mirror...and stopped dead. *Not* *yet...*Justice's words filled me as I stared at the stranger in the mirror.

Dark soulless eyes, bruises along one side of her face, and her neck. *Jesus!* I swallowed, feeling the pain of his hands once more.

I could count his fingers right here. My fingers trembled as I touched the deep purple lines that curled around my throat.

Marks along my body, black and blue, a graze that ran along my side. *How did I get that?* I wanted to remember...and yet, *I didn't.* No more...no more. I grasped the thick folded towel on the edge of the counter and looked down.

You've known some pathetic men in your life.

Pathetic. Men.

I clung to those words, tried to find the difference...between men like Elithien, and men like my father. I couldn't.

"You okay?"

I jumped at the sound of Hurrow's voice as the steel door slid closed. I hadn't heard him enter...hadn't heard a damn thing. Concern filled his eyes as he hovered in the doorway.

"I brought you some clean clothes. I have Rule going shopping later, to find you something better than our sweats to wear, unless you prefer he grabs some clothes from your place?"

"No." The reaction was instant. "Not my clothes."

Not my life. Not anything I ever had before.

I wanted none of it. None. Of. It.

My hand trembled, gripping the edge of the towel as my body started to shake. I felt desperate, *weak.* Detoxing from my scant hold on life. One that left me reeling...

Panic roared through me. My pulse thundered as the walls closed in.

"Hey there," Hurrow growled, lunging into the glare as I crumpled.

But he caught me, lifting me in one perfect sweep until I was against him, arms wrapped around his neck, my face pressed against his chest. I breathed in the scent of him, of darkness and death and terror.

Desire bloomed inside me like some deadly midnight flower. I wanted him...*no, I craved him.* To feel his strength, his power...*to feel anything.* "Kiss me," I murmured into his shirt. "Make me feel alive."

He froze for a heartbeat, then carried me into the bedroom. The edge of the bed groaned under his knee as he laid me down. Steel shimmered in his eyes. He was so perfect, so utterly perfect. All killer...all beast. Soft lips met mine as I closed my eyes. *All mine.*

His hands slid out from under me as the kiss deepened, taking the corners of my mouth and swell of my lower lip. I waited for his weight on my body and the unbuttoning of his shirt. I waited to be filled with him, mind, body...soul. But none of that came. He stayed clothed in his crisp white business shirt and perfectly pressed black pants, leaving me in nothing more than the fluffy white towel. Something sharp bit my lip. I flinched at the sting and tasted my own blood as Hurrow growled and pulled away.

"What is it?" I questioned, and licked the tiny cut.

His fangs lengthened, the pointed tips slipping over his dark red lips. He lowered that hungry gaze to my mouth, and the hairs on my arms stood on end. "Lie back now, Ruth," he ordered, his voice warped and strange.

Terror tore through me, but heat followed close behind, spilling between my thighs as the bedsheets crumpled under the sweep of his hand. An ache flared for a second as my muscles stretched taut.

"Don't bother trying to hide it from me." Hunger deepened his tone as his gaze traveled down my body. "I'll know the instant you're in pain."

He climbed on top of me, placing his splayed hands on either side of my head. But there was no weight on my body, not even a whisper of all the power coiled in his body.

I tasted it, though...tasted it on his lips as he sank lower. Sharp fang points gently dragged over my nipples, making me moan and quiver. The tight peaks puckered as he licked.

"Oh," I whimpered, and opened my eyes to look down.

White fangs pressed against tender flesh as I slid my fingers through his hair. I shifted my body, parting my thighs as he dragged my nipple deeper inside his mouth. This was what I wanted...this panic...this *need.*

Callused fingers skimmed the length of my stomach. He was so tender, so *light,* moving his mouth from the burn of my breast to gently kiss the deep bruise on my side. "Fuck me, I want you. I want you so *goddamn much.*"

"Then take me. Take all of me. Never give me back." The words spilled from my lips as he rose to my mouth once more.

"I will take you, Ruth." His eyes shone with promise. "I'll take you over and over, until you won't remember a time where it's not us...*all of us.*"

I sank into those words, widening my thighs as he kissed me deep and hard. And when the sting of my lip came once more, so did desire, sweeping through me as Hurrow sank lower.

The towel was tugged free. My entire body lay exposed. An unmerciful sound spilled from his lips as he kissed the rise of my public bone... then lower.

Tiny licks slid into the top of my slit. I bent my knee, my hand resting on the back of his head, until he pressed the length of those fangs on either side of my clit. Lightning tore through my body, making me jump.

"Don't move, Ruth," he cautioned, the sound vibrating against my sensitive flesh.

I bit down on my lip as he pressed those sharp points harder and *licked.* Danger and desire collided, making a hunger like never before. I lifted my leg and tilted my hips. "More," I whimpered.

Slick and sharp, he grazed those points along my crease and drove his tongue inside. The cry was sudden and shrill, tearing from my open mouth as I came. His tangled hair was taut under my fist as I bucked against his mouth. I was empty in that moment. No pain. No terror. No past or future, there was only Hurrow…and his love. I wanted more of it. I wanted so much more.

I uncurled my fist and cupped his head as he turned to kiss the inside of my thigh. There wasn't one wrinkle in his shirt… not one curl of his midnight hair out of place as he lifted his dangerous gaze to mine.

His lips shone, slick with my desire, then curved into a smile. "Sleep now, Ruth. Sleep and dream of me. I want you healed… and whole. I want you by my side when we go to take back your company once more."

Take back my company? The words swept in and swirled around inside my head as my thoughts slowed.

"But we can talk about that later," Hurrow promised as I closed my eyes.

The bed shifted, and my feet were picked up from the mattress one at a time as Hurrow carefully and expertly dressed me in his baggy sweats once more.

"Sleep," he whispered, and kissed my cheek as my thoughts slipped away. "We need you."

The covers were draped over my body before the *whoosh* of the door closing.

I was alone once more, slipping into slumber…as he whispered in my head.

Take back your company.
And your life.

7

RUTH

The house was silent when I woke. For a while, I didn't move, not to see the men who'd be waiting for me, or to return to the life I'd once had. I lay there pretending this was an endless void and wondered if I could stay here, in the quiet and the dim. If I could stay in the world within a world where the monster didn't hide behind the mask of a friend...*or a lover.*

A lover.

He had been a lover. I *thought* he'd been a friend. But he hadn't been any of those things. He'd been a betrayer. Warmth slipped from the corners of my eyes as Alex hovered at the edges of my mind, taunting me with the good times we'd had. But that wasn't how my thoughts of him ended, they never did.

BANG!

The gunshot echoed with the *whoosh* of the door. I flinched at the sound.

"Sorry." Samuel knocked and stepped into the room. "I didn't mean to startle you."

I didn't turn my head when he stepped closer and sat beside me. Tears shimmered, blurring the darkness.

"I should turn on the light." The bed shifted beside me.

"No," I snapped. "Please, don't…"

"Okay." The bed shifted again.

He smelled of soap, and…*bacon.* He smelled of bacon. My stomach clenched tight. Cold pressed against me. I fought the urge to scream and bit my lip. The sting was instant, searing through my lip with the faint taste of blood.

"Breathe in."

I inhaled.

"And out."

Hurrow.

Hurrow pushed the panic aside, the way he kissed me, the way he loved me. An image of Justice followed. *My Justice* as he held me against him in the shower.

"Breathe in."

I inhaled.

"Out."

Justice's anger rushed back to me. I'd upset him somehow. I'd made him angry…enough for him to leave. Elithien. The Vampire consumed me, taking me deeper than I'd ever known before, and then there was Rule. I turned my head and inhaled, finding the faint scent of deep woods berries and earth. I closed my eyes, carried away by the feel of them even if they weren't in the room.

"I think it's about time we had a chat." Samuel lowered the stethoscope. Silence fell until the doctor sighed. "I can't do this without looking you in the eyes."

The bed dipped once more as he rose. Padded steps sounded before the *tink* of a light switch. Glaring light flooded in from the bathroom, making me wince and glance away.

"Ruth, I want you to look at me."

He wasn't going anywhere, not until I heard what he had to say. When I met the doctor's gaze, I saw a man rested…a little, at least. Clean-shaven, wearing clothes that weren't his. He reached for my hand and I fought the need to pull away. Instead, I waited as he glanced at the door once more.

"We've known each other for a while now. Your father was a good man."

"No, he wasn't."

It was his turn to flinch as he forced a smile. "You're right. He was...*powerful.* But he was a good man in a lot of ways I respected. He was tenacious, demanding, and protective, and it's with those traits in mind I ask you for the truth. Do you wish to remain here...with these...*men?*"

With the Vampires. That's what he meant. Beasts...and *monsters.* A caress came across my mind, soft, careful...before it pulled away. I didn't need to guess to know who it was. *Elithien.* "No, Sam. These aren't the beasts out there. I'm safe here, safer than I ever was on the other side of the river."

"You know, they're still looking for you out there, your uncle...and the other men who worked for your father."

Fear plunged deep, chilling me. "Did you tell them where I was?"

"No. I haven't told anyone. My family thinks there's some kind of goddamn emergency in Winchester. They have no idea I'm still in the city."

It was that touch I couldn't shake, that feeling of *comfort.* That's what it was...Elithien was comforting, giving me a way out. *You've known some pathetic men in your life. I am not one of them.* Justice's words filled me once more.

"Did you hear anything I was saying just now?" Samuel gripped my hand. "I'd be remiss in my duty of—"

"I'm fine here, Sam. Honestly, I'm fine. I'm safe and protected." My voice trailed away, along with my thoughts. "Who on earth would come for me here?"

He searched my eyes for the truth and finally pulled away, satisfied. "Well, you're out of the woods now, so to speak. Your lungs are mostly okay, the risk of infection has dropped considerably. I'm going to leave some antibiotics, painkillers, and my cell number in case you change your mind about coming home. I'll call the…overbearing, protective one and check in with you twice a day."

"The overbearing one?" I repeated, forcing myself to smile. "Which one do you mean, exactly."

Samuel smiled for me, releasing his hold on my hand. "Be safe, Ruth…and for God's sake, walk outside the room and see to your protectors. They're all moping around, snarling and…cooking."

"Cooking?"

He smiled and jerked his head toward the doorway. "Ask *them*."

He rose then, wrapped his stethoscope around his neck, and touched my shoulder. "We'll talk soon, okay?"

The *whoosh* of the door came a second later, and I was alone…with his words ringing inside my head. My stomach ached and my thighs trembled, but I slid my feet from under the sheets and rose from the bed. The bright lights of the bathroom beckoned. On shaky legs, I took a step, then another, until I made it to the doorway.

Each step was agony. But the razor blades in my chest didn't cut as deep anymore as I sucked in hard breaths and used the toilet. I flushed, and turned to the basin, finding that haunted stare in the mirror again as I splashed water on my face and drank from my hand.

I needed out of this bedroom…I needed to remember I'd *survived*. Not just the cold brackish water of the river, but Alex…*I'd survived Alex.* I took one more look at the stranger in the mirror, then turned away.

Each step was agony as the muscles along my side clenched. But I forced step after step, bracing my hand on the doorway of the bathroom, then slowly made my way across the bedroom. My fingers trembled and my arms ached as I punched in the numbers on the keypad and waited for the door to open.

It did so with a rush and the lock click...the outside was just a step away.

Panic gripped me as I stared at the door's steel shine. I'd never once been terrified, not even in that alley years ago when the street-corner punks had come for me seeking retribution. I'd stood my ground. I'd fought and kicked and clawed their eyes out.

I'd done everything I could to stop from falling...and now here I was...*falling*.

The touch against my mind came once more, careful, barely there, like the slow, rhythmic breath of the one you love lying next to you at night. It was there...always there.

I pushed on, forcing my feet to move as the door opened in an instant, leading me to the hallway...into the house. *Outside.* It was the closest to outside that I'd felt in forever. Sawing breaths occupied my attention as the soft light in the hallway darkened to gray. I reached out, braced my hand on the wall, and tried to stop myself from falling. Breaths demanded my effort, the harsh rush filling my ears and brightening the gray.

Voices slipped into my hearing, followed by a *clang!* It was muttering...*snarling* even. The more I focused on the sound, the clearer the tone. It was Justice mumbling, coupled with the sweet smell of...*was that blueberries?* My hard breaths eased as that smell consumed my attention, twisting my belly and clenching my throat. My own body barked in hunger, forcing me to move. I licked my lips and stepped slowly forward as the last of the clouded gray seeped from my vision.

"Take her damn blood..." Justice mumbled. *"What kind of man does she take me for?"*

I closed my eyes and inhaled hard. He was pissy. Sunrise-kind of pissy for a Vampire, *just what I needed.* The smell of muffins clouded my anger, making me walk along the hallway until I reached the end.

"He's cooking," Rule whispered as he leaned against the wall outside the kitchen, arms crossed. "Been like that for hours. I hope you're hungry...*you'd better be hungry*, is all I can say."

I flinched at his voice and stared into the gloom. The empty living room stretched out behind Rule. Were the others gone already?

"It takes the threat of the damn Inner Circle to get them away from you, Ruth, and that threat has been and gone. They're around...waiting."

"Waiting for what?" I muttered.

He pushed off the wall and took a step toward me. "Do you really have to ask?"

Me...they were waiting for me.

A *crash* cut through the silence, followed by a string of mutterings that couldn't be good. I turned from Rule and slowly made my way toward the kitchen, my bare feet padding softly on the floor.

Justice was angry with me...and he had every right to be.

Even if I didn't quite understand why.

But I knew what I needed and it was more than blueberry muffins. I needed to stop this pain inside me...any way I could. The gigantic Vampire had his back to me, hunched over the stovetop, the oven door below his waist cracked open.

"Something smells delicious," I exclaimed. "I hope there's enough for me, I'm starving."

He froze, his hands gripping a muffin pan filled with some of the most delicious looking muffins I'd ever seen. Blueberries bled through butter yellow mix, reminding me of the bruises on my body.

"They do...and there is," he responded, slowly turning to give me the full brunt of his glare. "For a price."

"I will pay that price," I negotiated. "But first I want you to take me to the river."

His gaze widened and one perfect brow shot high.

"No."

The denial came from behind me as Elithien and Hurrow strode through the doorway.

"That can't happen." Elithien gave a shake of his head. "It's not safe."

Anger lashed through me, cutting like the crack of a whip. "Safe? It's not about being safe. It's about survival. *My* survival, and I want to go."

Movement shifted in the corner of my eye as Justice met Elithien's gaze.

"I have a right to see," I growled.

Nostrils flared as the glint in his eye sharpened. He never looked away, just nailed me with that stare.

"*I...want...to...see.*"

Out of that cutting glare came a whisper of fear. He was frightened. *No, he was terrified,* and for someone like Elithien, that *never* happened.

"Please," I pleaded, my voice shaking.

"You stay in the car."

I nodded. "I'll stay in the damn car."

"If it's not safe, we come straight back home. No arguing. No...*disappearing.*"

"I promise."

He took a step closer in the blink of an eye, to stop a hairs breadth away from me. "I'm barely holding on here, Ruth. I'm *barely* holding on."

I gave a nod, not trusting my voice not to crack.

"I'll drive," Hurrow insisted.

"After she eats," Justice countered. "Not negotiable."

My tears blurred Elithien's face. I tried to swallow the lump in my throat as Justice handed me a saucer with the biggest muffin I'd ever seen.

"Thank you," I sighed.

"We're *all* having one," Justice snapped, and handed each Vampire a muffin, one by freaking one.

First Hurrow took one before Justice held out the plate to Elithien.

"I'm not hungry," the Alpha declined, watching as I lifted the muffin and took a bite.

"I'll have his...*and* mine, brother," Rule piped up. "They smell divine."

We ate in silence. Rule and Hurrow demolishing theirs in three gigantic mouthfuls. I took my time, taking small bites and trying to swallow without letting the Vampires see me wince. Tension grew in the air, making the hairs on the nape of my neck rise until I took the last bite.

"I'll get the car ready," Hurrow announced, and left.

I waited for the tension to ease as I placed my empty plate onto the counter. But that didn't happen. They were quiet, *too quiet.* The eerie calmness set me on edge as Rule disappeared and Elithien stepped backwards, motioning toward the front door.

I sucked in a breath, taking my time as I made it out of the kitchen and headed for the living room.

"Here," Rule called, meeting me halfway across with a thick cable-knit sweater and a pair of boots. "In case you get cold."

He held them out, helping me as I slid the sweater on until the soft, cream-colored wool draped over me then he steadied me as I stepped into the boots. I waited for Elithien to grow tired of waiting and sweep me into his arms. But that didn't happen. Instead, he hovered, following me step by painful step until I eventually made it out the front door and into the night.

Three days I'd been recovering in the Vampires' den...*or was it now four?*

I couldn't get those days back. I couldn't get the old me back...I had to find a way forward. Hurrow opened the rear door of the Explorer and waited. Even though it was mere feet away, it may as well be clear across the river. My steps slowed as the pain bit deeper, making me catch my breath.

You can do it, Elithien whispered.

We know you can, Hurrow added.

Keep going. I turned my head to Justice as the Vampire watched me from the front of the four-wheel drive.

"One step after the other," Rule encouraged behind me. "I'll catch you if you fall."

I had no doubt about that. Even with this unyielding pain-in-the-ass attitude they were giving me, I knew one thing for sure...my Vampires wouldn't let me fall.

I held onto that and shifted my focus to the soft interior light of the car and the plush leather seats. Cold air plunged deep with every breath, until the burn settled in. The searing heat settled into my lungs as I reached out and grabbed the door.

"Well done." Hurrow motioned inside. "Now for the real work."

I slid inside, sucking in hard breaths as he closed the door. *Real work?* What the fuck did he call walking across the damn parking area in my condition? Car doors opened and closed in the four-wheel drive behind us. But Hurrow just slid behind the wheel as Elithien opened the opposite rear door and climbed in.

Steel shone in Elithien's gaze as Hurrow started the engine and pulled the car forward. We drove in silence, rolling through the familiar gates of the Vampire compound and out onto the familiar roads. The longer I was out here, the more I started to re-think this whole thing. It was too soon...too much, too...*everything.*

My nails dug into the stitching as we took the curve and lights glinted in the distance. This was really happening, this was really real. The outside world, the terror that waited. The more thoughts of the things that'd been done to me and the closer we came to those lights, the more the panic set in.

A faint glow from the city reached into the darkness. My gaze automatically shifted to the lights on the bridge...the same bridge that divided one half of the city from the other.

Goosebumps broke out across my skin the closer we came to the river. That deep pit of despair inside me seemed to grow wider and wider, until it was all I could feel. Hurrow took the last turn, hurtling us to where the Wolves played.

"Russell," I murmured. "Tell me he's alive."

Elithien stiffened, quiet as stone until finally he spoke. "He's alive."

"Can I see him?"

"No," he answered coldly. "It's not safe...not yet."

Not safe for me...or for him? I closed my eyes for a moment and tried to push the image of Russell from my mind, but no matter how hard I tried, he clung to me. "When will it be safe?"

Silence filled the car.

There was no answer this time and my heart grew heavy.

The faint throb of nightclub music pressed against the glass as we shot past the Hunting Ground and headed for the river. I reached with trembling fingers, and pressed the button. Cold air rushed in through the lowering window, scattering my hair as I turned my face to the wind.

The terrifying smell of water filled me, icy and deep, taking me under to where the darkness waited. Bright lights called to me across the river as Hurrow turned, taking us along the narrow dirt road at the edge of the water.

The river was almost empty, no mammoth cargo ships docked at port and blocking the way. Instead, smaller vessels dominated the water. Blinding spotlights were aimed at the draglines submerged in the water.

They were dragging the bottom...searching for

bodies...*searching for me.*

Cold whispered inside my mind. The kind of cold that once it found you...it never let you go.

"Your uncle is persistent, I'll give him that," Hurrow snarled.

I turned my gaze to the parking lot across the river. Watching the trawler as it inched past, a man stood on the walkway, dressed in a long, heavy black coat with the collar turned up...and for a second, I didn't recognize him...and then I did. "Is that Jerry?"

"He's been here every day and most of the nights. Watching...waiting."

He's been there? I fixed on the sight of him standing at the broken-down jetty, hands buried deep into his pockets. From here I could almost see that impenetrable mask of rage. It was the same look he'd had the day I said goodbye to my father...and accused my uncle of betrayal.

Cold anger.

Seething anger.

"He has men all over the city searching for answers. The police don't know what really happened...but your uncle..I think about now he's slowly starting to understand."

"He hates me."

"No...he wants to find you. You're his blood, after all," Elithien answered. "And if there's one thing the Costellos won't abide by...it's the murdering of one of their own."

I flinched at the words and jerked my gaze to the recon ship inching past in long straight lines, the words CROWN CITY POLICE painted on the side. Alexander...*where was he?*

"If we knew that, we'd be having a very different conversation right about now," Hurrow growled, and threw the Explorer into gear.

I wrapped my arms around my body and lifted my gaze to that lone figure standing on the walkway. "I've seen enough now. *Please,* take me home."

8

RUTH

Three days...*three days they've dragged the river for me.*
Three days...

The words consumed me as we drove back to the Vampires' den. I didn't see the sparkling lights of the city this time. I didn't even see the night. I saw that lone figure, shoulders hunched, fists buried in his pockets. I'd seen my uncle wear that long coat before. He called it his *brass balls coat.* You know, the one where you trembled so hard your balls clanged together like they were made of brass.

But I hadn't seen him wear it in forever...*but he was wearing it now.*

The coat spoke volumes. It wasn't something you wore fleetingly. Him standing there wasn't any drive-by check. It was one you hunkered down with, the one you heaved around on your shoulders. The one whose weight was secondary to its warmth.

My uncle had been there for days....and nights, it seemed.

That hurt me.

Tears slipped from my eyes with the pain. I lowered my head, shielding my eyes, until careful fingers grasped my chin and turned my head. "You don't have to hide yourself from us, Ruth. Not from your joy, or your pain. Lean on me...*use me*. Let me be the strength you need."

His silver eyes glinted in the darkness. Still, I couldn't move. I couldn't give him what he wanted. I was trapped by my own grief, nailed down by the kaleidoscope of rage.

I couldn't even give it to myself.

In an instant, the tears died away, leaving me staring at Elithien, my chest as empty as a pit.

There was a flinch in his eyes before he slowly lowered his hand. "Do you want out of these chains?"

I stared at him, trying to understand what he meant.

"Make your decision, Ruth. Only then come to me. Out of the chains, or drown in them."

His tone was so cold...as cold as the river.

"I want to see Russell," I whispered. "I need to know he's okay."

"No." Elithien turned away from me then and stared out the window.

Silence carried us home. Cold silence, bitter silence, and when we finally pulled up outside his home, Elithien was the first one out of the car. The hard *thud* of the car door shutting made me flinch, then he was gone, striding toward the front door of the house and slipping inside.

Hurrow neared cautiously, not meeting my gaze.

"What did I do?" I asked him.

"He only wants to help you." He reached for me, picking me up in one sweep of his arms. "We all do. But you have to want to help yourself."

He strode to the front of the house and stepped inside before lowering my feet to the floor. The thud of car doors echoed behind us as Rule and Justice came inside. I felt heavy as I slowly made my way back to the room. But it had nothing to do with the weight of my bones. It was my heart that felt the burden. My heart that pressed against the confines of my chest.

Confines that felt like the chains Elithien spoke of.

Silence swallowed me as I made the long, lonely trip back to the room. My eyes burned with unshed tears as I pressed the buttons on the keypad of Elithien's door. The Vampire had given me his bedroom...he'd given me his heart. But it was a cold heart...a *cutting* heart. It warmed to my touch but, without the warmth of my fingers, his heart remained cold.

I went to the bed and sat on the edge. The sheets were still rumpled, the smell of sex heavy in the air. He was cold, cruel, and in the space of a heartbeat, rage and anger cut through me. I hated in this moment...I hated *me*, this *weak*, spineless me.

Do you want out of these chains?

His stony, unflinching words filled me as I lowered my head and cried. Thick, heavy sobs gripped me, nearly stopping my breath as they cut deep. "Yes...yes, I want out."

Good, Elithien whispered. *Trauma is bondage, it will wrap you tight and take you under, you already know what that feels like. Let us help you...let us heal you...let us love you.*

Tears continued to slip free as shudders coursed through my body. A weight shifted inside me, and it was a hard shift...a *heavy* shift, like a door had cracked open somewhere deep inside me and light spilled through the darkness of my mind.

"I want to see Russell, too," I snarled, and wiped the stinging tears from my eyes. *"That* is non-negotiable."

In time.

It was the only answer he gave me. But it wasn't a no...and I could settle for that for a while. Exhaustion moved through me as I scooted higher up the bed, nudged off my boots, and slipped my feet under the crumpled sheets. This wasn't the cold, immaculate feel of my home, and for that I was grateful.

This place, amongst these pain-in-the-ass Vampires who didn't give me a goddamn inch, was feeling more like a real home day by day. Elithien was going to help me…he was going to save me, of that I was certain.

I lay my head on the pillow once more and breathed in the scent of him. That dark, erotic scent that invaded the darkest part of me. *Elithien,* his name hummed inside my head. How he was going to save me, I wasn't sure. But he would. I closed my eyes with the scent of him swirling around inside my head.

This time there were no dreams…and no nightmares. This time there was only peace and darkness as I slept.

9

RUTH

I woke to the hard rap of knuckles on my door. My heart leaped, slamming against my ribs as I rolled from the bed and stepped forward in the dark. For a second, I was lost, stumbling in the emptiness...until memories surged to the surface.

I was with the Vampires...I was safe.

*Knock...knock...*then a voice through the speaker near the keypad. "It's Kern, are you there?"

I stumbled for the keypad and pressed the button. "Yes...I'm here."

"Thank *Christ*. I've been banging on the damn door for the last ten minutes," he snarled, sounding bored and frustrated at the same time. "I've been given instructions to tell you that you're to shower and dress. New clothes are hanging in the closet and your escort is waiting for you in the living room... and hurry, will you? He's stinking up the place."

Hurry?

Stinking?

Escort?

I pressed the button once more and leaned close. "I don't understand, what do you mean?"

"Listen, Ms. Costello. If you want me to write it down for you, you're going to have to open the damn door. But the instructions are still the same. Shower, dress...get the Wolf out of my damn living room."

There was a *screech,* then silence. Shower, dress...and a Wolf?

Elithien? I called in the darkness of my mind. He was there, just a brush against my thoughts before he murmured, *Go, Ruth. I'll see you later.*

I stepped away from the speaker and glanced at the bathroom as the events of last night slipped in. *Do you want out of those chains?* The words returned, strengthening my spine, giving me the strength I needed.

My feet were firm and my knees didn't shake as I crossed the bedroom and turned on the light. My lungs didn't burn as much now, that piercing pain dulled to an ache. I glanced at the walk-in closet beside the bathroom and stepped closer.

One flick of the light switch, and I stared at a long row of high-end tailored suits. Lights glinted off the full-length mirror as I stepped inside. Rolex watches and diamond cufflinks. I'd seen prestige before...but nothing like this. There was a section of the closet closed off. I ran my hand along the cold surface. Steel, by the feel of it. Armor plated, I assumed. Whatever lay inside was precious to him. More precious than one-hundred-thousand-dollar watches and five-carat diamond cufflinks.

I left the closed section and turned to a section of the closet vastly different from the others. A long black dress brushed the floor, the material not satin or chiffon, but lace, the threads woven and gaping across the bustier. This was not a dress you wore outside the confines of your home. My flesh would press against the threads, nipples peeking free.

No, this was a dress of seduction...

This was a dress for sex.

I stepped closer and ran my hand along the fragile material. It had been intricately stitched by hand. Elithien had bought this for a purpose. Heat tore through me with the thought. Did he envision this on me? *Did this turn him on...*

A flicker of heat pooled between my thighs. I licked my lips with the surge of power...a faded remnant of the power I used to feel before, until I dropped my hand and stepped away. I grabbed a pair of black trousers and a soft cream angora knitted top before lowering my gaze to the sets of underwear placed neatly in the open drawer below.

He'd made space for me.

Not just space, sections and drawers and bedrooms and love.

I wasn't just a visitor anymore. I was part of his life. Tears blurred the clothes. I grabbed black lacy underwear and low-heeled black boots before I went into the bedroom and laid the garments on the end of the bed. Purpose filled me as I hurriedly yanked off my clothes and hit the lever for the shower. I was guessing Rule was responsible for the clothes. I glanced at the row of new bottles that lined the tiled shower shelf. Chanel Mademoiselle shower gel and high-end shampoo bottles that hadn't been there before.

"You've got damn fine taste, I'll give you that," I conceded, and reached for the shampoo.

I washed and scrubbed, taking a second to breathe in the decadence of the gifts I wouldn't dare buy myself, then stepped out of the shower smelling better than I had in forever. I dried, dressed, used the dryer on my hair until it was soft and still a little damp, and when I pressed the button for the door and stepped out into the hallway, I felt different than I had before.

Stronger.

Determined.

I made my way toward the living room and scanned the space, stopping as someone rose from the black leather couch, someone I wasn't expecting to see. "Arran?"

He smiled when he saw me. His soft brown eyes lit up and his perfect lips curled. "If it was anyone else, I'd say about damn time, but to see you looking like that, well...the wait was more than worth it."

My heart swelled as I slowly crossed the floor and opened my arms. He felt so good to hold...so damn good. Warm, and suffocating, swallowing me in his embrace.

"I was so fucking worried, Ruth...so fucking worried." His whisper was raw and harsh, choking. "You scared the shit out me, woman."

"I scared myself," I murmured into his neck.

"Right, yes." He seemed to gather himself and eased his hold. A sheen sparkled in his eyes as I stepped away.

There was a change in him, one I couldn't quite put my finger on. There was still the same cockiness...the same wicked, lopsided grin. But he didn't look at me with the same hunger he had before. He looked at me like a friend.

"We'd better get going, got lots to see," he exclaimed.

"Where?" I asked, confusion closing in. "What is this anyway?"

"You'll see." He just smiled and shook his head, stepping away in the direction of the front door. "And I've got instructions to feed you, as well. I hope you're hungry, I could eat a damn horse."

An image filled my head, Arran in his Wolf form in full flight, matching stride for stride with a massive black stallion. "I bet you could, too," I agreed, suddenly a little afraid of the beast he truly was.

I followed him toward the front door as Kern stepped out of the shadows.

"Thank God for that," the punk-turned-Vampire associate mumbled under his breath.

"You know, you're not that old that I can't give you a smack upside the head," I growled, stopping in front of him. "Learn some damn manners."

Arran just chuckled and strode out the front door, calling over his shoulder, "It's good to see you haven't lost that spark, Ruth."

I just stared into Kern's eyes, then turned and walked away. I'd met plenty of people in my life who didn't like me, who didn't like my name, or my face, or what my family did to earn their millions. Kern wasn't the first, and he certainly wouldn't be the last. When it came to me, I couldn't care less...but when the cruel remarks were directed at my friends, then I bit back...and I bit hard.

"Oh God," I muttered, following him out to his car. The Jeep...I'd forgotten about the damn Jeep, and the way he drove. "You sure this is safe?"

"What, you mean the car?"

"No, I mean you...driving."

Arran threw back his head and roared with laughter. "Well, seeing as how you're still damn mortal, I guess I'll stick to the speed limit—ish."

"Ish?" I cried, yanking open the passenger's side door and climbing in. "What the fuck does *ish* mean?"

He didn't answer, just grinned his wolfish grin and started the engine. The sun poured in through the window and spilled warmth along my skin. The day felt alien now, as though somehow, I'd traded my soul for the night.

The Jeep clunked into gear and jerked forward, jarring my teeth and tearing through my side. "Easy," I barked, and winced.

"Sorry," he apologized, then eased off the accelerator and took the turn gently.

"You still haven't told me where we're headed."

"Food, then a few places," he answered, lifting his hand and patting the top pocket of his crisp navy shirt. "I've got my list, so you just sit back and know I'll keep you safe."

He wasn't like the Vampires. There wasn't that predatory intensity that came with them. But underneath the smirks and the backhanded humor, I knew he was every bit as dangerous as my men. I sat back and watched the afternoon sun slant over the mountains and wash the ground. It was cooler now, not warm and bright. Winter was coming to Crown City, and with it would come the rain and the snow. The river would freeze in patches and there'd be a new problem to watch.

I thought about work as Arran drove with more care than he ever had before. I wanted to be back there, to hear the familiar roar of the ships, to have *purpose*. Sparks shimmered far off in the distance as we drove through the west part of the city and headed for the bridge.

My hand moved to the armrest, nails digging deep into the leather.

"I've got you," Arran reassured me, deep and sure. "You're safe with me."

Safe with me. I swallowed hard as the tires hit the entrance of the bridge. I put my trust in the Wolf and let him carry me back there...to the side of the city that'd once been my home. We turned as the street split into three and went left along familiar streets to the highway, then slipped onto the off-ramp.

I didn't know where we were headed, didn't know a damn thing. But as we turned again and headed along streets lined with cafes and shops, Arran pulled up in front of a run-down diner.

"Prepare yourself." he warned, and looked out the window, seemingly mesmerized by the grimy windows and checked plastic table-cloths that covered the tables outside. "You're about to experience Heaven."

He killed the engine and shoved the door open. "Wait here, I'll be back in a second. Honk if you're horny...I mean, if you need me." He shot a grin over his shoulder and climbed out.

Fear filled me as he closed the door behind him and

disappeared into the diner. I scanned the busy street and watched the door. True to his word, he strode out with a brown paper bag in one hand and two shakes in the other.

I leaned over, yanked the handle, and shoved the door open, watching as he juggled and slid behind the wheel. The heady smell of onions and meat filled the cab. My stomach let out a savage snarl.

"I know, right?" he grinned proudly. "Best ribs and burgers this side of the city. A rogue called Jacko runs the place, caters for those with big appetites."

I had no idea what rogue meant, but the smell was divine. Arran turned and reached between us, placed the food on the rear seat, then started the Jeep once more. I expected we'd drive to some kind of bar, or maybe head back across the bridge to his side of the city, but instead, he checked the mirror and swung the wheel, taking us back to the highway.

The engine growled as we slipped onto the on-ramp once more. We hurtled along, Arran's wild nature getting the better of him as he pushed his foot against the accelerator. I waited for the panic to rise to the surface, waited for that gut-clenching fear to take hold. But instead of terror...I felt *free*, reckless and flying.

I closed my eyes at the racing of the engine, until my body went one way and my belly the other, sloshing hard in my insides. I opened my eyes to the familiar off-ramp. It was the same one I took every day...twice a day, the off-ramp that led to residential suburbs, *my suburb.*

And as we sped along the streets, growing closer and closer, I knew that's where we were headed.

"Arran—" I started, but the words dried up in my mouth.

"It's okay." He glanced toward me. I must've looked like hell, because his eyes widened and his breath came hard and fast. "Stay with me, mortal...stay with me."

My gut clenched as he turned along my street and pulled the Jeep over against the curb...right in front of my house.

"Level one," he muttered, turned off the engine, and sat for a second. "You still with me?"

I couldn't move...couldn't speak. I could only stare at the place I'd once called my home. My car was inside...*Dad's car.* The sleek Bentley was tucked away in the garage. I wasn't in it the night *it* happened. It wasn't the shimmering navy paintwork that'd been riddled with bullets, nor was it those front seats smeared with Russell's blood.

I could still see the Chrysler as it pulled up against the curb, waiting for me that day, still see that last day as clear as the first...and all the days in between.

Arran reached between us and dragged the bag of food to the front. My stomach clenched at the smell of the food. I fumbled with the seatbelt, snapped the clasp, and clawed for the door handle as I spilled free.

There was nothing in my belly, nothing but dry heaves. Arran was beside me in an instant, his hand rubbing my back.

"It's okay. It's all okay. It's just a reaction, breathe deep. It's going to pass. That's it...*that's the way.*"

I tried to focus on his voice, tried to bring myself back from the brink of whatever hell this was. Finally, my stomach settled and I sucked in deep breaths as I straightened.

"Well, that went better than expected," Arran smiled.

I turned and glared at the curled corners of his mouth and shining eyes as I snarled, "Fuck you, Arran."

"That's my mortal," he cheered, and straightened. "Now for food."

I swore he almost skipped as he went around the rear of the Jeep and climbed back behind the wheel. I hated him at that moment, hated his smile and his food. I hated how when I straightened and turned toward my house, that I didn't feel that brush of terror anymore.

I climbed back into the Jeep and didn't object when he handed me a wrapped burger and a massive container of fries. I watched my house, watched it like I'd never watched anything before, and I ate. Slow, tentative mouthfuls at first, until a savage hunger swept over me. Then I attacked the food, chomping down in great big bites until the sauce ran down my chin and dripped down my fingers.

"Good, *huh?*" Arran grinned.

He always fucking grinned. I liked him more when he was threatening and moody as fuck. I grabbed the shake and drank down half its contents before I started on the fries. But by the time I was halfway through, my belly protested. I dropped the fry back into the container and shook my head. "I can't...I can't eat anymore."

"Pussy," he taunted under his breath.

"*Hey!*" I swiped at his head, laughing as he ducked and chuckled.

I didn't dare waste the salt on the tips of my fingers on the back of his head. I sucked and licked, pressing my spine into the back of the seat and watching, bemused, as Arran gobbled up the rest of my fries, as well as the double helping of his own and the four burgers he hid somewhere in that bottomless stomach of his.

"There's more, right," I asked finally. "More stops on this drive?"

"Two more," he answered, the laughter bleeding from his voice. "You ready?"

"No."

"That's what I figured." He started the engine and pulled the Jeep out from the curb.

There was a stillness now. A quiet stillness. It wasn't contentment, nothing so *nice,* but a detachment, one that stayed with me all the way as we got back onto the highway and headed for the city.

I knew where we were going as soon as we made the on-ramp. This was a cruel walk down memory lane. What I didn't know was...*why?* I suspected even if I asked, Arran wouldn't know. He'd been elected guardian, soother, ice breaker. *Protector.*

I didn't hate him...apart from Alex, I didn't hate anyone. As we turned off and headed to the heart of the city, where Costello Corporation towered above all else, I felt...grateful. I reached out and placed my hand on his as he shifted gears. "I'm glad it's you."

There was no spark of amusement in his eyes when he turned to me, but a glint of pride over a fierceness I'd never seen before. In this moment, he was not just a Wolf, he was a man... righting the wrongs of another man, paving the way with his snark and his laughter, warming my heart and easing my fears—and buying me lunch while he was at it.

"I had you all wrong, Arran," I said as he glanced at the road once more.

His voice was a little deeper, a little huskier. "No, you had it right the first time. You made the right choice. But I figured if I couldn't have you as a lover, then I'd settle as a friend. You're the kind of woman men want to be around, Ruth."

"Look how well that turned out for me."

"You will overcome this. You'll fucking rise like a damn phoenix. I can already see it happening. It's in your DNA."

We drove past the business center, right into the heart of Crown City and stopped outside the jewel itself. But there was something different about it. No cars lined the street outside the revolving doors. No security guards stood at the entrance. No lawyers, liquidators, no elected officials and start-up geeks clustered in the sleek foyer. The doors were closed, white notices flapped where they were taped to the glass.

My hand was on the handle before I knew it.

"Ruth," Arran called as I shoved open the door and stepped out.

The white page stuck to the glass called to me. The black wording was just a blur until I got closer.

NOTICE
This building is now closed
Costello Corporation PTY Ltd
Cessation of business trading October 26, 2021
Appointment of Administrator: Bishop and Partners
Contact by appointment only 555-987658

I stared at the notice, and felt the whole world sway. *This building is now closed.* "That can't be right."

"Ruth," Arran called again. "Come back in the car. "

It was gone...in what? *Weeks?* "I ruined everything my father ever worked for. *Everything.* Gone...just like that."

The edges of the notice flapped wildly, making me wince with every twitch. He took it all. Everything...just like he said he would.

I'd like to say we had some good times, Ruth. But you ruined it... you ruined it all. Alexander's words surfaced and with them came that grip around my throat, and that bitter cold as I sank deeper and deeper into whatever hell he'd intended for me.

"Okay, that is enough," Arran growled as he pulled me toward the open car door. "Inside."

I couldn't feel my body, couldn't see anything other than that notice, even as Arran started the Jeep and swept us away.

He drove in silence, sneaking glances at me. "This is bullshit. I can't do this."

"You have one more place." Empty, and strange, the words spilled from me. "Finish it."

Alexander had made good on his promise. He took it all... everything I'd worked for, and everything I owned. I had nothing if I didn't have my company. *I had nothing.*

"You sure?"

I nodded and turned my head to stare out the window. I didn't need to feel the sway of the Jeep as we headed for the water. I didn't need to smell the salty air. I didn't need to feel the cold as we drove to that abandoned lot once owned by Costello Corporation.

It was just the same as I remembered, dirt road, small abandoned office, single light pole outside.

Blink, it was darkness...and I wasn't in a Jeep, I was in a Chrysler.

Blink, Arran turned to watch me.

Blink, a small blue car was in front of us, interior light on, doors wide open.

Blink, there was nothing but memories. Nothing but police tape as Arran pulled the Jeep to a stop.

"You don't have to get out—" he started.

But I was already yanking the handle and stepping out of the car. I was already staring at the calm waters of the river. *The river...*

Do you want out of those chains?

Elithien's words haunted me. Chains...that's what they were, every memory and every scar. Chains that held me under, chains that dragged me down. I lowered my gaze to the dirt parking area. In my head, I still saw it, the Chrysler's door open, silver-rimmed bullet holes piercing the black, my bodyguard lying there, coughing up his own blood.

Chains.

Chains.

Chains around me pulling me down. My fists curled, nails

driving deep into the flesh of my palms as I lifted my gaze to the sky and screamed. Hot...*burning,* the sound seared along my throat and raked the air with bloodied nails. Until it was over.

Until the sound was gone, and that quiet...*desperate* need was all that remained. Darkness was coming, barreling down on me. The light from the lamppost flickered and buzzed, splashing weak yellow light on the ground that slowly brightened.

I blinked into the glow, finding the lights of the harbor already twinkling in the night sky. But not from the Costello docks...not anymore.

The ports were barren. Ships just sailed by. They weren't even dragging the river for me anymore.

It was as though I'd never existed.

You'll rise from the ashes, like the damn phoenix you are. It's in your DNA.

I turned to find Arran wide-eyed, staring at me from across the Jeep's hood. "Phoenix, you said?"

He swallowed hard. "Yeah, a damn phoenix."

Darkness shimmered at the edges of my vision. I turned to the small, run-down office with its barred windows and faded notice of NO CASH KEPT ON PREMISES, and I was drawn to the edge of the building, where the faint evening sun didn't reach. Something moved within the shadows, something *darker.* A void. One that made me gasp.

"What is it?" Arran was all Alpha in an instant, surging forward to stand between me and the shifting shadows.

"Do you see that?" I whispered, and lifted a trembling finger to the edge of the building where I swore eyes watched me. "Right there."

"It is me, Wolf." Thunder rippled out from that patch of emptiness.

"Kapre?" Arran called, then jerked a panicked gaze over his shoulder to me.

Fear claimed him, giving off a faint bitter tang in the air until he steeled his spine and turned back to the void...a void that stepped around the corner of the building and slithered into the night, just a little closer to us.

It was shadows...shadows and terror all wrapped up in a faint outline that grew sharper against the dimming sun. "I wanted to see the mortal for myself."

Arran shifted as the thing grew closer. It was taller than a man, bigger than a Wolf, with eyes that held the night. My protector took a step forward, drawing the *beast's* gaze. "Are you here to harm her?"

The inky creature took a step closer, gliding forward without making a sound. "Harm her?" The words rolled through the air and slipped inside my head. *Harm her...harm her...harm her...*

"Unseelie," Arran warned, stepping into the beast's path.

I didn't cry, didn't tremble, didn't even move. If death came for me now at the hands of this creature, then so be it. I was free from the terror, free from the past, the present, and the future. "It's okay," I said as I stepped forward, around Arran and away from the light.

The inky beast just looked down at me, while I stared up as night closed in. "Are you afraid of me?"

"Yes."

The beast stared at me for what felt like an eternity, driving that midnight stare into my very soul. "The mortal is lucky... weak right now...but she will be strong. I have no doubt about it. Take care with her, Wolf. I'll be watching."

As if it was pulled by some force, the mammoth midnight creature slipped backwards, blending into the shadows of the building once more. I stared into the gloom, watching as the shifting shadows stilled, then I waited a little longer, until the night grew cold around me and the wind gliding off the river fluttered my hair.

Finally, I turned. My knees trembled as I hurried to the open passenger's door. I climbed inside, yanked the seatbelt across me, and nodded. "Okay, I'm done. Please get me the fuck out of here."

He wasn't a Wolf in that moment, he was a man…just a man, like most men. One who didn't know how to react when a woman was hurting. So he drove, taking me back over the bridge to our side of the river once more, and as night swept down with raven wings to cloak us in darkness, we headed to somewhere I wasn't expecting at all.

The Hunting Ground.

10

RUTH

"Here?" I cut a careful glare at Arran. "This some kind of ploy?"

"No ploy," the Wolf insisted, and pulled up alongside the curb outside the shifter nightclub.

The dancers had already started inside. The beat was slow and erotic, humming through the window. It reminded me of another night, when my emotions had gotten the better of me, a night when I was swept away in desire...until it all went horribly wrong.

"They're waiting for you inside," Arran advised.

I hadn't noticed that he'd made no move to climb out of the car, that the engine was still running. His focus lay straight ahead, staring at the spot where the headlights met the road.

"You're not coming in?"

A shake of his head, and a hint of a smile. "Not this time," he answered. "I've got other things to attend to. But you're safe in there, Ruth. You're always safe."

As a friend. He didn't need to say the words, I'd felt them all damn night. It was in every sad smile and every careful brush of his hand. It was in his words. Friends, just friends and nothing more. I reached over and placed my hand on his as he gripped the gearshift. "I'm glad to have you in my life, Arran. Very glad."

He just gave a nod, and that sad smile reappeared. I turned, yanked the handle, and stepped outside, letting the heavy beat of the music wash over me. I didn't wait for an introduction. I knew exactly who *'they'* were. My Vampires…my protectors.

My guardians.

I took a step forward, feeling a sense of freedom. This afternoon had been hard. *No.* Hard was an understatement. This afternoon had been fucking torture. But a freeing kind of torture, a clarifying torture.

But it wasn't my house that haunted me, or the parking lot beside the river where I almost lost my life. It was the notice on the window of my family's building that stayed with me as I pushed the door inward and stepped inside.

The bouncer stepped forward and lifted a hand before I met his gaze. "Don't tell me you're still giving me a hard time?"

The gruff, hard expression softened, and a smile replaced the frown. "Not you, Ms. Costello, you're free to come in."

"Wonders never cease," I muttered, and stepped down the stairs to the dance floor.

My atomic blonde dancer was back, dressed in a sheer black lace bodysuit and impossibly high heels. She dragged her shimmering white hair over her shoulder, caught my gaze as I passed, and gave me a wink.

It wasn't just the Vampires' den that was starting to feel like home. It was these streets, this nightclub…*this side of the river.* Never in a million years did I ever think I'd say those words. Not before that night in the alley…just shows you how fucked up my life has become.

"They're in the black room," the bartender informed me, lifting a hand and pointing to a door at the rear of the club.

I followed, feeling a flicker of amusement. *What could they possibly want here that we couldn't do at their place?* I pushed through the door and stepped into a pitch-black hallway. Tiny white lights lit up the space a bit at floor level, splashing against matte black walls. "What the hell?"

There was a single door at the end of the long hallway. Just one door, cracked open and waiting. I glanced over my shoulder and kept on walking, slowing my steps as I got to the door. "Elithien?"

"In here. Close the door behind you."

I stepped into the dim room as panic pushed to the surface. *It's okay, nothing will hurt you.*

Elithien was a brush across my mind, a sweeping sensation of power and protection all at once. He carved through me like wildfire, taking my breath...pulling me into him until he was all I wanted...all I needed. I closed the door and blinked into the gloom. There was a light in the back of the long room, a light that flickered and danced. The smell of sex clung in the air, sultry and heavy. I flinched at a low moan...*a woman's moan.*

"Do not turn around." Hurrow's command was cold...*forceful. So unlike him.* "Do not make a sound. Do you understand me?"

"Yes." A woman breathed quietly...so damn quiet.

It was the first time I heard her. The closer I came, the brighter the flame. Rows of candles ran along the tiled floor, leaving an orange glow to flicker against bare legs. Long, lean, *gorgeous* legs.

"What's going on?" I asked as she came into view.

A woman.

Facing the wall.

With her hands tied behind her back. Trussed up in lashings of rope.

Rope that criss-crossed the entire length of her arms.

Rope that pressed against tender flesh, making it plump between the strands. So soft, so...*erotic.* My heart stuttered, then raced as I lowered my gaze to the rope cutting between her legs, pressing the mid-thigh leather skirt hard against the curve of her ass, and panic mingled with heat. I licked my lips, breathless. "What's going on here?"

"It's okay." Elithien rose from a seat on the opposite wall and crossed the room.

What was this...some kind of sex play? Some kind of *introduction to what he liked?* My knees were shaking...making me stop in the middle of the room. "I'm not into women, if that's what this is."

"What?" Hurrow barked. *"No!* You think we...?"

"It's you we want, Ruth," Elithien murmur reassured, stepping closer. "Only you. All this...*for you.*"

I turned my head to look at her once more. Bound, *exposed.*

"You want out of those chains, don't you?" Elithien came closer, so close he brushed my body with his. But not once did he touch me. Not once did he make me yield. "You hunger to be free. If you let us help you, we can show you how to have just that."

"Freedom." Rule shoved off from against the wall and stepped toward me.

"But only if you want it." Justice growled, staring at the back of her. "It has to be your choice."

*No...*the word swept through my head but it didn't reach my lips.

"The same chains that give you terror can give you the freedom you crave." Elithien instructed. "All you have to do is trust us. Can you trust us, Ruth?"

I was consumed by the raw, *desperate* maleness of them. Still, I was drowning inside, slipping under the surface, weighed down by the weight of my own terror. I turned to the woman standing silently against the wall. I saw what this was now...this was no betrayal, no invitation to taste another.

This was an introduction, this was a cracked-open door. All I saw was her body...the marks on her flesh, the hard arch of her shoulders, breasts straining against her black lace bra. "You want to hurt me?"

"Hurt you?" Hurrow shook his head. "No...*never.*"

"Does this hurt?" Rule queried, standing beside the woman. I hadn't even seen him move. He reached out and gently tugged on the rope until it pressed taut around the base of her throat. But it wasn't choking, not anywhere near enough to cause her distress.

Just pressure.

Just...*the sensation.*

The woman let out a moan, and whispered, "No."

"Touch her," Elithien directed, that steely stare seizing mine. "See how the rope binds but doesn't hurt...see how it crosses over her chest." He turned his head toward the woman. "Chelsea, turn around."

She did as he instructed and soft brown eyes glazed with desire met mine. The rope cut across her breasts, two taut strands pressing against her bra. Her nipples were hard and puckered, dusty peaks straining between the lacy strands. I followed the rope as it spanned across her stomach before diving between her thighs.

"You can touch me if you want," she invited.

Touch her? My mind swam and swirled. All my emotions...all my grief...*all my chains.* They swirled around me, filling me with fear...and terror. I shook my head and took a step backwards. "I can't...I can't do this."

The walls closed in around me, until the flickering candles started to blur. I was in the water once more, the pressure around my throat...*choking.*

"I'm sorry." Tears blurred my gaze as I stepped backwards, then turned to race for the door.

I made it along the hallway, and slammed out the door onto the dance floor. The music throbbed, making the panic worse.

"Ruth," Elithien called behind me.

I was in his arms before I knew it, pressed hard against his chest, his arms wrapped around me.

"It's okay," he whispered. "It's all going to be okay. We'll figure this out...*we'll find a way.*"

But how could someone fight the monsters in my head... how could someone save me from my past?

How could someone...even someone like Elithien, save me from myself?

Footsteps resounded around us as my Vampires closed in.

"We'll take you home," Hurrow soothed, and gripped my hand in his.

The steps were a blur, the bouncer inside the doorway, too. I was whisked through the darkness and into the four-wheel drive. I wanted the darkness. I wanted the night. I wanted the safety of the steel doors of my bedroom...and most of all...I wanted that white notice on the front of my building out of my head.

"You're safe now," Elithien assured calmly, holding me in the back seat of the car. "You're safe."

11

ELITHIEN

I pushed her too hard...drove her to the edge before she could handle it.

Too soon.

She still shuddered in my arms, and stifled sobs made choking noises in the back of her throat that eventually turned silent.

Too goddamn soon.

I closed my eyes, and held her close to me, hating every fucking thing this world had to offer.

*I'll fix it...*I pushed the words toward her. *I'll fix you. I promise.*

She said nothing, just slowly pulled away to stare out her window. I'd rather listen to her sobs than suffer the goddamn silence, rather take her blows than feel her warmth slip away from me. But that was what was happening now. She was pulling away from us, withdrawing into herself. There was nothing I could say now...nothing that would undo what I'd done.

*I'm sorry...*the words floated through my mind. But still, I couldn't trust myself to speak.

I'm...

So.

Fucking.

Sorry.

Her shoulders sagged and her hand rose, fingers touching the cold glass. It was all about her now, every move...every decision. My every fucking need...*to protect...to avenge.* The car slowed as we pulled up at the house. I yanked open the door before we rolled to a stop and stepped out of the car.

The wind picked up as I closed the door behind me, carving right to my goddamn soul. I dropped my hand to the buttons of my jacket, worked them free, and shrugged it from my shoulders as I opened her door.

She was so goddamn small, stepping out of the car and into my arms. I lowered my head, slid the jacket over her, and inhaled the perfection of her. She smelled like onions and burgers, salty fries and sad laughter. "Let's get you settled."

She forced a small, sad smile, and nodded. "I'm just tired."

She slipped free of me, just like I knew she would. Pain roared to the surface, stinging like the lash of a whip as she grasped the jacket around her shoulders and stepped away from my touch.

Hurrow looked at me, waiting for my nod. Of course I'd send him to her. I motioned for the Vampire to go to her, to take her hand...to give her what she needed, and watched as they stepped up to the front door and slipped inside.

Headlights splashed around me, bathing me in luminescence as Justice and Rule pulled the Explorer beside me and killed the engine. I waited for them to climb out...waited for the glance in my direction...waited for them to shoot a glance to one another before one of them worked up the courage to approach.

"You going to stay out here?" Justice inquired. "Want some company?"

I shook my head. "No...*thank you.*"

"You want me to pour the Scotch?" Rule offered.

"Sure." I gave a nod, trying my best to put them at ease.

But it wasn't working. They just *hovered,* until the vibration in my pocket started. I shoved my fingers inside and yanked the damn thing free. I didn't need to look at the caller ID. I knew exactly who was calling.

"Yes."

That one word said it all. Underneath my simple command was everything I dared not speak. *Give me something here...before I go insane.*

"We found him."

I stared into Justice's gaze. "Where?"

"Tracked the piece of shit all the way to Guatemala, then lost him."

"Lost him...how the fuck did that happen?"

There was a curl of Justice's lip as his wicked fangs lengthened. I swallowed the rising rage, pushing it under the stony exterior.

"Your boy either has a fuckload of money to spend or friends in *very* high places. This wasn't just *any* disappearing act, Elithien. This was ghosting like you've never seen before. I have my best team on this."

I lifted my wrist and stared at the Rolex. "How long ago?"

"Three hours. My men are still scouring the city. If he's still there, they'll find him."

"The Wolves..." I started.

"They won't give up, won't rest. They will hunt this motherfucker down, Elithien."

"Spare no expense," I insisted. "None. Whatever you have to do."

"I'll stay in touch."

I ended the call and dropped my hand.

"We should be there." Justice met my gaze.

"The Breeds will take care of it." I forced the words, desperate to fight my own feeling of helplessness as I shifted my gaze to the open door of the house. "They'll do what needs to be done. Our place is here…right where she needs us to be."

"What, so we can sit here and watch her crumble?" Justice shook his head and clenched his fists.

"If that's what she needs, then that's what we do." Even as I said the words, they rang false.

A woman like Ruth didn't crumble, not really. She might fall…might hit the ground and skin her knees. But someone like her didn't stay down for long. She'd find a way to get to her feet. If not through pleasure and release…then we'd find another way.

The cell phone vibrated once more in my hand. I glanced at the caller ID this time, finding the word *WAREHOUSE* flashing across the screen before I pressed the icon. "What is it?"

"It seems you and I have a problem," Shrike announced.

The hairs on my arms rose as the quietly controlled Unsleelie's voice washed over me. "We do?"

The money…something's happened to the money. The panic filled my head.

"Your bodyguard isn't just alive. He's now awake…*and he's asking for her.*"

I clenched my jaw until the *crack* tore through my head, and forced the words. "That's impossible."

"Apparently not."

"You assured me…"

"I said I'd keep him alive. How was I supposed to know the sonofabitch was fucking stubborn?"

I winced at the words. It seemed when it came to Ruth, most males were prepared to do almost anything to have her in their lives…and when they couldn't…well…they wouldn't be alive long enough to worry about that, would they?

"I think it's best you come," Shrike *suggested.*

There was nothing demanding about the request…but an Unseelie like Shrike didn't need to command. Words were sparse from the Fae, but when they spoke, it meant you were to listen...and read between the lines.

"I'll be there," I replied, and hung up the call before lifting my gaze to the others. "You go on ahead. I'll be back soon."

They just nodded, leaving me to stride around the rear of the Explorer and climb into the driver's seat. I pressed the button, started the engine, and pulled the four-wheel drive around, heading for the warehouse once more.

Guatemala...

The place nagged at me. What would a walking dead man like Alexander Sewell be doing in a place like that...especially when he was on the run?

The Breed would find him. If anyone could, it'd be them. I paid them enough to do it. Hunters like those didn't come cheap. Genetically enhanced, lethally trained, they were special operations like none that had been created before. Military... government, and owing allegiance to no goddamn Inner Circle. They were *outside* the damn Circle.

Beasts for hire.

Weapons of choice.

You name it, they were it; Fae, Vampire, Wolf, and creatures no one wanted to know about...not until they needed them, at least. They were dangerous...*a dangerous breed indeed.*

I grabbed my phone and slid my thumb across the screen before I pressed the contact and waited for it to be answered. I didn't need to wait long.

"Yes, sir."

"Have the jet fueled and ready. Be prepared to go wheels-up within thirty minutes from my next call."

"Destination?"

"Guatemala," I answered, and hung up.

I was heading there, just as soon as I received the call, and there wasn't a damn thing alive that'd stop me. Nothing at this moment was more important than finding the lawyer. I clenched my grip around the wheel—*nothing.*

City lights sparkled in the distance. But I didn't see them. In my head, I was another country away, one with bright painted buildings and fairly quiet nightlife. The kind of place where a man like Alexander could spend eternity...*at the bottom of a shaft.*

I turned the wheel and gunned the engine, taking the corner hard as I tore past the row of strip clubs and bars Phantom handled. The street was filled with them, just one of many. The Wolves handled more than most realized, with eighty percent of the city's bars and sex workers working for them.

They were honest, and protective...and fucking brutal when it came to providing a safe work environment for their employees. More than one john had gone missing after leaving a mark on one of their girls. Word had spread...now business was booming, in a safe, honorable manner...and we just needed to keep it that way.

I hit the turning signal and braked, pulling up hard at the automatic gates until they opened enough to drive through. The warehouse was obviously closed, the windows darkened, security cameras mounted around the exterior of the tall building.

Anyone would think the place was deserted...and they'd be wrong.

I pulled the Explorer up at the set of outside stairs that led to the external door. Only three people had the combination for that door...and as I shoved open the car door and felt the hairs rise on the back of my neck, I knew two of us were here.

I locked the car and climbed the stairs, all the way to the keypad. The tiny red light flashed to green with the eight-digit combination. I jerked the handle and was inside in an instant.

Jesus. The sour stench of desperation and rage hit me as I stepped inside, and for a second, it was all I could do to keep from turning away...and leaving the male behind. He wasn't supposed to live. I strode along the hallway to the bank of rooms at the rear of the building. *He wasn't supposed to survive...*

A *crash* ripped along the hallway, followed by savage snarls. There was a bark of dominance but that only seemed to rile the...*beast* up. The walls shook...I stopped dead in the middle of the hallway. *The walls fucking shook.* The tremor spilled through the floor and into my boots.

I lifted my gaze from the shuddering floor of the sold brick fucking warehouse to the end of the hallway as the air became unnaturally still. Hairs on my arms stood on end as I sensed the...*predator,* and he sensed me.

I turned my thoughts inward to the power of my Immortal being, and tasted the air.

The beast turned his attention to me.

Yeah...that's right. I'm here, you stubborn fucking human.

A growl slipped through the air, and at the end of the hallway, a door opened. One of the Fae stepped out. A towering brute of an Immortal. Thick muscled shoulders strained the white collared shirt he wore. There was blood...a lot of blood, like an arterial splatter, that ran along the side. The ghastly sight only grew bolder as he sensed me behind him and turned...and connected with my gaze.

"Elithien," the Fae warrior growled.

"Ruin," I responded, my gaze dropping to the arc of crimson that cut across his shirt.

I didn't need to be a crime scene expert to know what had happened. He'd hurt the bodyguard, probably forced the bastard into chains. It must've been Ruin I'd sensed as I stepped inside the warehouse.

Ruin that had made the hairs on my arms stand on end.

Ruin that had made the damn floor tremble and quake. "I hope you left him somewhat intact for me to question." I jerked my gaze back to the thick stream of blood as the door opened once more.

"That's not his blood." Shrike's deep rumble spilled through the air. "That's...*mine.*"

I stared at the towering Unseelie as he stepped out behind his second-in-command and shook my head. All that thick, heavy muscle and that smoky shimmer his caste had were like a fucking shield. Magic clung to him, dark magic...*Unseelie magic.* "No...that can't..."

A sound came from inside the room...like the yawning gate of Hell opened wide and all the bleakest atrocities spilled out. It was a forbidding sound, a sinister, threatening sound. A *promise* to all those who stood in his way. And as that snarl rebounded from the walls and engulfed the building, Shrike lifted his hand and cupped the base of his neck.

He was a powerful Immortal. *A terrifyingly powerful Immortal.* One I'd seen on the battlefield...only once. And once was all it took...to know my place was as his ally and *not* his enemy.

My gaze drifted to the door...and to the creature that waited inside for me.

A creature that should *never* have existed...

"I *want* to see her," that *thing* inside the room growled, and the clank of chains followed. I could feel the tension spilling out from inside the room, feel it come *alive.* "Ruth...Ruth Costello. I *can smell her on you.*"

Rage pushed to the surface, that savage part of me that made me closer to beast than I was to man. I forced myself to move, striding closer as Shrike shook his head.

He stepped forward to meet me and lifted one massive hand to my shoulder. "You don't want to go in there."

"It's why you called me, isn't it?" The words were a little too cold...a little too *Vampire.*

Whatever waited in there for me was my problem to take care of....my problem to *solve.* I'd solve it...regardless.

The Fae commander gave a slow nod and stepped to the side. Darkness drew around him like a cloak. Piercing midnight eyes shone from the powerful gloom as he took a step, stopping at my side. "For what it's worth...I'm sorry."

The words didn't instill a whole lot of confidence, especially when Ruin followed close behind him, leaving me with whatever waited inside that room. It didn't wait long...issuing a guttural command. "Come in and face me, Vampire. See what you have done."

I stepped closer, gripped the door handle, and smelled the blood. Black smeared across my palm as I twisted the handle and pushed the door open wide.

He stood at the rear of the room, hands shackled with inch-thick steel. The links ran to two points on the wall, then down, leaving his hands splayed out from his body...*so how in the hell did he damage a Fae like Shrike?*

The bodyguard's head was bowed as he stared at the floor. He was shirtless...the black pants he was killed in were strained across powerful thighs. If he was considered a military weapon before his transition...then there was no word for what he was now.

*Formidable...*the word came to mind as he slowly lifted his head. Darkness shone in the cruel glint of his midnight eyes. Moonlight spilled through the small windows high above, bouncing off the hard planes of his cheeks like sheets of glass.

There were no words to describe the feeling inside the room. I clenched my jaw, forcing myself to stand still and meet him face to face, to see what he'd become. *Bloodthirsty. Merciless...Inhuman.*

His chest rose as he inhaled hard. Shadows shifted all around him, gathering higher, making him appear to *consume the room.* His fingers grew, hanging limply in midair from the shackles. So help me God, as I stood there, the tips of his fingers tapered, claws grew from his nails, and turned as black as midnight. That darkness raced like rot to claim his hands, then his wrists, consuming his forearms like some kind of disease. *Unseelie.* The word pushed to the forefront of my mind. Muscles across his chest tightened as he strained against the shackles. "Is she...is she alive?"

"Yes."

The glint in his eyes shone that little bit brighter, like he'd somehow captured the night and drew it into his soul. I had to remember not *who* he was...but *what* he was. What *I'd made*.

He'd been born mortal...but he was so far beyond that now. Kapre's blood moved through his veins. The Unseelie creature was the single most deadly creature of all the Fae.

I'd known one drop of his blood would save the bodyguard...but two might kill him.

I'd hoped for two...*I'd fucking banked on it.*

Then I could console her, tell her we tried our best...that death had staked its claim and his soul was at rest. I'd hold her while she cried. I'd kiss away her tears. I'd be safe with the knowledge that I was a man of my fucking word...

But this...this fucking male...had a whole fucking quart of Kapre's blood flowing through his veins. *A whole fucking* quart!

"Has she asked about me?"

*Lie...*the thought rose to the surface, but pity reared its pathetic head. "Yes, she's asked about you."

A hardness swept across his face. "Did you tell her I was dead?"

I didn't answer, only stared as the man slipped away. He changed, morphing into something terrifying, something I was unable to put into words. That glint in his eyes turned savage, and his body seemed to swell, driving muscle against steel.

"Did you?" he growled ferociously as he grew to swallow the room...and the walls began to shake. "Did you tell her I was *dead?* Did you look her in the eye while you lied to her? *Did you tell her...DID YOU TELL HER I DIED?"*

The floor trembled and the night seemed to quake. There was something savagely *unhinged* about him, something no

ATLAS ROSE

longer human...something not even Fae. He was every unmerciful...terrifying fear come to life.

"Yes," I admitted. "I told her you were dead."

He stilled then, like time itself no longer mattered. Slow, hard breaths came, almost silent, as those cutting words drew blood.

Relief washed over him, twisting his face into a mask of agony. "Good...good. I don't want her seeing me like this. I don't want her anywhere near me. I'm not...not in control of myself."

"Don't worry," I answered coldly. "I'll be sure to keep her as far away from you as possible."

He just nodded, and lowered his gaze to the floor once more. I turned on my heel and strode toward the door.

"But you...you so much as lay a breath on her she doesn't like, then we're going to have a problem."

My hand trembled as I gripped the handle.

"I don't like you," he declared. "And I know you don't like me, so let's not pretend."

"Yes...let's not pretend," I responded, yanking open the door and striding out of the room, leaving the beast, my own fucking burden, behind.

I made my way to the CCTV room and the large office the Fae used as their meeting room. Rage seethed inside me, first the fucking lawyer and now the bodyguard. It was starting to become difficult to remember a time when my life wasn't turned upside down by the mortal woman.

The kicker was...I'd do it all again, just to have her, to hold her.

If the mutated guard thought I'd hurt so much as a hair on her head, then he didn't know me at all. I stepped through the rows of darkened monitors and made my way to the glass door at the end of the room. Movement shifted inside...Shrike...*and Phantom?* The Wolf lifted his head as I opened the door and stepped through. "Did I miss something?"

Shrike just nodded toward a seat. "We wanted to wait…"

"But you know me," Phantom grumbled. "I go right for the fucking throat."

I readied myself for the onslaught as I closed the door and took a seat at the head of the table. But I didn't let the position go to my head. We were all equals here. In Crown City there was no turf war. It came down to respect…and honesty, and if that meant we were brutal in our delivery, then that only strengthened our bonds.

"If we said we weren't worried about drawing attention, Elithien, then we'd be lying," Phantom explained, and leaned back against his seat.

"The last thing we need is the Inner Circle on our doorstep," Shrike added. "And things like that…" he pointed to the rear of the building, "are bound to get back to them."

"I understand," I said, nodding, as my own fear bloomed.

Alliard's death was fresh…so fucking fresh, and even though the Inner Circle cared little about mortal details, if word got out we'd betrayed them—then they might care very much indeed.

"The mortal woman," Shrike started.

Anger punched to the surface, cutting like a sword. "No. She stays. I take full responsibility."

"Then you need to finish this…you need to keep it quiet. Things have to go back to normal." Phantom held my gaze. "No more cops, no more Costellos. Change her hair…*Hell,* change her *name* If you have to. But she can't be who she is over here, E. Or she might be the death of it all."

"The lawyer?" Shrike cut in.

"In fucking Guatemala. The Breeds are on it."

"Villain?" Phantom's brow rose.

I gave a nod.

"Shit. He's a vicious bastard. The lawyer's as good as dead."

Not before I get my hands on him. Then he'll wish I'd thrown him to the fucking Wolves…

"Then it's just the bodyguard," Shrike muttered with a wince.

His hand automatically went to his neck. Did he still feel the bite? I had no answer for that one...and we were well past a bullet to the head.

I rose from the table, leaving the other heads of the Immortals behind, and strode from the room...and the building, heading out into the night. I didn't shake that uncomfortable feeling as I climbed into the Explorer and drove home. I didn't shake it at all. If anything, it seemed to grow as I drove through the winding roads all the way back.

Did you look her in the eye while you lied to her? The bodyguard's words haunted me. *Did you tell her...DID YOU TELL HER I DIED?*

"I only wish I had," I mumbled, and pressed the accelerator to the floor. "It'd be better for all involved."

But I hadn't...and my Ruth was waiting...

12

RUTH

He wants to hurt me. The words resounded inside my head. I wasn't naive, nor was I a goddamn prude. I'd had my fair share of kinky sex, a little hair pulling, a nice slap on the ass. But there was nothing sexual about rope burns to my wrists, or a knot against my throat.

Nothing about that turned me on in the least.

I looked at myself in the bathroom mirror. Gaunt cheeks, dark circles around my eyes, my body was different now, all jutting bones and sagging skin. I looked old...older than I ever had before, and I felt it, too. I didn't look like I used to.

Do not turn around. Do not make a sound. Do you understand me?

Hurrow's command surfaced as I gripped the basin. I closed my eyes, recapturing the cold, stony tone. He cared nothing for the woman in front of him. He barely saw her, barely even registered she was there. But he wanted her there. *No, he needed* her there—for me.

Do not turn around.

Would he use that same icy tone on me? Would he be the monster under the mask...for me? I still felt his lips on my body, his big hands as they slipped my panties down. I still felt the scrape of those fangs on the throb of my clit.

Desire made me swallow hard. But it was a cruel desire, one mixed with sadness...one etched with fear. *Do not make a sound.* A shudder swept through me, catching my breath. I knew he wanted me...knew he'd fight for me. I knew he'd even kill for me. They were, after all, killers.

Could he speak to me like he spoke to her?

Could he demand...

And take?

I shook my head, opened my eyes, and looked at my own reflection. "I can't do that. *I won't do it.*" I lifted my hand and touched the base of my throat. In an instant, the panic washed over me again. My heart thundered and my knees turned weak. The white walls inside the bathroom started to blur.

My chest tightened and my heart hammered, beating so fast I couldn't catch my breath. I reached for my throat as the darkness moved in. "Hurrow." His name tore from my lips as the panic mushroomed.

Heart attack. The words rose in my mind, and that numbing cold moved in.

My teeth chattered and I clawed at the edge of the basin as I started to fall.

A cold breeze swept over me and strong arms caught my fall, lifting me, cradling me.

"I've got you," he soothed. "You're safe, Ruth. You're safe."

Still the panic swallowed me, blurring the bright lights until we sank into the shadows of the bedroom once more.

"You're okay," Hurrow insisted as he lay me on the bed.

But I wasn't okay. I wasn't anywhere near okay, and as much as I tried to claw my way out from under the rock, it still pinned my leg. All I could see was the woman from the bar, her hands bound behind her, the rope between her thighs, and that look of desire in her eyes...that *need.*

In an instant, that image turned into something else, a moment that blazed neon bright in my mind. The last moment I was happy...the last moment I was safe. I was in the car with Russell, we were driving back from my home, and my thoughts were filled with the Vampires. "All I wanted was you."

"Ruth?" Hurrow questioned, and knelt on the floor to stare up into my eyes. "You with me, here?"

I tried to nod, tried to do anything but struggle against that rock pinning me under. That last moment...that last goddamn moment and I was frustrated...pissed off with myself, and my...*damn phone.*

A red light blinked in my mind. "I forgot to charge it, my phone." I lifted my gaze to Hurrow, but in my head, all I saw was that red fucking light...

Ruth. Call me when you get this message. It's urgent.

The message from Ace flashed into my mind as the panic melted away. "The message." My heart boomed in my ears. "I forgot about the goddamn message."

"What message?"

That panic of being tied up was pushed to the side. My heart thundered for another reason now. It was all I had to hold onto...all I could see. That blinking red light from my phone in the car and that message...*it's urgent.* "Ace. The message from Ace. He needed me, and I forgot all about him."

Lightning moved in his eyes. There was a twitch at the corner of his mouth as Hurrow straightened. "Who the hell is this...*Ace?*"

"Relax, Tarzan," I calmed him. "He's a hacker friend of mine. I found a USB from Judah and Blane when I thought they were the ones behind the attacks. It had a file I couldn't open, some kind of encryption, Ace said. He'd had the thing for a couple of months. I assumed it was a dud, or one he couldn't open."

"So why the damn message?"

I sucked in a deep breath and my panic vanished. My mind

---

was racing now, mingling with that sense of falling. I wasn't falling now...I was floating, suspended by my past, as I answered, "I don't know. But there's one way to find out."

"Do you think that's safe?" Justice asked from the doorway.

I jerked my gaze to the shadows, to where the towering male stood with his arms crossed over his expansive chest. "It is if I have an escort..."

Silence filled the air as he stared at me with that stony gaze. I'd hurt him before in the shower. Whatever I'd said struck some kind of nerve. I still felt the sting, like an exposed thing, pulsing and aching. If you'd asked me a second ago how I could understand him better, how I could somehow bridge this gap between the mortal and the Immortal, I wouldn't have known where to begin.

But I knew I had to start somewhere.

This felt like that *somewhere* could be this. Common ground...a *purpose* between us. "I could find a way to meet with him, if you're willing to help me?"

Justice pushed off the wall. The heavy thud of his boots on the floor filled my ears as he strode toward me. He commanded the space, *swallowed* the space, until Hurrow stood and moved out of the giant's way.

"I'd be nothing but honored to be your shield," Justice assured me. "But I'm not taking you *anywhere* until we know who this Ace is...and we meet on our side of the river."

I shook my head. "He's not..." the words dried up with the glare from Justice.

"He is if we say he is," the Vampire declared. "From now on, Ruth, everyone is vetted by me...or Hurrow. No one comes anywhere near you without going through one of us. Am I clear?"

Heat rushed to my cheeks, and with it came the flare of anger.

But there was something else...

The way he looked at me.

The way he leaned his body toward me.

The way he drew my scent in with every hard, savage breath.

He dared me. Dared me all the goddamn way.

Fuck me...I liked it.

"Fine," I snarled, trying to push that lick of desire away as he rose, still looking down at me. Jesus, I'd never been so turned on.

I couldn't command him, that's what it was. I couldn't command and demand and *expect him to fall in line.* There was no *'in line'* with the Vampires, no yielding to my demands. We were two immovable forces...one of us had to give.

"So, if you still want to do this, I'm going to need to speak to this...*Ace.*"

Hurrow smothered a bark of laughter and shifted his gaze.

"Something *funny?*" I asked.

There was a shake of his head as Hurrow took a step backwards. "I'm going to leave you two to...work this all out. Call if you need backup."

If I needed backup? I clenched my jaw as the Vampire hurried out. But Justice waited, Mr. Cool, Calm, and Biting. "I suppose you want his name, date of birth, and Social Security Number?"

"Do you have that?" he asked, one brow rising and shifting the leather patch over his eye.

"No, I don't have *that,*" I growled. "There's only one way we're going to get anywhere near Ace for you to stare him down with whatever it is you're doing." I waved my hand toward him.

"And what *exactly* am I doing?" he queried, leaning close once more.

I was drawn to his lips and the hard ridge of his jaw. I was captivated by the *hardness* of him. The icy cold exterior. *Just fuck me already.* Jesus, I felt like a damn teenager. "Nothing." I forced the word. "You're not doing a damn thing."

A smug nod, and he straightened, satisfied. "Now, you were saying…"

"Pekingese," I answered. "That's how we make contact."

"Pekingese?" he repeated.

"Did I stutter?"

It was his turn to be dumbstruck, his turn to look at me with a whole fresh expression. I clawed hold of that tiny spark in my belly. Blew gently with a desperate breath. I wanted that fire to fill me once more. I wanted that *burn*.

"Pekingese," he said it again for good measure. "Sounds like a damn rodent, but let's do it."

It wasn't a rodent. It was the only way Ace would ever let me contact him. "I need a computer and access to the internet."

One wave of his hand, and I stood from the bed. My knees trembled for a second before I found the steel in my spine and marched to the door. The Wolves' nightclub lingered in the back of my mind as I stepped up to the keypad and punched in the code.

Heavy footsteps echoed behind me. I wondered if this is what she felt when the ropes around her body bit tight. Did she feel that rush of vulnerability? Did she feel that tremor of being solely reliant on another?

I strode through the doors as they opened, and the *thud* of the front door filled the air as we went down the hall. Elithien was like a storm rolling in, dark…*dangerous,* filled with turbulent destruction. He lifted his head, catching sight of me, and stopped in the middle of the living room.

Something passed between us, fear…apprehension. He was rattled…that was easy to see.

"You okay?" I headed toward him.

"Fine." He forced a smile, but he wasn't fine…but whatever it was, he wasn't sharing.

"Trust goes both ways, Elithien." I held his gaze. "It starts here."

Justice shifted behind me in an attempt at drawing the Alpha's gaze. But his didn't move from mine. Instead, Elithien swallowed hard and spoke. "The men I hired to find Alexander have hit a dead end...in Guatemala. Do you have any idea why he's gone there?"

Because he was once my lover...and until recently, there was still hope between us. Enough for him to share at least that much. But there wasn't hope between us...and he never shared a damn thing with me. Even at the end...when I'd felt his hands around my throat. "No, he's never mentioned it."

"Did you have access to any of his personal files? Maybe there's something we can use."

"We have that hard drive from his apartment," Justice added. "I have one of the Wolves working on it."

Hard drive.

Apartment.

Guatemala.

The walls of the house closed in. My breath lightened, coming hard and fast.

"But that's not all," Justice continued. "It seems there's a hacker friend called Ace that tried to reach out to her. Something about a Pekingese."

"You mean the dog place, Paws and Things, right?" Elithien was talking to me.

"You...know it?" I responded as that night returned to me and, with it, that feeling of being watched.

"Yes, the hacker's strange...but approachable," he answered, lifting his head to Justice. "Which makes him dangerous." He stepped away. "Justice, make sure he's put through the test."

The test?

But Elithien was gone...without bothering to explain what he meant by that. I turned on my heels and faced the towering Vampire. "Test...*what test?*" He just gave a shrug, which only pissed me off. "Don't just shrug at me. *What damn test?*"

"Call it a litmus test for any male that comes near you," he answered.

"And what exactly is the deciding factor of this...*test?*"

"Me," he clarified with a smug smile. "If they can get past me."

I winced as that spark of fire inside me turned to a flame. "Your fangs are showing, Vampire," I snapped, and walked out of the office...putting as much distance between me and the overbearing Goliath as I could.

But it didn't work. He just shadowed me, like I knew he would.

My life wasn't my own anymore. Nor my acquaintances or my friends, not that I had many of those left. But Ace was someone I could trust...someone I protected from the rest of my life. He didn't see the name, or the flashy cars...he saw me. The woman. I needed that now, more than ever.

"He's my friend," I said quietly as Justice followed me into the study.

"Then he's got nothing to worry about," he stated, stopping behind me.

He was close...*so damn close.* The hairs on my arms stood on end. I had never felt like this before with anyone. *Anyone mortal, anyway.*

I waited for the brush of his fingers along my arm, *craved* for the seduction, the thrill of knowing they could have any other woman in the world standing right here...but they wanted me.

Me.

Ruth Costello.

But instead of the drag of fingertips across my shoulder and down my spine, the towering Vampire just lowered his head to the back of my neck and turned his head to murmur, "When I fight *with* you, then I fight *for* us. Because if I didn't care, then I wouldn't bother."

With a draw of breath, he straightened and stepped around

me to the desk, where a laptop waited. His fingers moved fast as he leaned over the keyboard. I couldn't take my eyes off him. The way he entranced me amazed me, the way they all entranced me.

I could love them for a lifetime and still I'd never truly know them.

Not their thoughts or their purpose.

I didn't know anything about them…and all of a sudden, I realized they knew everything about me. There wasn't a moment in my life they didn't see in my memories. I caught my breath. I was as vulnerable to them as I was to Alexander…but still…

Still they grew hungrier, more predatory…

More determined to keep me safe.

If I didn't care, then I wouldn't bother.

Justice straightened and lifted his gaze from the screen to me. Heat sizzled between us…savage and unmerciful. In the steely shine of his eye, I saw how much I affected him. The tips of his white fangs peeked out as he licked his lips. "Keep looking at me like that, female, and we're not going to meet anyone tonight, friend or otherwise."

That was no threat…*that was a promise.*

I forced myself to move, rounding the desk as Justice dragged out the chair. His fingers brushed the tops of my shoulders as I sat. One smooth drag and my hair cascaded over one shoulder, leaving my neck bare.

I tried to focus, punched the website name into the address bar, and waited for the site to load.

"Pekingese training for beginners, huh?" he read, and let his touch travel over my shoulder and down my arm.

My fingers stopped, and my eyes closed of their own accord. My heart was racing, skin shivering in the wake of his fingers. "I can't…I can't concentrate when you do that."

"Then maybe you'll remember that the next time you look at

me like you want me to fuck you right then and there. Because one more glance, Ruth...one more *fucking glance,* and I'm not going to use all my fucking strength to hold myself back."

Jesus. My heart thundered, panicked and exhilarated, filling my head with a deafening rumble. My body didn't know if it wanted to run for its life or rip my clothes off and drop to my knees in front of him.

I bet he was fucking hard, too...

No. *No.* I squashed the thought and forced my eyes open. "Glad we got that straight."

Got a question about your Pekingese? Join Harvey and the Crew. I clicked on the forum and started typing, using all the codewords that Ace would trace. "Come on, Ace. Don't let me down."

The forum was alive tonight, hackers and meets taking place in the blink of an eye.

I'm looking for Horne...

Nothing. The chatter kept rolling until there was a *beep.* Lights flickered on a box at the side of the keyboard.

"What's that?" I asked, and stopped as the screen lit up.

"Nothing, just your boy sending out feelers." Justice leaned over me, punched some keys, and the screen settled. "He's good, I'll give him that."

"Good?"

Justice glanced down at me. "He just hacked our system in less than five seconds, so I'd say that's pretty damn impressive."

"Hacked your system. You mean he knows who you are?"

"Oh, he knows alright. Or he knows what we want him to know, anyway."

A charge of fear mingled with excitement as the forum screen lit up.

Horne: Same place, same time. If you are who you say you are, then you'll know exactly what to do.

I sucked in a deep breath. He was the first person I'd reached out to, the first person after being dragged from the river. My thoughts turned to Russell, and that heaviness filled my chest.

Ace was the first, but he wasn't the only one I wanted to see. All I had to do now was convince Justice to take me to see my bodyguard…and hope to God Elithien never found out.

13

RUTH

"I thought you said only *your side of the river?*" I muttered, and stared through the rain-splattered windshield at the doggy cafe across the street.

"Color me intrigued," Justice shrugged, and watched the cars.

I glanced at the clock for the fiftieth time and tried to still the shakes in my legs. I didn't want to be here...I didn't want *Justice* here, not on this side of the river, not near mortals, in general.

I turned my head and placed my hands on my knees, forcing the bouncing to stop. Justice's long midnight hair shone in the glow of the streetlights. Leather muted the shine, casting a glow against his trench coat.

"It's time," Hurrow declared, and reached for the door.

I waited for a second, leaving him to climb out and scan the road around us before I pulled the handle and shoved the door wide. This wasn't going to end well, either way.

"I want you to point him out to me." Justice moved around the front of the Explorer. "But do not approach."

Now he was making me jumpy. The wind picked up,

flapping the long black coat behind him as he reached out and grasped my hand before we walked across the street. In a heartbeat, I was back in my world once more, walking hand in hand with this powerful male. Heads turned as we stepped up onto the sidewalk.

He glanced at the sign above the cafe, but I couldn't stop staring at him…and I wasn't the only one. A couple walked past, a fluffy golden retriever pulling him on a leash as they climbed the stairs of Paws and Things. The guy gave Justice a wide berth, but his partner stared…*hard.*

There were more. A young woman turned her head, glancing over her shoulder as she passed. But Justice was seemingly oblivious.

"You do know everyone is staring at you, don't you?" I whispered.

"I'm well aware," he answered softly, glancing at the dark alleyway next to the pet cafe. "But thanks for pointing it out."

I shook my head as he lifted my hand and kissed my knuckles, turning his full attention on me. "Don't tell me you're jealous?"

There was a hint of a smile. One that made me almost forget the darkness that clung to my mind.

I was…just a little.

He jerked his head to the cafe and let go of my hand. "Let's go inside. You lead and I'll follow."

I did as he asked and climbed the stairs to the dimly lit cafe. Tiny wet paw prints shone on the polished timber floor as I stepped inside.

"Did you bring your furry comp—" the waitress started, her words dying in her mouth as she caught sight of Justice.

"Furry, no. Companion, yes," I replied, scanning the tables for the empty booth toward the back. "But I see my table, thank you."

I moved deeper into the room, stepping over dropped

leashes and sleeping dogs. The cafe was filled with the low drone of chatter. I scanned every face, searching for Ace's purple-haired friend. Would she remember me? I hoped so.

My foot jerked to a stop and I lurched forward before a strong hand stopped my fall.

"Oh. My. God," a woman groaned.

I turned, finding Justice sweeping the tail of his trench coat out behind him as he sank to one knee beside me.

The woman at the table next to us just stared. She gripped her coffee cup in midair, red lipstick staining the edge of the white enamel, as Justice reached down, untangled the leash from my heel, and lifted his gaze to mine. "You okay?"

"Yes." The woman beside me answered, not even concerned she wasn't the one he'd asked.

Her companion was no better. An older woman, with faint gray speckling her dark hair, peered at him over the top of her glasses as he rose to his full height. "Oh my. You are a big one, aren't you?"

That surge of pride and jealousy came once more as he met their gazes and gave a small nod. "Ladies. Please, enjoy your evening."

"We sure have now," the closer one declared as Justice grabbed my hand. She cast me a glance, brows rising. "You sure are lucky."

"Lucky?" I answered, forcing a smile. "I dunno about that. There's three more like him constantly hanging off me. They get under your feet, mostly."

Her mouth dropped open as I turned and strode toward the back of the cafe.

The low, throaty chuckle behind me just made me furious. They were under my skin now. Buried deep inside, like a shotgun blast to the heart. I was protective...and jealous.

Mine.

The word raged through my mind. I wanted to shout it to the world and bare my teeth. Jesus, they really *had* gotten to me. *Mine.*

His hand brushed my spine as I slid into the booth. One glance at his face, and I groaned and looked away. "Stop smiling, Justice."

He still smiled. His dusty pink lips stretched and curled. I wanted to reach over the table and grab his face. I wanted to take back control over this tug-of-war with my heart. I wanted my life to go back to normal. I wanted to feel powerful again, to be the type of woman that, when someone saw Justice standing next to me, they realized we were a perfect fit.

But right now, they didn't see that. I caught my own reflection in the warped stainless steel shine of the kitchen door. A navy blue baseball cap hid the dark circles under my eyes if I pulled it low. The thick, oversized sweater from Rule hid what little curves I had. Combine that with black leggings and sneakers, and I couldn't be further away from the woman I once was without swapping my damn body.

The problem was…I didn't know that woman anymore.

I didn't know her power. I didn't know her strength. My damn knee bounced, *bounce, bounce, bounce, bounce.*

"He'll turn up," Justice reassured me, scanning the other tables. "If he wants to."

I jerked my gaze to him. "Why wouldn't he want to?"

A flare of pain carved through my chest. Just one more rejection in a long list. I was starting to rack up a nice tally. But Justice didn't answer, just sat back and folded his hands as the waitress neared the table.

"Can I get you both something to drink?" She smiled at Justice.

"Coffee, please," I answered.

"None for me," Justice said, staring at the wall.

She gave a nod, then slowly stepped backwards, knocking into the corner of a table before she turned and scurried.

"And you wonder why I said our side of the damn river," Justice grumbled.

"Is it like this...all the time?"

He shifted his head and met my gaze. "Worse."

The waitress hurried to our table and placed the fresh cup of coffee in front of me, along with a tiny stainless jug of milk, before casting a panicked glance toward Justice and retreating.

My heartbeat deepened as I stared into the silver shine of his eye. I didn't see a monster when I looked at him, not anymore. I saw the man who'd pulled me from the river, who'd snapped a power pole in two like a matchstick as he screamed of retribution.

I saw the man who undressed me, the one who bathed me in the shower...*who cared for me.* And who *seduced me.*

The harder my heart thundered in my ears, the more he captivated me.

He drew me in...like a moth to a flame. That silver shine in his eye never wavered as he held my stare. I knew the kind of signal I was giving...that desperate, clingy fucking vibe. I knew how I must look to everyone in this damn cafe. Damaged, desperate.

He slowly reached across the table and covered my hand with his. In an instant, my body calmed and my knee stilled.

You're safe with me, he whispered in my mind. *You're always safe.*

I saw myself then...for just a brief moment. But I wasn't here in the cafe, I was back home...*back in their home,* standing in the shower, my red hair dark like blood. Need raged through me. Hunger for something more than blood.

Hunger for something...*sacred.*

In that moment, I realized I was the thing he craved. *I* was it...*me.*

With a flicker of a sad smile, he pulled the image away from me, leaving me floating in the darkness of my own abyss once more. I filled that with the heat of the coffee as I sipped.

"Now do you get it?" he whispered, holding my gaze.

I was his redemption, his heart to protect. I was everything he'd been searching for but hadn't found—until now. I was the woman who went to war with him. I was the one who would survive *because of him.*

The same chains that give you terror can give you the freedom you crave. Elithien's words surfaced as I broke Justice's gaze. *All you have to do is trust us. Can you trust us, Ruth?*

"He's not coming," the Vampire growled. "It's been twenty minutes. He's not coming."

"He'll be here." I swallowed my own words and scanned the faces of those inside the all-night doggy cafe. "He'll be here."

We waited for what felt like hours, watching every face that came and went until an hour had passed.

He wasn't coming. Not now...maybe not ever.

Had he found something on Elithien's computer that scared him? Whatever it was...this didn't feel right.

"Okay, we're done here..." Justice decided, reaching into his trench coat and grabbing his wallet.

The crisp bill was slipped under the edge of the saucer before he pushed to stand. He stood in front of me, watching the entrance, as I slipped along the booth seat and rose.

Disappointment filled me as I followed Justice past the slowly emptying tables and outside into the night. I'd thought for sure I could depend on Ace, thought of all the people who knew me, he'd be the last one to leave me high and dry.

It looked like I didn't know people half as well as I'd thought I did.

I inhaled hard and shivered in the bitter night air, following Justice as he turned and strode along the sidewalk toward the alley. The screech of brakes pierced the early morning air. I caught sight of two cars skidding as I froze.

The *crash* was deafening. Glass shattered and screams followed, piercing screams, *wailing screams.* Screams that made my blood run cold as Justice took a step forward, drawn by the call of desperation.

Warmth slammed over my mouth as I was grabbed and yanked backwards. I stiffened as fingers mashed my lips against my teeth, trying to yell. But Justice was staring at the car crash as a feeling of dread claimed me. My feet skidded as I was dragged across the pavement. I plunged back into that water, that freezing cold water pushing all the way into my nose and my mouth.

Back in the terror.

Back in the dark.

My knees shook, my insides turned to water. I wanted to wet myself, or throw up, gag, and heave, and scream...I needed to scream. The sound clawed at the back of my throat, ripping with savage claws until I trembled.

It was just a shudder.

Only a shudder.

And that overwhelming disconnect swallowed me, tearing me from my body. Short, sharp pants came faster...*and faster... and faster,* until Justice turned his head. He found me. Steel shone in his eye as I was dragged into the shadows, and in an instant, he turned from the man into the monster.

Air buffeted my face as he moved faster than I could track. Whoever had me was ripped free and flung into the air.

Still I didn't move. *I couldn't move.* I stood there, panting and heaving. The world swirling around me in one massive kaleidoscope of darkness. *No air...no air...no more. No more. I was drowning. Drowning.* Sinking into the darkness. My pulse out of control, deafening my ears.

A sound came. Deep. *Muted.*

It came again, this time louder. A rumble that spilled over me, but not through me.

I couldn't catch it. Dazed. *Stunned.*

"Ruth, can you hear me?"

The heavy *thud* of something hitting the ground followed.

One brush of his hand shattered the spell. Fingers on my arm...*touching me.* I screamed then. An unmerciful sound ripped from my body, shattering the ice inside.

"GET OFF ME!" I clawed and kicked and thrashed. *"GET OFF ME! GETOFFME!"*

Surprise widened his eye. His hand dropped away, leaving me in that tempest rush of fear. Until he moved slowly and forcefully, gripping me, pulling my body against his, and pressing my head to his chest as he murmured. "It's okay. I'm here...I'm right here. It's Justice. Ruth, it's Justice."

But the screams kept coming, burning the back of my throat as I slammed my fists against his arms. I closed my eyes, and still I couldn't stop it, couldn't stop the sound fighting with the wail of sirens as the street began to fill with emergency vehicles.

"No more...no more...no more! Nomorenomorenomorenomore..."

"It's me, Ruth." A deep growl rumbled through his chest. "It's me. It's just me. You're safe. You're safe now, with me."

His hand cupped the back of my neck, fingers kneading the muscles. My head was pulsing, sending sparks into my eyes... and pain followed. Gnawing, grinding agony that stripped me bare.

But it was his touch I clawed hold of. His strong fingers, pressing, finding tender knots in my muscles as he worked them free.

"What the fuck?" came a mutter from behind us.

Justice whipped his gaze over my head. "You fucking move and you're a dead man."

The screams ended, and my fingers found purchase on his

trench coat. I gripped him, crushing the leather in my fists, and I didn't care.

I didn't care.

He was my anchor in that moment, the only thing keeping me from sinking. The only thing that let me breathe.

"You okay now?" the rumble spilled through me.

I blinked into the darkness at the tall lanky guy dressed in a black hoodie, and slowly his features cleared. "Ace?"

"It's me," he answered. "Jesus, I didn't mean...*what the fuck happened to you, Ruth?*"

"*Don't fucking look at her* I'll snap your goddamn neck," Justice threatened.

I sucked in hard breaths as the wail of sirens ended. Blue and red lights strobed, filling the air.

"You know this fucking idiot?" Justice barked as he slid his arms from around me and crossed the shadows in one massive stride. "What kind of fucking man terrorizes a woman like that?"

He was like a tsunami...*unstoppable,* grabbing Ace, hauling him into the air, and lifting his feet from the ground.

There was a second where I thought we were done, where Justice would keep squeezing and squeezing until Ace's long legs stopped kicking in the air. I'd have one more dead friend on my conscience then...and I was quickly running out of friends.

Until, with a savage snarl, Justice dropped him, watching with a cold, calculating gaze as he crumpled to the ground in the darkness...in an alley meant for me.

"Ruth?" Ace's strained voice cut through the air. "Ruth, I'm sorry. I...*had to be sure.*"

"Had to be sure about *what*?" I forced the words through the terror. "You scared the shit out of me."

"About him," Ace gasped, and lifted his head to stare at Justice.

He tried to control his breaths as he shoved against the

ground, wobbled for a second, then found his balance. "Do you work for them? Is that it? Is that why you have her?"

"Work for *who?*" Justice snarled.

Only then did Ace look away, dropping his gaze to the shadows on the ground. He took two small steps, knelt, and grabbed something, a laptop, small…compact.

A green glow spilled across his body as he opened the laptop. On the screen was a CCTV image of traffic lights and two cars crashing in the middle of the road. I stiffened, and swiveled my head, to find the same two cars parked across the intersection while Ace's fingers flew across the keyboard.

"The DMV? You hacked into the goddamn DMV?" I muttered.

I was trying to keep it together, trying to stop that darkness from swallowing me whole. My body trembled and my will was weak. I tried to slow my breaths, tried to focus on the rushing in my ears.

"I needed a diversion, thought I could get you away fast."

"You thought wrong," Justice glowered.

"No shit," Ace winced, closing the laptop, and rubbing his throat. "Look, I'm sorry. I didn't know you'd react like that. Normally, you'd just kick my ass. But you still haven't answered my question. Who the fuck do you work for, dude, and don't lie to me. I have friends who know *exactly* who I'm meeting, and where. They'll go to the police if I'm not back."

"Friends, huh?" Justice took a step forward, watching as Ace flinched. "And who exactly did you tell those friends you were meeting?"

They didn't like each other, that was easy to see. But Ace glanced at me, searched my face, and straightened his spine. He took one slow, tentative step forward until he stood eye to eye with a Vampire who outweighed him, out-muscled him, out-trained, out-gunned, out-every-thinged him.

Yet Ace never moved. This nerdy guy who I'd known for

what seemed like forever never moved. *"Do. You. Work. For. Them?"*

"If you tell me who *'they'* are, I can answer you yes or no," Justice growled, his lips curling, his white fangs glowing in the dark cold night.

"The Circle. Do you work for the Circle?"

It was Justice's turn to flinch. The curl of his lips slowly sank as he stared into Ace's eyes. "And just where did you hear that name, *mortal?*"

The file...the file on the USB. "From me," I cried, and clenched my fists, trying to still the shakes. "He got it from me." I jerked my gaze to Ace. "You opened it, didn't you?"

"Hell, yeah I did" he answered. "And the shit I found in there made my fucking skin crawl. Did you know they killed him, killed that famous Vampire?"

"What Vampire?" Justice questioned, and the hairs on my neck stood on end. "Choose your next words carefully."

Everything stopped moving in that moment. There were no cars on the street. No splatter of rain on the roof. No distant chatter of voices from the cafe. There was nothing. Just us. Just Justice as he fixed that merciless stare on Ace.

"The one they call Alliard" Ace mumbled. "You murdered one of your own."

Justice rocked backwards, like someone had punched him in the face. "How the fuck do you know all that.!"

"I cracked a code embedded in a file and traced it all the way to a server off Russia. I found all kinds of things on that server. Some of it scared the shit out of me, and brought fucking assholes with baseball bats to my door. I've been hiding ever since...until you. You, Ruth. Jesus Christ, I thought they got to you, too."

"And you have a record of this information?" Justice moved closer, making Ace flinch.

"Yeah, yeah, I do" my friend replied. "So you're saying you're not...not with that Inner Circle?"

"No," Justice denied, easing back. "And the next time you decide to grab a woman and drag her into an alley, you might just want to think long and hard about that. You're damn lucky I didn't snap your goddamn neck."

"I needed a way to get to her without you." Ace rubbed his throat again and looked my way. "Sorry, I guess I didn't really plan that out. You look like hell, by the way. Actually, worse than hell."

Justice let out a snarl. "Ruth, can I please teach this asshole some fucking manners?"

I swallowed the flare of pain when I remembered Ace's words. He was right. *You would've kicked my ass...*the words stung as they resounded. I sure would have...before.

"The file, Ace. Just give us the file." I held out my trembling hand.

There was a small bark of laughter as he shook his head and glanced from me to Justice. "You don't think I'd have it with me, do you?"

No, he wouldn't have it with him. That wasn't how an unpredictable, narcissistic, insecure genius with a computer worked.

"Where?" my Vampire growled. "And you'd better not be jerking my chain. I'm running out of patience...*fast.*"

Ace seemed to pale before he swallowed hard. "It's at a house...not far from here."

"Then be my fucking guest." Justice motioned toward the street.

"I have my own transportation," Ace declined.

"Perfect." Justice smiled. But it was an off-putting smile, one that made your stomach clench tight. "You lead and we'll follow."

Ace glanced from the Vampire to me. Of all the ways tonight could've gone...I was betting this was one he hadn't planned for.

One small nod, then Ace clutched the laptop against him and stepped backwards.

I waited for Justice to stop staring daggers after Ace before I whispered, "He's not going to trust us if he fears us."

"If he fears us, then it might just keep him alive, never mind trusting."

I reached for him, grasping his hand. He was so cold, ice cold, standing there watching as Ace scurried away into the darkness.

Only then did he turn to me and lift his other hand to graze his thumb along my cheek. *I would've killed him.* He didn't need to say the words, they echoed through his touch. There wouldn't have been a thing I could've done to stop it.

I needed out of here. Out of this side of the city...out of this skin. My body still trembled, that terror lapping the surface, desperate to spill free. I had to hold on...for just a little while longer.

"I know," I sighed. "Let's just get this done. I need to go home."

14

RUTH

"You've got to be shitting me," Justice exclaimed as a piercing yellow headlight nearly blinded us.

Ace flew out of the alley, head down, his lanky body hugging the aged scooter as the piercing whine of the motor filtered faintly into the cab of the Explorer.

"I said he was smart…I never said he was rich," I countered as Justice started the engine and pulled away from the curb.

We gained on the scooter, even as he wove in and out of traffic. The dominating four-wheel drive was a predator gaining an inch, then a foot…and finally a car length as Justice drove with savagery and skill. His fists strangled the steering wheel, gaze fixed on the back of the scooter and the back of Ace as he sped through the busy streets and headed for the more economical suburb of the city.

Turn after turn, I watched the scooter hug the corners and weave across the streets as it fought to gain ground. But there was no fighting. Not when Justice was involved. Headlights shone against red brick apartment buildings. Most of them were taken up by the university students, and when the students were on break, the place was almost deserted.

Apart from those who liked to live like a hermit on a dime that is. Ace slowed the scooter and mounted the curb with a hard jolt that I felt to my bones. It was one of these deserted buildings he aimed the scooter for, pulling up hard against the building.

The Explorer took the curb more easily, its ground-eating tires swallowing the jolt with little more than a shudder, and Justice pulled in behind Ace as he climbed off the scooter.

"Stay in the car," the Vampire ordered. "Any problems, I want you on this horn, okay?"

"Okay." I winced as he shoved open the door. "Justice...don't kill him."

The look he gave me was one of disappointment and exhaustion as he closed the door.

"Justice," I called as he strode off into the white glare of the Explorer's headlights.

I thought of following, of standing guard for Ace. God knows, he needed it. But that panicked feeling still clung to me, making me feel weak and afraid. I reached for my mouth, fingers scraping across my lips. I could still feel his hand over my mouth and that uncontrollable terror of being unable to move.

That was the worst feeling in the world.

It wasn't fear. Fear made you move, fight or flight. It gave you motion, and with motion, you had a fighting fucking chance. But not being frozen. That made you a target...*that made you weak.*

I was weak. I'd been weak when the gunshots rang out that night. I'd been weak when Russell begged me to run, and yet...I couldn't even move. Maybe I'd never broken free from that.

I was still there.

Still staring as the life flickered and then dulled in Russell's eyes.

Still hovering at the edge of the pontoon with Alexander's fist around my throat.

Still dragging my heels against the sidewalk as Ace wrenched me backwards into the dark.

Still numb. Still a victim.

That was one thing I'd never been...

Tears blurred the headlights as shadows moved inside the apartment. I fixated on the towering outline of Justice as the other form moved frantically through the apartment. I had to get control of myself. I had to stop this...avalanche from swallowing me time and time again.

I had to find a way out of this suspended feeling, this weak, *powerless* feeling.

I had to find...

I had to find freedom.

Somehow.

The woman from the club came back to me, her arms tied behind her back. Body bound by rope. But there wasn't that look of fear on her face. There wasn't that terror of being trapped.

Not like I felt every waking minute since I was dragged from the river.

I needed to get out of here. I needed to get back home.

Home to Elithien...and that fucking question. That same damn question.

The same chains that give you terror can give you the freedom you crave. All you have to do is trust us. Can you trust us, Ruth?

Trust them. I lifted my gaze to the silhouettes. Could I trust them?

Trusting them with my life was one thing.

But trusting them with my vulnerability was another thing completely.

And yet that darkness pushed against my mind.

The apartment door opened and Justice walked out. Black

trench coat flapped in the wind, that look of savagery contouring his beautiful face. My hands trembled as that panic spilled free as my Vampire slipped in behind the wheel and caught my expression. "What is it?"

Say it. Say you need out of this. Say you have to do...something. Anything. I had to try anything. "I'm ready." The words spilled free. "I'm ready to try."

He was silent. His chest expanded with a deep breath. Tension built in the air to dance along my skin. There was a need in his eyes, a vulnerability of his own. One that'd been building from that moment in the shower.

Trust.

That's what it came down to...*trust.*

Gears shifted with a clunk. Justice lifted his hand over my head as he gripped the back of the seat and reversed the Explorer out the parking lot into the street. I was cocooned by him. His hand was against the seat, his scent in my nose, his power rising in the space of the cab. He drove with ferocity, the engine racing, needles redlining. The dashboard lights beckoned.

"Hold on to me," Justice murmured. "Hold on, baby. Just hold on."

He saw more than I'd realized, saw my bones were disconnected from my body, saw my soul desperate for flight. We raced through the night, spearing back across the bridge until I was on my side of the river once more.

Still we didn't slow, not when the glint of the city lights dwindled in the side mirror or when that unmistakable pale fog rose up to swallow the Explorer whole. Headlights splashed against the windows as he pulled up hard outside the house.

My fingers shook so badly I had to claw for the handle with both hands. But Justice was there in an instant, yanking open the door, and pulling me into his arms.

"I have to walk." Strained words tore from my lips. "Justice, I *need* to walk."

If I was going to do this…I wasn't going to be a victim, not anymore.

One nod of his head, then he held out a hand. I sucked in deep breaths and climbed out of the car. My knees trembled as I walked to the front door. But it was opened before I had a chance to grab the handle.

"What happened?" Elithien searched my face as I entered, but he turned on Justice like the Alpha he was. "She's pale…and shaking."

"She had…" Justice started.

"I'm fine," I snapped, as Hurrow and Rule strode toward me, concern etched in their eyes.

"Like fucking hell you're fine," Hurrow disagreed, and shot Justice a glare that could level a building. "You want to explain this to me?"

"I'm done," I explained. "I'm done feeling like this. I want out. Out of this skin, out of this feeling of being trapped. I want out, Elithien. *I. Want. Out.*"

He held my gaze. Anger raged in his eyes. Cold, savage anger that simmered under his cold facade.

"I need you to help me." I clarified. "I need you to help me… trust again."

It was like I'd hit him with a sledgehammer right in the center of his chest. He swallowed hard, then took a slow step forward and lifted his hand to my cheek.

I leaned my head into his, and for a glimmer of a second, I saw my way out…*with them.*

"I have information—" Justice started.

"It can wait," Elithien interrupted coldly, without shifting his gaze.

"But it's about…"

Elithien's fingers stilled as he turned his head. "It doesn't matter how important it is. It can wait."

And it would...it'd all wait.

Life...*death*.

The damn USB and all its festering secrets. Nothing else mattered as Elithien took my hand and requested, "Come with me."

Something in my chest fluttered. A bird, heart smashed, broken winged, raked its claws inside me as it fought for freedom. But it didn't find it. Instead, I swallowed that feeling down as I followed Elithien into the living room and headed toward his bedroom.

"Wait," I hesitated, breathless as I stared at the stainless door. "Not in there."

"We're not going in there." He gripped my hand. "Trust...remember?"

He turned at the last moment, taking me to that room with the four-poster bed...and the leather seats that lined both the walls. The room I knew well...the room where I'd danced for them.

But I'd been a different woman then.

A bolder woman.

A powerful woman.

"I don't—" I started.

But he didn't stop, just walked through the bedroom door, pulling me behind him. The others followed, closing the door behind them.

Candles were lit along the shelf against the wall. A sweet, seductive scent filled the air. But I was too nervous to place it. "What are you going to do to me?"

"Nothing you don't want. How's that for an answer?" Elithien murmured, and slid the middle panel of a closet door aside.

Ropes sat entwined on a glass shelf inside. Some colored,

some deep reds that shone as Rule hit the soft overhead lights. I flinched, and the room plunged into shadows again, leaving nothing more than the soft flickering candle glow.

"Will this hurt"? I couldn't take my eyes off the shine of the entwined strands.

"Not if we do it right," Elithien answered, lowering my hand and staring at the newly wound strands. "Remember, this is all for you. You're in complete control here...complete and utter control."

He's done this before...

Jealousy flared, cutting through my panic. I turned my head and met his gaze.

All for you, Ruth. The words floated through my head.

I remembered how cold they were to the woman at the club, how they took no pleasure in her...how desperate they were to help me. With that memory, I lifted my hand. "Do it."

There was a tiny shake of his head and small smile. "Not so fast. First there are rules. We start off small, we discuss each increment before, and, as corny as it sounds, we need a word to know when you want to stop."

*When he hurts me...*the thought panicked me. I said the first thing that came to mind. "Russell."

Elithien flinched, the pale candlelight kissed skin turned ashen. "You sure...you can have any word." *Pick another,* his tone said.

But I wanted it. Wanted it because it made me feel safe. Because I had something to atone for and that hollow feeling of loss still waited inside me, along with his face. I owed him that. I dragged in a harsh breath and whispered, "I'm sure."

My Vampire forced a smile and leaned in closer. "Any other male might be jealous at the thought of his mate crying out another man's name."

"Then, like you said...I won't have a reason to use it." I fought the tremble in my voice. Something surfaced in his gaze. Confusion. Fear...*a secret.* Something he was keeping from me.

"Pick one." He jerked his head toward the ropes.

Hurrow and Rule moved forward, striding toward me, but Justice never moved, leaning against the wall across the room.

I followed the movement of his head and stared at the blood red color of the rope, but I didn't move. I didn't want the moment over...not by a long shot. I wanted to know why the fear...why the secrets. I wanted to know him as well as he seemed to know me. But instead, this wasn't about his secrets... it wasn't about him at all.

It was about me. "The red one," I whispered.

Justice turned his head and looked away as Elithien grabbed the entwined strands and dragged them free. "It's silk...so it won't burn, but it also has little give."

I swallowed hard and nodded.

My skin was on fire, fingers trembling against my thighs by my sides.

"First your hands, nothing else tonight." he said, his gaze boring into mine as he grabbed the bottom of my sweater and lifted it over my head. "I'm going to tie the rope around your fingers and wrists, okay?"

My head jerked a little as I nodded.

"Breathe, Ruth," he reminded me, dragging my gaze to his sad smile.

"We're right here," Hurrow murmured, reaching out to take my hand.

My knees were shaking, my breath trapped in my chest.

"Your word is our command." Rule stepped beside me.

I trembled, flinching with the brush of Hurrow's fingers as he gently lifted my hand to his lips.

Red slipped over my other thumb as Elithien looped the rope around the base of my knuckle and wound the two strands around my wrist.

My heart thundered at the sensation. That panicked feeling surfaced as he worked the rope in a figure eight around my hand and then around my wrist, over and over.

A kiss on the side of my neck drew my focus away. Rule trailed his hand over my shoulder and turned his head to murmur against the panicked throb of my pulse in my neck. "Fuck, I love seeing my clothes on you. But I like it even better when they're off."

The strand jerked as Elithien straightened. It was wrapped around one hand like a fighter's strapping, leaving my other hand free.

"You okay?" Elithien asked.

My pulse pounded as Rule kissed my neck, drawing my attention back to the trail of his lips, pulling me back from that edge of terror. I swallowed hard and answered, "Yeah. Yeah, I am."

Elithien slipped the strands through the loop and dragged the rest of the rope through. Tightening and working over the strands around the base of my fingers and at my palm before he tugged it through again.

"Is that too tight?"

I shook my head as he slipped his fingers under the strands before he jerked the rope, tightening that bite of the strands around my palm.

But there was no moving, no unwinding...unwrapping. No getting out of this.

Lips raced along my neck, hands gripped my waist. Rule was against me on one side, Hurrow on the other. They closed me in, trapped me like the rope around my hand, and as my panic started, Elithien moved, stepping to the side, dragging my hand behind my back, and jerking it upwards with a jolt.

My breath caught in my chest...and that terror closed in once more.

Fingers skimmed the lower edge of my shoulder blade.

"You're safe here." Hurrow moved to my front, those dark eyes boring into mine. "No one can hurt you. No one can get to you. You're surrounded by four Vampires who'd kill everyone in this entire city if it meant you'd be safe."

"God, you're beautiful," Rule sighed. "Raw and vulnerable. Talk to me, *feel me, Ruth*. I'm right here, we're all right here."

I closed my eyes as the rush of panic swept through me. *Russell,* his name filled my head, but it never made it to my lips. All I could feel was the pounding of my heart...and Rule's lips as they trailed down my neck.

This wasn't me...not anywhere near me. Not this desperation, or this fear—

The roped jerked higher.

"Your other hand," Elithien softly commanded.

There was no pretense now, no careful planning. Just *a demand.*

Still, I found my hand rising, and that pounding in my chest took on a new tone...*a dangerous tone*. My heartbeats stuttered as I reached my free hand behind my back. I bit my lip at the feel of the rope around my fingers.

"Talk to me," Elithien urged from behind me. "Tell me what you want me to do."

A deep, inhuman growl filled the room, making me open my eyes to find Justice across the room.

"He doesn't like it when I command you," Elithien explained.

White fangs peeked from my protector's lips as he leaned against the wall. The muscles of his jaw bulged as he stared at me. This was torture for him, his own private hell, his own punishment.

"He wants to be the one to touch you," Elithien disclosed as he wound the bonds around my other hand.

My pulse raced, sending tremors through my chest.

"And he'd tear my fucking throat out to do it," Elithien continued.

My breath caught at those words. He would. Justice was a predator, a savage, merciless male. *If it was anyone else...* Justice whispered through my mind. *Any male other than one of us, they'd never draw breath again.*

He craved to caress me...to have *his* hand work the lashings around my fingers. Elithien jerked the strands, wrenching my other hand higher against my back. My muscles were taut, hands feeling the bite of the rope against my skin.

I couldn't move my arms, couldn't pull away, couldn't push him away.

I couldn't push any of them away.

I couldn't escape anything. *Helpless...*

Rule's head turned away from me, and I felt the absence of his lips.

I was easing into them, tracking every touch...and every whisper. It was the only thing holding the darkness at bay. Rule stepped away, and Hurrow followed, allowing his hands to fall from my body.

It was only Elithien now...because Justice hadn't moved a muscle, not since he strode into the room.

"Tell him what you want, Ruth. End his fucking torment," Elithien whispered in my ear before he brushed his lips down the line of my neck. "Tell him to come to you. Tell him to get on his knees. Tell him to take your pants off and lick between your thighs. Tell him to move...before the Vampire forgets I'm his Alpha and does what mated Vampires do."

This moment had been building between us, impatient and ravenous. That tug of war of desire that surged inside me like the tide. I wanted it done. I wanted it over. *I wanted him on his fucking knees.*

More than anything...I wanted him inside me.

A charge of electricity tore through me. I swallowed hard, my gaze pinned by Justice's ravenous eye. "Come to me," I pleaded. "Justice, for Christ's sake, come."

15

RUTH

There was a second when he didn't move...where the room trembled in silence after my plea. Then in an instant, Elithien let out a soft, throaty chuckle behind me and Justice broke rank, practically leaping across the room.

Hunger glinted like the honed edge of a sword as he stopped in front of me and stared into my eyes. "Say it, woman. Tell me what the fuck you want from me."

"I want you on your knees." The words were barely more than a sigh.

There was a twitch at the corners of his lips. "Are you sure? You don't sound convinced."

My arms trembled, muscles aching. I squirmed against the bindings...until Elithien's voice slipped into my head. *Don't fight against them...they aren't where you need to find freedom. Search for it, Ruth. It's inside.*

I lifted my head, meeting Justice's gaze once more, and forced the strength into my voice. "Yes, yes, I'm sure."

He slowly sank in front of me until his knees hit the floor. Jesus, the sight of him yielding like he was the one lashed...and I held the rope in the palm of my hand. Heat flared through me, catching my breath.

"Tell him," Elithien whispered.

"My pants," I ordered in a rush. "Take them off. I want you to kiss me...I want to feel your lips on me...*and your fangs.*"

A primal growl slipped from Justice. His body trembled, but his hands stayed by his sides as his shoulders rose and fell with a long, deep breath. He fought himself, fought to take it slow as he lifted those big hands to my body and slid them along the outside of my thighs.

I shuddered, aching and needing. God, did I really have this giant at my whim? He could kill me in the blink of an eye...hurt me before I had a chance to draw breath and here he was...*waiting for me to tell him what to do.* "My jeans, take them off."

His hands moved higher, sliding under the edge of my knitted sweater, and worked the button free. One slow slide of the zipper, and he dragged my pants free, leaving my panties. I lifted my foot, letting him tug my boot free, then my sock and one leg of my jeans before moving to the other side.

"Kiss me," I urged, watching as he pushed my discarded clothes aside and stared at my thighs.

He was so gentle, his big thumbs running a line up the middle of each thigh. He moved closer, his hard lips brushing my thighs. I wanted this...wanted it for me. "Slide your finger under the edge of my panties," I directed.

He followed instructions perfectly, one finger gliding under the string of my black lace bikinis... then lower as he moved further between my thighs.

"Under." I closed my eyes. "Under more. Touch me."

Heat rose like an inferno, sweeping me away in the flames. The hotter I burned, the more I liked being at his mercy...until his hands stopped. I opened my eyes. "Don't stop...*please, don't stop.*"

He pulled away and rose from the floor. For a second, I thought it was over, and that cold empty darkness waited for me on the horizon, an abyss of terror...of that helpless feeling that stole the heat from between my thighs.

Justice reached out, trailing his finger along the outside of Rule's soft cotton t-shirt, stopping at the tip of my breast. I shuddered, hardening and tightening, until, with a savage grunt, Justice moved, gripping the bottom of my shirt and splitting it right up its middle to hang in tatters from my shoulders.

Panic claimed me, tearing a whimper from my lips. I tried to pull my hands free, but it was useless.

"Are you back there?" Justice growled, reaching for the neckline and jerking his hands.

Cotton bit into the back of my neck.

"Do you feel that water?" he asked as he yanked the sleeves, ripping them until the ruined shirt fluttered to the floor at my feet. "Feel it wash over you, *bite* into you. Do you feel it rising up to claim you?"

He opened his fingers, splaying them wide across my chest, his thumbs pressing against my throat.

That terror returned, and in an instant, I was there, standing on the edge of that boardwalk with Alexander standing in front of me, his hands around my throat. That look of disdain...that *sickening* look of disdain finding me once more.

My breath caught as that suspended horror washed over me.

"Do you feel helpless, confined, *weak*," Justice continued, pressing his thumb against my throat and triggering that feeling.

My lips trembled, my breath raced until I couldn't catch it.

"That's the way," Elithien encouraged, the bite of the rope digging in. "Work through it. You're safe here, you're so fucking safe. No one is getting in here, it's just us."

Through the sheen of tears, I found Justice once more.

"Touch me...fucking touch me, take me...*love me.*" My words were thick and throaty.

Still I was the one trapped in that darkness. I was the one tied and held down. I was the one who couldn't get free no matter how much I fought. Because in the end I was weak and pathetic.

He sank to his knees once more, keeping that pressure on my throat with gentle brushes of his thumb. He lifted his other hand, his fingers skimming under the elastic of my panties once more. This time, there was no hesitation, no tremble in his hands. This time there was only the slow slide of his fingers.

"The bed," Elithien murmured, lowering my hands from behind my back. "Take her to the bed."

With a predatory snarl, Justice lowered his hand from my throat. Red rope shimmered against his black collared shirt as my hands fell to his thick shoulders, throbbing and aching. The muscles overstretched. He lifted me like I was nothing, carrying me to the bed and sinking to the fresh silk sheets. Candlelight shimmered around the room, growing against the darkness as he laid my head in the middle of the bed.

All I saw was him and that deep, sullen intensity in his eyes and in that instant, I realized I'd never asked him what had happened to him. But as I lifted my hand, the red rope falling across my breasts as I cupped his cheek, I knew I *would* know him.

I'd know them all...as intimately as they knew me.

"Fuck me, you're beautiful," he groaned, looming over me.

He ran a big hand down my arm, trailing his fingers so gently across my skin, until he reached and captured my wrist. Elithien was there as Justice passed one roped wrist to him, then the other.

"Not too tight?" Elithien dragged my hands over my head, securing them against the headboard.

"No," I answered, my breaths hard and fast again.

I was stilled gripped by the darkness, still clutched in its claws, still suspended by that immobilization. My body felt like lead, weighed down and heavy. But as Elithien tugged on the rope, stretching my body taut so my legs dangled off the end of the bed, I let that feeling wash over me.

Trust...that's what it came to.

Trust with them.

Trust with myself.

Justice slipped his finger under the strap of my bra and pulled it low, freeing my breast with a jiggle. His mouth was there instantly, tongue lapping the tight peak, making me shudder.

Long white fangs captured the front as he moved his head and, with one savage jerk, he bit straight through the middle. My bra sprang back, falling to the sides and exposing my breasts.

"Jesus fucking Christ" Justice sighed almost reverently.

His tongue found a nipple, fingers found a breast. I tried to pull against the binds, desperate to touch him, but I couldn't move. I could only lie there as he moved from one breast to the other, taking his time...doing what he wanted.

Silk sheets whispered as he sank lower. "Now, where was I?" he taunted.

It wasn't really a question. He knew exactly where he was, crooking his finger under the elastic of my panties, pushing my thighs wider apart with a massive forearm.

Trust...trust had never felt so good.

Through the crack of terror inside, Justice came alive. He commanded me, controlled me, confused and cradled me, slipping one hand under my knee as he eased my thighs further apart.

I lifted my head from the mattress, watching as he sank lower, his fingers skimming the heat of my core. This was a fall, I knew that now. That long slide into falling in love with him.

He was the one who'd saved me from that guard at my office, the one who'd snapped a power pole in two in rage.

The one who'd stood there while I spiraled out of control, slamming my fists against his chest.

He was the immovable, towering mountain, and I was the careening car skidding across the white lines, headlights splashing against the stony cliff face.

And as he pressed his lips to that heat between my thighs, I felt that *crash*.

Glass shattered in my mind with a moan. One jerk of his hand, and he snapped the thin elastic, tearing my panties free... leaving me bare.

Bare for them...

Bare for myself.

"I love you," I announced, lowering my head to the mattress as I stared at the ceiling. "I love all of you."

Tears slipped from the corners of my eyes and trailed down my temples to seep into my hair. Movement came from between my legs as Justice lifted his head. I could feel him aching for my gaze, desperate for that connection.

In the stranglehold of my past, I finally found what I was looking for...*a way forward.*

My throat thickened, straining, trembling, as I found the steel in his focus. Shock spilled across the hard planes of his face until, with a small, quiet voice, he said, "I love you, Ruth. God help me, I love you, too."

A deep, hungry growl swept across the room. One... two...*no,* three deep, ravening calls bounced against the walls and filled my mind.

"I'm about to show you just how much," Justice finished, lowering his head.

One hungry lick and he had me shivering. His fangs pressed against my tender flesh.

"God, you smell good," Elithien moaned, standing beside the bed.

He watched Justice as he slid his finger along my crease, parting me to dive in. His hand moved from my knee to slide under my ass, lifting my hips from the bed to collide with his mouth.

"I could bite you," Elithien hinted, sending a shiver of exhilaration along my spine.

I knew them now, knew the games they played, knew the fear and desire that danced between us.

That was the game.

"Justice could bite you. Couldn't you, protector?"

Fangs pressed against my clit, making me throb. Fire lashed as he left those weapons in place and danced the tip of his tongue around the numb. I jerked with the sensation, the darkness making way for a different kind of need now.

A savage need, primal and confusing, tormenting and immoral. I forced my legs wider, jerking against the bonds as an inferno rushed over me. I lifted my leg and hooked my knee over his shoulder. My hands twisted and turned against the bonds to grasp the rope.

This wasn't sex...*not anymore.*

This was different. This was terrifying and exhilarating. This was falling...falling so hard, end over end, as Justice dragged my clit gently between his long, wicked fangs and deeper into his mouth.

"Not yet," Elithien advised as I rocked my hips harder against Justice's mouth.

A finger found me, sliding in with the wetness. Justice let out a possessive snarl that made me cry out, the rope shaking under the strain of my hold.

My protector moved lower, licking deeper before he rose. Then he gripped his black shirt and tore it free, buttons pinging somewhere across the room. His hands were a hasty blur, working the button of his pants and jerking the zipper down.

He slammed back onto me, driving his thick, hard length between my thighs. My breath caught with the shock, then a whimper tore free.

"Harder," I managed to gasp. "Justice, *harder.*"

His hands gripped my hips, body driving deeper inside me, making me spiral out of control.

"Mine," the Vampire barked as he leaned forward, his hands on either side of me. His leather patch gleamed, shimmering with the hard, brutal thrusts as he staked his claim. *"Mine."*

I was his...I *belonged* to them.

Mind...body...*soul.*

My cry mingled with the hard slaps of flesh on flesh. Still I held on, mesmerized by this mountain of a man above me. He fucked me brutally, with perfect tenderness. Controlled and beautifully monstrous, crowding me with his body.

"Do what you want with me," I whispered, giving him all of me, every tremble, every desperate need. "Do whatever you want."

Stars glinted in his eye as he bucked his hips forward, burrowing deep, then stopped. White fangs shone in the amber candlelight. He lowered his head, his hard breath blowing across my neck as a long, perfect moan tore free.

He waited like that for a heartbeat. My words were ringing in my ears, desperate and pathetic. Until, with slow movements, he dragged his hand over my head and worked the bindings around my wrists. Elithien stepped forward, removing them so that my hands dropped against the mattress, burning and throbbing.

In a sudden rush, Justice pulled away from me, sliding one arm under my knees and the other under my back as he lifted me from the bed.

I'd told him he could do anything with me...whatever he wanted.

And he did, carrying me out of the room and along the hall to his bedroom.

One I'd hadn't been in before, furnished with deep reds and blacks that crowded my vision in the corner of my eye. But all I saw was him as he turned me sideways.

"Lights, bathroom," he called, staring into my eyes. "Dimmed."

The bathroom slowly brightened.

"Lower," he commanded, and the darkness deepened.

He sat me on the edge of a mammoth bath, kneeling against the cold tiles as he reached across and pressed the drain plug into place before turning the faucets for the water. The room was filled with the rushing sound as the bath slowly filled.

A moment later, we were sliding under the water together, chest to chest, the smell of him all around me and, as I closed my eyes, I knew this was what he wanted to do with me.

He wanted to take care of me.

He wanted to protect me.

The door to my past closed a little, leaving nothing more than a glimpse of the darkness.

The darkness that would always be held at bay...*when I was with my Vampires.*

16

RUTH

"I'm pruned," I said, lifting my hand from the water and staring at the wrinkled skin on the tips of my fingers in the dim bathroom lights

"You're fucking perfect," Justice disagreed behind me, his arm draped around my middle. "Pure fucking perfection."

I wanted to stay like this forever, to stay within these walls and their arms. I'd never get bored here. Never be hungry for anything other than their lips on my skin and their hearts finding the parts of me I'd kept hidden my entire life.

Trust was new and tender, downy soft, all flushed pink skin and new limbs. It was the tremble that raced across my body in the wake of a caress, or the thrilled speed of my pulse when they whispered all the things they wanted to do to me.

But even the perfection of this bath couldn't last forever. The water grew cold, and a faint shiver raced over my body before I murmured, "You have to tell him about the USB."

"I know," Justice sighed, turning his head to kiss behind my ear.

My body trembled for a whole different reason. He trailed

his thumb along my arm and rubbed my wrists and fingers. "You sure you're okay?"

It was the fifth time he'd asked, even after checking every finger and kissing every knuckle. "I'm positive. If anything, I feel...*lighter.*"

"Good. Fear weighs us down for far too long. But I want you to know you don't have to do this on your own." He lifted my hand, cupping it in his own, my fingers cradled between his. "A real woman can do it all by herself, Ruth. But a *real* fucking man won't let her."

And that was the difference...right there.

I would never have to suffer in silence.

I'd never have to cry into my pillow alone.

I'd never have to stand in the darkness again...unless it was with them.

I was starting to understand him now, starting to realize what had upset him in the shower before.

My entire life, I'd been last...last with my father, last with Alex. But not with Justice...or *any* of them. They'd always put me first, even before their very nature. They'd fight their beast...and they'd do it all for me.

I had to do the same for them, had to fulfill my end of the bargain and put myself first. As that realization dawned on me, for the first time since I'd woken from that night, I felt not so out of control.

I was safe, cocooned in their love.

That gave me the strength to pull myself upwards, letting the water from the bath run down my body. Justice watched me, his gaze lingering on the way my breasts moved as I stepped over the side of the bath.

"Woman, just know, there's no way I can give you up now. I'll be a good Vampire and wait my turn with the others, but I won't like to share. I like the smell of me on your skin...and between your legs."

Heat blossomed inside me, rising like the sun on a perfect day. I stood, toes curling into the thick bathroom mat, and found myself smiling. "I think I'm going to like this game very much." I grabbed a big fluffy towel from the rack. "It's nice to see you squirm, Vampire."

He stilled for a second before following me with a splash of bathwater and soft thuds of his bare feet. "Squirm?"

I strode out of the bathroom and into his bedroom...*our bedroom now.*

"Squirm?" he repeated. "Woman, you're going to drive me crazy, I can already feel it."

I could only smile and wrap the extra wide bath towel around my body as a knock came at the door. Rule cracked the door open, his careful gaze sweeping across my body before it moved to the naked giant looming in the bathroom doorway. "Meeting in five. We don't have much time."

I glanced over my shoulder at Justice as he gave a nod and answered, "We'll be there."

The door closed and Rule was gone, just as quickly as he'd come. It was time to tell Elithien what Ace had found...and time for him to understand what the Inner Circle had done to the man he considered a brother.

"I have to be with him," I said.

"I know."

I lifted my gaze to his and that unspoken communication roared between us. For all the savagery these Vampires possessed, they felt just as keenly as any mortal, and this would cut deeper than any blade could.

"I'll find you some clothes," Justice declared, and crossed the room to stand naked and dripping in front of a large bank of dressers.

His muscles rippled, sleek and powerful, as he yanked out a drawer and shuffled underneath my clothes to find something perfect...for me. Whatever he found would be miles too big, the shoulders hanging halfway down my arms. But I'd wear it with pride, and I'd inhale the scent of him that clung to the fabric and stand fast with whatever came for us this night.

Because we stood *together*, our unusual little family as dangerous as any in existence as we faced whatever came for us this night, and as Justice turned, clutching a soft, deep blue sweater in his hand, I knew this was how it'd be for the rest of my life.

Whatever happened from this moment on, we'd find the strength in each other to overcome.

Because that's what real men did.

Vampires included.

"It's perfect against your hair," he commented, crossing the room.

I shivered with the chill as I let the towel slip from my body, knowing exactly what he wanted. Red marks crossed my wrists from the rope. But they didn't hurt, just peeked out from the ends of the blue wool sleeves as Justice tugged the warm sweater over my head and let the rest cascade down my body.

"The pants are another matter," he grumbled, his gaze dropping to the sweater's hemline that just reached the underside of my ass. "Fuck me if I don't want you just like this."

His heavy hand trailed down the sweater along the outside of my hip until his fingers brushed against my skin. He ran across them, dipping low until he found the juncture between my thighs.

"Later," I reminded, my heart speeding at the thought.

I lifted my hand and cupped his chiseled jaw, feeling the power in those jaws. His fangs glinted as he gave a hint of a smile. Jesus, the things he could do with those, and there I'd been thinking they were all about biting.

I'd had no fucking idea.

Footsteps echoed outside, heading toward the study. I

stepped closer, and rose up on the tips of my toes to kiss him before pulling away. "It's time."

I left him then, hating every second as I crossed to the door and pulled it open. I hurried, slipping into Rule's bedroom two doors down. The Vampire was a bit smaller, his sweats still hung badly, but didn't balloon like Justice's would've.

Besides, Rule had an immaculate collection of designer suits and piles of sweats. But as I opened his closet, I froze. The clothes had been rearranged...and next to his own gray flannel and soft cut-off sweats was a smaller pile of soft cotton t-shirts and pants that were exactly my size, as well as some designer jeans and a few low-key shirts. Clothes that were so very different from anything I'd worn before.

These were baggy and soft, no longer slim cut and no power suits. That wasn't me...not the new me. I smiled and reached out, grabbing a pair of lacy underpants he'd laundered and tucked into the side, then hurried, slipping them on before a pair of boot-leg jeans.

Doors opened down the hall in the direction of the study. I straightened the sweater, and hurried around his bed to the door, meeting Justice as he opened it. His gaze swept over the new clothes and he gave a hint of a smile. "He's always better at knowing what someone needs."

"Drink?" Rule stepped out of the bar and into the hallway as we approached. He took one look at my clothes before he smiled proudly. Two glasses were in his hand, with ice cubes clinking, swimming in perfect amber.

I took one and walked to the open study door, leaving Justice and Rule to follow. Elithien was standing against the desk, arms crossed as he waited for the rest of us. His gaze swept over me and dropped to the marks on my wrists as a shiver of excitement tore through me.

He wasn't like the others, not as warm...not as *yielding*. He was the Alpha, the leader...the one whose shoulders carried the burdens. He was the one they all turned to, the one who spoke and whose orders were followed. The one who looked at me with blatant carnal desire.

And in the wake of that stare, I came alive.

"The mortal is a hacker," Justice started, and moved behind the desk, his gaze fixed on Elithien as the leader stared at me from across the room. "He's good, military-trained good. He found files on a USB Ruth gave him. Files that contain information of how the Inner Circle found out about our plans with Alliard...and had him murdered."

Still that stony gaze never flinched from mine, even as the words found their mark.

"It's bad, E." Justice booted up the computer. "I'll leave you the files to go through. But suffice to say, the Inner Circle knew all about Alliard's plans..."

"Who," Elithien questioned. "Who killed him?"

"Black Fox."

There was a twitch at the corner of Elithien's lips before he gave a nod. Hurrow shifted, standing in the corner of the room. Rule just drained his glass, turning my attention to my own. I lifted the glass and sipped, letting the burn slide down the back of my throat.

"The Breeds?" Hurrow asked.

"No." Elithien gave a shake of his head before he broke my gaze. "I'll take care of that on my own."

I wasn't sure of all the players here, all I knew was that for tonight...they were done. Rule reached up and massaged the back of his neck.

"We'll finish this tonight," Elithien instructed. "Go, sleep."

Justice's fingers flew across the keyboard before he straightened. Hurrow cut across the study and stopped at my side, grasping my hips and pulling me close. He kissed me, deep and slow, reaching up to trail his fingers along my cheek before he pulled away. "Sleep well, Ruth. No nightmares tonight."

"If there are, then we'll be waiting," Rule assured, and followed.

After Hurrow left, Rule and Justice stopped to kiss me, Justice's gaze piercing as he stared into my eyes. An unspoken communication passed between us before he eventually left, as well, and we were alone.

Elithien and I.

"Will this get you killed?" I spoke when they were gone, voicing the words they couldn't.

He didn't answer, not at first, taking his time to slowly stride toward me and take the glass from my hand. "I sure hope not. Not now I have something that's finally worth living for."

He led me out of the study to his bedroom, stopping only to punch the code into the keypad.

Steel doors opened with a *whoosh* and we were inside, sinking back into the darkness of the familiar bedroom. But it was different tonight. It was just us, my body no longer battling pneumonia. He dropped my hand long enough to switch on the light on the nightstand.

"I just want to hold you," he murmured as I reached for the bottom of my sweater and pulled it free. "If that's okay."

"It's more than okay." I dropped the sweater as he unbuttoned his shirt and let it drop to the floor. His pants were next, leaving him naked as he switched off the light and crawled into bed. I followed, sinking into the pillow as he pulled the blankets around me and settled.

"You are my reason for surviving," he murmured against me. "But *they* cannot live, Ruth. Not now…"

"I know," I whispered as his arm slipped around me. "You don't have to be strong all the time for me. You can let me in. Let me soothe you." I shifted in the bed, turning to face him, and lifted my hand, fingers against his cold cheek. "You can let me be strong for you like you're strong for me."

"Yes," he said, swallowing hard, eyes glinting in the dark as his voice turned thick and throaty. "I guess I can."

This was the life I'd signed up for, a life that was a battleground.

But as I closed my eyes, I knew it'd never really been any different.

Just the players had changed.

And as Elithien grew still behind me, I snuggled in...and tried to sleep.

17

RUTH

I couldn't sleep. Dreams chased me into the gray of restless slumber.

Will this get you killed?

My own question haunted me, making me open my eyes and stare at the ceiling.

I was safe here, alive, protected, *loved.* But now those I loved were vulnerable...and that I couldn't tolerate. I shifted in the bed, turning to find the murky outline of Elithien in the dark, as outside those bomb-proof walls, I felt the sun rise. He loved, this man, loved hard and fast. He loved cruelly, like he was the only one who mattered and maybe for a long time, that had been true.

But things were different now.

He *was different now.*

Hurrow was his second, his sword at his side. The one who had his back. Justice was his protector. His scarred, unmerciful destroyer. The one he sent when blood needed to be spilled, no matter the cost. Rule was the one thinking three steps ahead of them, cars, clothes, everything else these mafia monsters owned. I was starting to see how they worked together, how this formidable band of warriors survived.

They survived together.

But whatever was on that USB was threatening that. My breaths deepened, the only sound in the room. There was no rise and fall of Elithien's chest as he sank into whatever pit that waited for him, no steady throb of his heart. I lifted my hand and reached out, my fingers finding cold bare skin. I tried to reach him with my mind, through that connection we shared now...but there was nothing.

No Elithien...no Vampires.

Just emptiness...just questions.

Will this get you killed?

"Fuck," I whispered, and slowly rolled over, letting his arm slide from my middle as I rose from the bed and grabbed my boots.

A four-digit code later, and I was standing outside his bedroom door as it closed behind me. The house was quiet... eerily quiet. But I knew I wasn't the only one up, and with sleep lingering out of reach, that left only one thing for me to do.

Find answers.

I moved to the study and hurried to the desk as I tugged on the boots and yanked my zipper up. "Come on, are you gonna make things easy for me?" I muttered to the computer, wiggling the mouse and tapped the space bar, watching as the screen came to life.

Password?

"Shit." I stared at the blinking cursor and straightened.

There was no way I was going to even attempt to decode a damn password. I lifted my gaze, catching the glint from the Explorer's keys. "There's more than one way to get what I need." I snatched the keys from the desk and made my way through the house, then grabbed my baseball cap from the bar and headed for the foyer.

There was a whole other side of the house I hadn't explored yet. A side that held exactly what I needed…sunlight seeped in through drawn shutters to spill along the hallway. But there were no sounds of movement as I walked along the hallway, peeking into another sitting room and a long bank of what I assumed were bedrooms, their doors closed.

"I thought you were asleep."

I flinched at the sound and spun as the young tattooed punk stepped out of the shadows. He was dressed already, dark blue jeans, white collared shirt. His hair was slicked back, his deep-set dark eyes boring into mine.

"Too wired for sleep," I answered, and picked apart his manner.

He didn't like me, didn't want me here, that was easy to see. He was awkward, cold and snarly, like he didn't know how to act around someone like me. I was too…*powerful* for him, too in-your-face, like we were night and day and I was the day.

"What do you want?" he asked.

"Money," I answered, and caught the flinch. I knew exactly what he was thinking. Me, Ruth Costello, rich bitch of Crown City, asking for a handout. But it was no handout. "I'll repay it, but I can't very well go and withdraw money from my account right now, not without an ATM card."

"I'm fighting myself here. I don't know if I should lock you in your damn room like a petulant child, or open the front door for you myself…and hope I never see you again."

"Ouch," I snapped, finding that bite in my tone. "Jealous, are we?"

He took a step closer, and this time, I never fucking moved. *You touch me motherfucker, and I'll end you.*

"I don't like you. I think you're reckless and stupid, and I think you, above anything else, will get them killed. You're a liability, a dangerous, albeit pretty, liability."

My heart was pounding, my jaw clenched as I leveled him

with my gaze. "You think I give a fuck what you think of me? I've had worse indigestion than you. I'm here because I *choose to be here.* I'm no one's fucking prisoner...and no one's goddamn liability, either. Now, unless you want me for a serious fucking enemy, you can choose to either help me, or get out of my goddamn way while I help myself."

"Fine." He reached into his back pocket and withdrew a wallet. "How much?"

"How much do you have?"

He stilled then, a twitch of annoyance at the corner of his mouth before he slowly met my gaze. It wasn't really a question, not one that needed a spoken answer, just an answer of cash. He slowly opened his wallet and grasped the wad of bills inside. "I'll expect this returned."

"With interest." I grabbed the money from his hand and turned to leave.

"Where are you going?" he asked. "Not that I care."

"To find answers," I snapped, and left the other half of the Vampire den behind.

Morning sun washed across the dark gray Explorer parked at the front of the house. I hit the lock button and climbed in behind the wheel, then fumbled with mirrors and levers. Once I had everything adjusted from Vampire-size, to me-size, I started the car. "This is too damn big." I mumbled out loud.

Then I yanked on my seatbelt and shoved the four-wheel drive into gear. My damn hands trembled as I spun the wheel. It felt like years since I'd driven. I thought of Dad's Bentley as I made my way slowly toward the bridge and the 'other' side of the city.

It wasn't my side anymore, not my people, and not my business. Apart from Ace, not even my friends. I thought of Russell as I slowed the four-wheel drive and made my way across the bridge. He was alive. That was all I knew, alive and taken to some place where the Fae took care of him.

The Fae.

Kapre.

I shivered and reached for the temperature control as that inky beast stepped straight out of the shadows of my mind. My pulse sped with the memory, my hands trembled on the steering wheel before I gripped the damn thing hard and turned onto the highway.

The mortal is lucky...weak right now...but he will be strong. I have no doubt about it. Take care with her, Wolf. I'll be watching.

The shadowed creature's words drifted back to me. Wherever Russell was...he was being treated by this Kapre, and others like him. I gripped the wheel and pressed down on the accelerator. I had a feeling being *treated* by them didn't involve hot soup and a warm cloth across his brow.

He was alive. That was all I knew.

Alive...and right now that was what I held onto.

I gripped the wheel and checked the mirrors before changing lanes. The traffic grew heavier the further I drove, until I saw the off-ramp and left the highway behind. Familiar houses and packed streets passed as I turned, then turned again, making my way to the cheaper apartment buildings where Ace lived. One scan of the building and I caught sight of the scooter he'd ridden last night parked hard up against the wall.

I slowed the Explorer and pulled into the parking lot. He wouldn't be happy to see me, not after last night. But I was beyond niceties...or giving a fucking damn.

No movement came from inside the ground-floor apartment as I pulled into a slot and turned off the engine. I opened the door and slowly climbed out, tugged my cap low, and scanned the buildings around me.

My damn heart thumped, panic hovering over my shoulder like a fucking bully. I locked the doors, my damn fingers slick against the remote as I made my way to the sidewalk and the front door.

Two hard knocks and I waited. I craned my head, listening for movement, and waited a bit more before lifting my knuckles to the door again, then I stopped. The blinds shifted in the window beside me as someone peered out.

"Ace, it's me," I called, before the blinds swung closed and footsteps sounded.

The door was pulled open before Ace stepped partially out and scanned the parking lot behind me.

"It's just me," I assured him. "I promise."

"No fucking Vampires?" he grumbled.

"Daylight, remember?"

He gave a huff, and fixed bloodshot eyes on me. "You scared the shit out of me."

"Sorry," I apologized, shifting nervously and lowering my voice. "I have nowhere else to go."

That stopped him dead and his scowl lightened before he inhaled hard. "Come on inside."

I'd never been to his place before, not once in all the years I'd known him. Ace was private...borderline-obsessive private, hence the websites and the forum, and the weird Pekingese obsession.

I stepped inside and found myself face to face with a fluffy tan animal standing in the middle of the hallway.

"Don't worry...it's stuffed," he grunted, stepping around me and picking up the toy.

"Why do you..." I started, staring at the damn thing tucked under his arm. "You know what? Don't even bother to explain."

"Statistics say you're safer if people who break in think there's a dog in the house," he grumbled, and moved into the small living room.

"I think they mean something bigger...you know, something that can do some injury, like a Pit-Bull."

"You mean like your friend from last night?" He placed the

stuffed toy on the sofa and turned. "Thanks for that, by the way."

Fuck being sorry. "You brought all that on yourself," I responded. Even standing there just looking at him, my knees trembled a little with the memory.

"What the hell happened to you?" he asked as he took a slow step forward, stopping when I flinched.

I lifted my head and met his gaze. "Too much. But I'm not here for that. I need information."

"The USB?"

"That and other things."

He seemed unsure, shifting from one foot to the other as he scanned me from top to bottom. "They're bad people, Ruth, the worst of the worst. You do know who the Inner Circle are, right?"

"Not a fucking clue," I answered, remembering how Elithien had paled at the mention of their name.

"They're the supposed leaders of each breed of Immortal. More than kings...like judge, jury, and executioner all rolled into one. Vampire, Wolf, Fae...and others who govern their own kind. All the money they earn on the other side of the river goes to the Circle."

"And the Vampire Prince, Alliard?"

"They had him killed. Apparently, they didn't like his vision for a new Immortal world, one that involved integrating into ours."

Ours? "You mean mortals'?"

There was a nod of his head. "That's what was on that USB, the contracts, the plan...a fucking video of the execution."

I stiffened...my stomach clenched as fear moved through me, leaving ice in its wake. "You mean they killed him."

"In gruesome fucking detail," Ace agreed. "That's what was on that USB, Ruth. Those...creatures are fucking dangerous, especially to someone like you."

"What does that mean...*someone like me?*"

"They'll draw you in, Ruth. They'll use you, hurt you, they'll make you fodder for their brutal fucking war and when they're done with you..."

No. No, that's not true...not Elithien. Ice filled my veins as I shook my head. "Not them," I insisted. "They're different."

"I hope so," he said as he took a slow step forward. "For your sake. But I'm not sticking around to find out. I'm clearing out of here today, going to head to some place I can lay low. I don't need those fucking beasts knowing I even fucking looked at their communication."

My heart pounded. He was going...leaving me, my last fucking friend. But I understood, as much as it hurt.

"You've changed." He stared at me. "You're more real now... more real than you've ever been before. It's more than the baseball cap and the jeans. I hope you survive this, Ruth. I hope you come to your senses and fucking survive."

He turned then and stepped toward the door, a not so subtle hint we were done.

"I'm not finished yet...I need one more piece of information. You get me this and you never have to hear from me again."

"As cruel as it sounds," he sighed, "I very much hope so. What is it?"

"I need the location of a warehouse...one run by the Fae."

"You've got to be shitting me," he muttered, picking up his laptop. "You really are looking to get yourself killed, aren't you? Or worse, turned into one of them."

18

RUSSELL

I lifted my head, senses on fire as I came awake in an instant. Chains rattled, the links were taut, stretching my arms out as far as they would go as I stood there in the middle of this cell...for what felt like an eternity.

A hunger moved through me. But the need didn't rumble in the pit of my stomach...it pressed against the back of my throat and burned a hole in the middle of my chest.

It was a craving like I'd never felt before...a *sickness*, out of control, one I turned into hate of those who held me captive. *Come for me*, I sent the whisper out into the dark, to the creatures that came for me, the ones who shoved foul tasting food in my mouth and commanded me to eat.

I ate alright, then waited until the big one came close enough and opened my mouth, taking a chunk of his fucking neck, instead. They looked at me differently after that...*and they never came inside.*

"Come for me, so I can make you bleed," I whispered. Fists clenched, teeth ground as my jaw tightened, until that yearning trembled...and a new one made itself known.

One that pricked my skin.

One that made me draw breath, searching for what had made me come alive.

There...

A sweetness...urgent and destructive...a compulsion that pushed aside the rage. I stared into the darkness and pulled against the links. Power raced along the steel and into my body.

Come for me, I whispered in the darkest depths of my mind.

I sucked in a hard breath, drawing that hint deep into my lungs, and whimpered. *Jesus fucking Christ.* That slow, heavy thud deepened, rattling the cage of my chest. I clenched my fist and yanked against the inch-thick steel around my wrists. But there was no room for the movement, no give in my body or the steel...*or the magic that hardened the links and coated the walls.*

This was no ordinary cell for criminals...and I was no ordinary fucking inmate—not anymore.

Footsteps sounded, heavy...moving fast. I tracked the sound as that longing moved through me, one I couldn't quite place. That sensation came again, like a thirst I couldn't quench. I licked my lips, my tongue thick, pressing against the roof of my mouth. I turned my head and glanced at my hand, the fingers splayed outwards, the webbing stretched taut. In the pitch black, I watched as the tips darkened...and claws grew.

Half-beast, they called me.

Half beast...and all fucking monster.

Save him! Elithien...save him! That scream had sealed my fate. Her scream...her voice.

My eyes snapped open.

Senses on fire.

Her...voice...

Bad blood ran through my veins. Black as ink. Deadly as poison. Fae blood...*Kapre blood.* Fragments of memories lingered in the back of my mind, tiny snatches of time. Terrifying moments filled with screams, blood, and pain when they'd dragged me from that car and into this hell.

I was alive...and yet alive wasn't how I felt.

I was changed...predatory...*ravening,* a beast to be put down...a creature made for nothing more than what I had right now...*a cell...and chains—forever.*

Footsteps came once more, this time faster...*panicked.* I could feel them...those dark, foul creatures called Unseelie, feel their infernal desires...feel their power move through me, like we were somehow all connected, and yet, even they called me an abomination.

Kapre, one of them had whispered as he'd stumbled from my cell, eyes wide, hands fisted in front of him. *Kapre.* That name had stuck in my mind, wedged tight like a snapped stick, the splintered ends drawing blood. *Kapre*...not my name...*but what I was.*

That scent came again, dancing on the tip of my tongue as I closed my eyes and inhaled. Ferocity and malignance were sweeping through my body like a fire out of control. Panic filled me, making me snap my eyes open and jerk against the chains. My heart thundered, that stampede of terror filling my head as that sensation grew stronger.

I couldn't stop it now, couldn't buck against the chains or stop my feet from slipping on the floor as I tried to get away. That hunger was ravening...dangerous and unmerciful.

Ruthless...

The lock gave a *clunk* before the door to my cell was wrenched open. I hadn't heard them...*I hadn't—*

"You don't fucking move, you hear me?" the savage one barked from the doorway, his midnight eyes drinking in the shadows. *"Do. I. Make. Myself. Clear?"*

I could only nod...only give into that weak part of me.

I was coming apart at the seams, unravelling inside as the *boom* of footsteps echoed along the hallway, racing toward us. Voices spilled through the air...words I couldn't seem to catch, until the one they called Mojin barked, "No, I don't want you to touch her! You want to start an all-out fucking war with the Vampires? Shrike...where the fuck is Shrike?"

A low growl answered before Mojin turned his head and met my gaze. All of a sudden, he saw me...saw the panic in my eyes and my veins popping out on my skin. "Fuck me...you can feel her, can't you? You can fucking *feel* her." He took a step backwards, his eyes widening. "Are you her mate? Jesus Christ. You're fucking triggered."

"Help me..." the words clawed my throat as they tore free.

Instinct raged inside me, desperate for me to tear these chains from the wall...and annihilate anything that stood in my way...and that included six-foot-seven mountains like Mojin.

I stiffened as that sensation cut through me. In a heartbeat, I knew the reason for the torture...

I knew it all.

I felt her...

Near...

"Ruth..."

The piercing tone of a cell phone ripped through the air, making me bare my teeth and let loose an inhuman fucking warning. Mojin swiped the screen and lifted the phone to his ear, never once taking his eyes off me.

Russell?

God...my name...she called my name.

My muscles spasmed, my spine cracked as I straightened. The links...the links weren't strong enough. I could feel them bend, feel them weakening...feel her calling me like nothing I'd ever felt before.

"Phantom." The Unseelie almost wept with relief. "Ah, we have a situation here. Arran...the Wolf, yeah. I know him. I'll have one of my men meet him out front...and Phantom, *tell him to fucking hurry.*"

*I'm here...*she called. *I'm right here. Come to me...Russell, if you can hear me, come to me!*

178

I swiveled my hands and gripped hold of the chains as Mojin slowly lowered his phone and turned his full attention on me. "You're gonna be a good little half-breed now, aren't you? You're not gonna cause me trouble...not going to make me have to fucking put you down."

A roar ripped from the deepest depths of me and tore through the room. Every instinct I had was on fire. The steel girders welded into the walls howled as I pulled against the chains. There was no fighting her, no more than I could fight what I was. I closed my eyes and tried to draw away from her power. But I could no more fight the night. *"What's... happening...to....me."*

"You, my friend, are one damn step away from succumbing to the trigger she gives you...and doing a spectacular job of it, I must say. Fuck me, your arms. Your fucking arms."

No, that desperation raged. She didn't want this. Not what I am, not what I'll always be...The thought of her seeing me like this filled me with dread. *Fight. Fight it.* I closed my eyes and drew on every ounce of strength I possessed. The walls shuddered and the floor shook. I opened my eyes and stared at the ceiling. In my mind, she smiled, her sad, sweet smile as she told me she liked me *as a friend.*

But it wasn't love...it wasn't anything like love.

Not tender moments and heady romance.

She didn't want me...and fuck me, I wasn't going to have her chained to a beast...

Not one like me.

Fire filled me, cold savage fire that spewed from the darkest part of me. A black fire. A ravenous fire.

"Jesus fucking C. You're fighting it, aren't you? That can't happen...*that's not supposed to happen.*"

The fucking Fae's voice faded into the background. All thought was about her, about how she *deserved better than this.* Those midnight flames reached higher, burning away every good thing I'd ever known...and in the middle, was her. Her face. Her lips. Her fucking smile.

And that desperation to save her grew inside me, just as clear now as it was when the gunshots rang out and I took a bullet to the chest.

Save her...

Save her.

"No fucking way." Terror slipped into the Fae's voice as I opened my eyes.

I didn't dare turn my head.

I couldn't stomach to see that burn as it raced from my fingers to my arms.

I already knew what I'd see.

Shadows. *Darkness. A beast.*

Russell! she screamed somewhere outside this compound. *I'M COMING FOR YOU!*

19

RUTH

I punched the looming electric gate. The steel rattled as I lifted my gaze to the CCTV camera that tracked my every move. "Okay, so you're not gonna just let me in, are you?"

The place was enormous, almost as big as the warehouses at the shipping yard. But there were no towering cranes hauling containers from cargo ships here, or the frantic dance of forklifts as they raced back and forth...there was nothing at all.

The place was locked up like Fort Knox. And it was quiet.

Too damn quiet.

The longer I stared at the closed roller doors and the external stairs that led to a door high up on the wall, the more I was convinced this was the right place.

It smelled...*wrong.* Like someone had taken every dark, seedy, ominous scent of the night and rammed them up my nose at once. My damn eyes watered and my throat thickened like a whimper was trapped inside. I winced and took a step backwards, fighting an overwhelming urge to flee. The Explorer was parked on the road behind me, the driver's door open, the key in my hand. All I had to do was turn and stride toward it... all I had to do was give into this feeling of dread.

But the moment I searched for the reason why, that stony-jawed, all-American soldier's face came back to me. I remembered Russell as he drove me to that diner on the edge of the city and introduced me to that sickly sweet mess he called... what was that again?

They call it Campfire Delight, that throaty chuckle came back to me. "That's it...Campfire Delight," I murmured as the camera on the warehouse swiveled and tracked my every move. "Okay. I can play this game."

I scanned the tall eight foot fence topped with razor wire, and thought of leaving. I could come back with Justice...yeah, he'd get me into this place. The damn Vampire would get me the moon if I asked for it.

The moment I thought of him, a surge of desire cracked like a whip. But it wasn't the Vampire that pushed into my mind. It was the reason why I was here...*Russell.* The bodyguard wore at me, always there in my mind...never far from my thoughts. His last words still rang inside my head.

Don't hurt her...

My breaths deepened and that fucking ache of loss found its way home. I swallowed that pain, let it quake inside me, and turned, following the fence line toward the vacant lot of land. Tufts of yellow grass stuck out of rocky ground. There was nothing here, no hint of life, other than the movement of the camera. But still, there was *something.*

A shiver raced along my skin as I hugged the steel border, leaving the Explorer behind. I kept walking, my gaze drawn to that door high up on the side of the warehouse. Whatever they held here wasn't anything they wanted others knowing about.

Money, that's what Ace said this place held. *Money and Fae.* I slowed at the corner closest to the road and ran my gaze along the long side that ended at a row of abandoned concrete buildings. This whole place seemed...*empty.*

Streets of emptiness. Graffitied concrete buildings and

smashed streetlights. This place was meant for darkness. I glanced over my shoulder at the waiting four-wheel drive, and started walking forward again.

Cold danced along my skin with the first step. My heart started pounding and my knees went instantly weak. I was pushed and pulled all at once, like a turbulent tide thrashed inside me. The further I walked along the fence line, the stronger the feeling grew. Something was out here. Something both terrifying and exhilarating, something that made my heart pound and sweat break out along the nape of my neck.

Ruth...

A deep growl washed through me. I froze and jerked my gaze over my shoulder, swearing he was right behind me. My heart lunged with the sound, smashing against the cage of my chest as I whispered his name. "Russell?"

But there was no one behind me. No cars parked beside mine, not a whisper he was here at all...apart from a nagging feeling in the pit of my stomach. It wasn't the first time I'd felt something I couldn't see...and in a frenzied heartbeat, I was taken back to that moment in the alley and the rush of desire as Elithien left me sated and heady from our first connection... right before the alley was filled with punks carrying bats and a need for retribution.

It was that same icy feeling in the pit of my gut, that warning I'd pushed to the side, thinking it was nothing more than my mind playing tricks on me...and that warning had come back in the moments in the Chrysler when we drove to the slipway and Russell's headlights splashed over Charlotte's car.

I'd felt it then...just as I felt it now.

A warning...*fear.*

Ruth.

My name tore through me once more. Only this time, my bodyguard's voice was clear as day, and savage as hell.

"Russell," I called. "I can hear you." I turned, scanned the vacant lot all around me, then turned back and kept on walking.

With every step, that feeling only grew stronger. The more I felt it, the more desperate I became. My strides lengthened, boots crunching on the stony ground, carving a path through the long grass. "I'm here..." I called as a shiver tore along my spine. "I'm right here. Come to me...*Russell, if you can hear me, come to me!*"

A blood curdling howl tore through the air, coming from the warehouse...it was a bestial sound, *a terrifying sound.* Deeper than a growl, more commanding than a roar. The air quaked and the ground trembled as the awful call was pierced by the racing of an engine and the piercing squeal of brakes.

I jerked my gaze toward the sound, finding Arran's Jeep launching over the gutter and flying through the air toward me. *No...no, not yet.* I stumbled backwards, desperate to find what I came here for.

"Russell!" I screamed. *"I'M COMING FOR YOU!"*

Movement came in the corner of my eye. A mammoth beast of a man with long dark hair and a face filled with thunder headed toward me from the rear of the warehouse. His steps never slowed as he hit the looming steel fence...*even when he passed right through it.*

Death. That's what death looked like.

The huge, menacing creature slowed his steps and jerked his head toward the Jeep as it skidded behind me. Rocks pinged against metal, making me tear my gaze from the terrifying male as the Jeep stopped in the middle of the vacant lot and the driver's door flew open.

"Ruth!" Arran roared, the dangerous gaze of the Wolf scanning the warehouse and turned back to me. "What the *fuck are you thinking?*"

I turned my head as panic rose inside me. That creature saw

him...no doubt he was heading this way. Arran would fight that gigantic beast...he'd fight it to protect me—*and he'd lose.*

A cold shiver of dread tore through me.

Anyone would lose...*against something like that.*

But the second I turned my head back, my gaze finding the spot where the creature had stepped through the fence, I found it empty. A scan of the lot turned up nothing. No scowling, formidable creature, not even a shadow he left behind. There was nothing. Nothing but a tall fence and a quiet warehouse... and one *very* pissed off Wolf headed my way.

"Ruth," Arran snarled, dragging my futilely searching gaze away.

I'd never known terror like this. It wasn't just the idea of Arran going fist to fist with that *Fae,* but, as I shifted my gaze, finding a Wolf in full flight as Arran pounced and grabbed my arm...the realization that *he* was every bit as terrifying as the Unseelie I was so afraid to find.

"Are you okay?" His gaze raced over my body, then held my gaze before he barked, "Fuck me, you almost gave me a goddamn heart attack!"

"He's in there, isn't he?"

Arran froze, sucking in hard breaths, those amber eyes boring into mine. "Ruth...*no.*"

"I knew it." I ground my teeth and found the rage inside. "I fucking knew it. I want in, Arran. I want to see him."

"Not going to happen." He shook his head.

"Arran!" I jerked my wrist from his, took a step forward, and growled, "I *want to see him!*"

That cold edge of fury dissolved in his eyes as he answered, "That's not my call, even if I wanted to take you to him—which I don't...I fucking couldn't."

"I don't believe you."

He gave a shrug. "Believe what you want. You want to see the bodyguard so bad, then you take it up with your keeper."

I flinched as though slapped. So that was it? "Elithien is *not* my keeper."

"No?" The Wolf backed away. The Jeep's engine was still running, faint white smoke still spilling from the exhaust.

I warned you. The words were written all over his face. "I'm no one's property, Arran."

"You're mated to a den of fucking Vampires, Ruth. What did you think was going to happen?"

"The same thing that would've happened if I'd lain with you, I'm guessing," I answered coldly.

He threw his hands out. "We're all fucking beasts. There's no denying our very nature."

Wasn't that the kicker? They *were* beasts, no matter how perfect the smile, and expensive the suit. I'd forgotten that while the rope bit into my skin...and their lips traveled down my neck. I'd forgotten which side of the river I was on.

"I have to escort you back," Arran informed me. "Elithien will have my fucking balls if I don't. Besides," he shifted his gaze and scanned the warehouse, "this isn't a place where you want to be, Ruth. Not at all."

I glanced at the warehouse...

"Don't run, Ruth. You don't want me throwing you over my shoulder. I might like that a little too much."

Heat tore through my body and filled my cheeks. I whipped my gaze to his. "You wouldn't dare."

He grinned...those perfect white teeth showing.

He would...I had no doubt about that. But as that flicker of anger burned deep, I realized he wasn't the one I should be pissed at. It should be *my fucking keepers*...the damn Vampires. "Fine," I snarled, turned on my heel, and charged back through the long grass once more.

"Fucking Vampires and their goddamn secrets," I ranted, slamming my boots into the ground. "They have no idea who the fuck they're dealing with. I'm not some goddamn pushover.

If they wanted a bimbo, then they picked the wrong fucking Costello. Judah…yeah, they should've picked Judah instead."

The faces of my family drifted to the surface of my mind. But I wasn't ready to deal with all that. Not yet, anyway…I needed to fight one battle at a time. As I climbed into the open door of the Explorer, I lifted my gaze one last time to the warehouse. "I'm coming for you, Russell. Vampire or no fucking Vampire…I'll be back."

I started the engine, shoved the four-wheel drive into reverse, and flipped Arran the bird as I backed out. I couldn't hate him…not for coming to my defense, or for protecting me… but I sure could be pissy about it.

Shit, I was beginning to sound like the damn Vampires. I drove home, or back to the cell block, as it was starting to feel, and Arran filled my rear-view mirror every bit of the way. I grumbled under my breath, turned off the engine and climbed out. Then turned, to find the Jeep parked at the edge of the driveway as I marched up to the front door and strode inside.

"Back so soon…did Gucci not have the heels you were looking for?"

"Fuck you, Kern," I growled, striding up to him as I yanked the wad of bills from my pocket. "Your money back. It's all there if you want to count it."

"You bet your ass I will." He held my gaze as he grasped the money from my hand.

Fire rose inside me. I wanted to yell and scream. I wanted to punch a hole in something.

I wanted a drink…*yeah,* I *needed* a goddamn drink. I stomped to the bar and grabbed a tumbler from the shelf. A shaking hand and a spill of Scotch later, and I lifted the rim of the glass to my lips. The burn was delicious, spilling down the back of my throat to find the fire already in my belly. There was plenty to add to, a whole fucking inferno raged down there.

I turned, pressed my back to the counter, and stared at the

closed door...*of that room*. My heart started pounding, the *boom...boom...boom* filling my head. Without thinking, I pushed off, strode toward the door, and turned the handle.

Shadows and the smell of sex waited inside. It was cold in there, the chill licked my skin as I stepped slowly inside. My gaze was drawn to the closet, knowing exactly what was inside. The thunder in my chest deepened, my breaths jagged and harsh. I took another swallow and drained the glass.

God, I needed more.

More courage to be in this damn room...*knowing what we'd done here.*

I glanced toward the bed...the red silk rope was still tied to the headboard. I could still feel the bite, still feel the struggle, still feel the terror as that consuming feeling washed over me.

And in the wake of that cold disconnect, they were there, fingers touching me, pulling me back from that edge of despair. They'd showed me a way through the pain, shining a light in the darkness.

If I was honest, that light still shone inside me today.

I felt different...*not like the old me...but a better me.*

A truer version of me, one who didn't need the Bentleys and the designer suits. One who felt just as good in jeans and an oversized man's sweater. Still, as I stared at that rope, I found myself reaching for that desire, that feeling of being *owned*.

I fucking *liked* not being in control.

I liked that they did what they wanted.

I liked being vulnerable.

A small bark of laughter tore free. The old Ruth would've run kicking and screaming from the idea. The old Ruth would've kicked vulnerability square in the balls. But there was a softness that lingered inside me now. Like a deep cut that still oozed. I wasn't sure when the cut started, maybe it was after the death of my father, maybe it was from that night.

All I knew was, the cut was here to stay...and the poison that welled inside needed to come out. I couldn't go back there, not to the darkness and the defeat, not to that feeling of consuming dread.

I had to find a way to press against that wound, and keep pressing until the poison spilled out and drifted away. I crossed the room and leaned over, grasping the ends of the rope in my hand and balancing it over my knuckles.

The color did look good on my skin...it looked very good indeed.

20

RUTH

I paced the damn hallways, walking every inch of this side of the Vampire den over and over while I waited for the sun to fall and my Vampires to rise. The first sound was a growl.

A fucking growl.

Followed by another...and then another, from room to room. I stopped dead in front of the sofa and crossed my arms over my chest, waiting for the door to fly open and hell to be unleashed. My eyes burned, but not as much as my belly. The bottle of Scotch was empty, but my senses weren't dulled—if anything, they were sharper.

The door to Elithien's room opened and the Vampire strode out. My heart stuttered and almost stopped dead when I saw him. He wore a midnight blue suit, the jacket slung over his arm, the pants hugging every inch of his long legs and perfect ass, and a crisp white shirt unbuttoned at the top.

I swallowed hard, and let my gaze reach higher. Midnight hair shone fresh from the shower. *Fuck me, he was gorgeous.*

But he never once looked at me, just strode into the kitchen and yanked open the refrigerator door, and for the first time, I realized I'd never asked about how they actually...*fed.*

The second door opened and Hurrow strode out, dressed in black pants and a high-necked sweater.

"Going to a funeral?" I joked as he met my gaze.

The scowl he wore only deepened.

Okay then...so I really was in some serious shit.

Justice was next. The Vampire's gaze shifting to me in an instant as he searched my face and then my body, noting the empty glass in my hand before he looked at the empty bottle on the bar.

Rule followed, striding out of his bedroom and giving me the barest hint of a smile before he followed the others into the kitchen. The silence was fucking thundering, like the anxious beating of my heart. I did nothing wrong...*I did nothing fucking wrong.*

Until finally, Elithien came out of the kitchen and threw his jacket on the back of the dining chair newly tucked away. Only then did he meet my gaze...only then did those perfect fucking lips part. "Did they touch you?"

A chill swept through the room with the ice of his tone. There was no playing here, no getting out of this...no getting out of anything. "No."

He inhaled, eyes glinting, as pressure built inside my head, like all of a sudden, the Scotch hit me, making my thoughts turn fuzzy and my head swim. All I saw was the glint in his eyes and the press of his lips. The harder he pressed, the more my thoughts seemed to grow weaker...

Until it clicked.

I jerked my gaze upwards, my jaw clenched so hard my teeth ached. "No...*no, fucking way.* Get the *hell out of my head.*"

I shoved him, fighting against wave after wave until I was drowning. I had to do something. *There is freedom in chains...*his own words pushed to the surface of my mind. I flung them at him, screamed them inside my head...and broke the spell.

My steps were a blur, my heart booming in my ears as I

lifted my hand and struck. The *slap* was brutal, finding the cheek I'd caressed only hours ago. "No...*all the fucking way no.*"

His hold was gone in an instant, tearing away so hard my knees buckled until I fought to stand.

"No?" He repeated, that cold, merciless glint in his eyes raging.

"*No.*" I sucked in a breath and felt my world tremble...my world in the eyes of this man. *A man I loved.* "I appreciate all you've done for me, I really do."

"You *appreciate it...*" he repeated.

God, that tone was like claws through my heart. I swallowed, and tried to clutch the ounce of steel lift in my spine. "I do...I really do. But let's get one thing straight here. You don't *own* me..." I lifted my gaze to the others who stood silent in the background. "None of you do. No man...no *Vampire* will control my existence ever again. You want me in your lives...then we stand together. I *will not* walk behind you. I will fight alongside you. Now you speak of trust like it's easy...it's not fucking easy. It's time *you* start trusting *me.*" I fought the quiver in my voice. The shake that told them everything was riding on this...and they held all the fucking cards. I met Elithien's gaze. "I want to see him."

He shook his head, those dark eyes not shifting from mine. "No."

"I. Want. To. See. Him."

There was a spark of fear in his eyes...before the battle continued. "Hell no."

"Hell fucking *yes.*" I lifted my hands to my hips. "I'm not asking your permission on this. You won't help me...then I'll find someone who will." I lifted my gaze to Hurrow.

"You...*wouldn't...dare,*" Elithien snarled.

"Try me." I jerked my gaze to his once more and put the *bitch* back into my tone. It was so fucking easy...like riding a damn bike. But under the ice lingered that stab of pain, one that cut far too deep for me to be that person I once was…now there was only pain.

I felt myself pull away from him, felt that cold shiver wrap itself around me and pull the hurt in close. I thought I knew Elithien, thought I'd finally found someone who not only respected me, but encouraged me to be me…

I guess I was wrong.

That fucking stung. I flinched and looked away. I think my time here is—

"You do know he's in love with you."

My body froze, mind racing. "Who?"

"You know who. If he crosses the line with you, Ruth…if he lays one fucking hand on you…"

I turned back to him, finding that cold, undead *Vampire*. Oh and he was cold…chilling, actually, right down to the fucking core.

"Never forget you are ours." Jealousy raged, making those perfect white fangs slide out from between his lips. It looked good on him…*everything looked good on him.* "You are bonded to us…you *stay* with us."

"He tried to save my life," I argued.

"Tried and failed."

"So did *everyone.*" He winced with the reminder. "I died in that water, Elithien. *I fucking died.*"

"And for that," he strode closer, lowered his head until our lips almost brushed, and stared into my soul, "I'll hate myself for all eternity."

"I still have to see him. I still have to make sure he's *okay* with my own eyes. I have to make this right," I begged. "Please…"

His breath danced across my lips. I could…almost taste him.

"You don't go there…you don't go anywhere *near* there. You want to see him, fine. I'll bring him here."

"Fuck me," Hurrow grunted, and looked away.

I shifted my gaze as my Vampires looked away. "What?" I questioned as fire found me once more. "Don't tell me you're scared of one fucking male...all four of you?"

"You really have no idea, do you?" Elithien straightened, keeping my gaze. "Well, looks like you're about to get your wish. You'll find out soon enough."

"What's that supposed to mean?"

He stepped backwards. "Hurrow, Justice, you're with me. Rule, don't let her out of your damn sight."

"Wait." I watched the three of them stride toward the front door, leaving me behind. "I'm supposed to come with you. I'm supposed to see what's in that warehouse."

But they were gone, not even leaving the echo of their steps behind.

The Explorer started, and the wheels spun as it backed out of the driveway in a cloud of dust. They were gone in an instant, leaving me staring at the open door...wondering what the fuck just happened.

"You get under his skin." Rule spoke from across the room. "I don't know what you do, but in all the hundreds of years I've known the man...no one affects him like you do."

I turned back to the open front door as my heart sank. "As he does me."

I stood like that for what felt like an eternity, listening to the birds squawk and settle for the night, and under my bravado, that small voice whispered...*what if he's right?*

"Was I wrong?" I asked, and turned back to where Rule was standing a second ago.

But he was gone.

Just like that.

"Fucking awesome."

I sat on the sofa, crossed my legs, then re-crossed them, rising a few minutes later to rearrange the throws and the pillows. I thought about searching the cupboard for a little more liquid courage, decided against it. Pacing, *yeah pacing*. I walked the hallways and snarled at Rule as he gave me a smirk. I was about to snarl at him again when headlights cut through the darkness and flooded the living room with light.

It was him.

Him...

My breath trembled...senses on fire as the *thud* of a car door rang out... then another and another. Behind me, Rule growled, a long...inhuman warning. One that ripped through my soul. I took a step forward as moving shadows cut through the headlights and headed toward the door.

Hinges howled as the door was shoved open, making room for him to squeeze through, but there wasn't enough room. Not in the damn doorway...or in this house and, as the heavy thud of his steps rang through the foyer and headed toward me, I knew there'd never be enough room ever again.

Not in this world...

Not in *my* world.

Blue eyes captured me as he walked into the living room, flanked on either side by Vampires. He looked rough, in sweat stained clothes, and dark stubble replaced the clean-shaven chin. He looked like he hadn't bathed, hadn't eaten...hadn't seen the outside, in days. His hands were behind him, and for a second, I didn't understand why...until it registered. Heat rushed, and an ache followed, one that tore through my chest. "You cuffed him?"

"They stay on," Elithien growled, leaving no room to negotiate.

"It's okay." Russell held my gaze. "I *want them on.*"

"You want them on? I don't understand."

He was colder, unflinching and stony. Those blue eyes I knew so well glinted like glass. This wasn't the Russell I knew. He was different...*Fae*.

Pale skin and deep red lips. God, he even looked like one of them now, right down to the almost-snarl when he looked at me. No, this wasn't my bodyguard at all.

He'd been Trouble's man. A bodyguard Dad respected back in the day. I hadn't remembered Russell at first in the hospital all those months ago...*fuck*, it seemed like a lifetime ago now. I hadn't remembered until he took care of me after the punks left me for dead—and the Vampire who'd saved my life in slaughtering them.

But Russell had been there, always quietly in the background, trying his best to look...*helpful*.

He didn't look helpful now. He looked sick, with ashen skin and gaunt eyes. He'd lost weight, although definitely not size. My gaze drifted over him, taking in his longer hair now, not the usual clean, shaved-around-the-sides look he always wore.

I took a step forward and they flinched. Justice took a step forward, breaking rank to lift his hand. "Ruth..."

"He's not going to hurt me," I snapped, and turned back to him, watching the spark in those blue eyes harden. "Are you?"

He just inhaled as I stared into his eyes.

Are you? The question roared through my head. *Say it...say you won't hurt me.*

But there was no comfort from him. No reassurances that he was the same man I once knew. There was nothing but that *unfathomable silence.* God, I was so fucking stupid not to listen when Elithien tried to warn me.

I was so fucking mortal, wasn't I? Bleeding-heart, pathetic piece of shit.

"Do you remember what you said to me in the hospital when I woke up bruised and in pain?" I murmured, desperate to see a flicker of warmth in his eyes. "Do you remember why you told me you were there?"

He didn't answer, not even a shake of his head this time as I took another step forward, ignoring the daggers from Elithien's gaze and the outstretched hand from Justice as he moved with me, placing himself between me and my bodyguard.

Still, that didn't stop me speaking, or moving to the side to meet those blue eyes. "Do you remember?"

"Yes," he growled, then stilled. Hard breaths expanded his massive chest. "Yes, I remember."

"You told me you'd asked to be there," I murmured as that moment came back to me with blinding clarity. "You told me you'd asked to stand guard, and that nothing was going to come through those doors without my say-so. You told me I was safe with you."

Corded muscles in his neck strained as I stepped around my towering giant of a Vampire and lifted my hand. The pounding of my pulse was deafening, swallowing every other sound in the room as Russell flinched.

Panic flared in his eyes, his hard breaths turned to pants. "Don't," he pleaded. "Don't come near me."

I stopped dead, registering the tremble in his voice. He was scared of me...scared I'd—

Look at what you did...all this because you couldn't let him die in peace.

The words surfaced before I knew it.

He wasn't scared of me...*he hated me.*

Hated me for what I'd done.

The thought was a knife to my chest. A moan came to life in the back of my throat before I swallowed it, and drank in the pain in his eyes. "You hate me...you truly hate me. God, what have I done to you? What have I done?"

His eyes widened. "*No,* I don't hate you."

But it was too late. I saw it all now, saw it through the shimmer in my eyes, saw it as the tears welled and spilled free, sliding down my cheeks. "It's okay. I don't blame you for it. Hell, I brought it on myself."

A growl tore from Elithien before he jerked his hostile gaze to Russell.

"Don't." I shook my head, dislodging more slick tears before I turned away. "Don't you blame him. This is on me."

Nothing is going to come through those doors without your say-so, Ms. Costello. You're safe here with me.

Safe.

Safe. He made me feel safe, and I turned him into a monster. I shook my head and forced the words around the lump in my throat. "I don't *ever* expect you to forgive me for what I've done. I can assure you...I won't forgive myself."

I left him there, left him cuffed and in pain. Left him because I didn't know what else to do.

The house blurred all around me as I strode from the living room and headed to the rear of the house, until a savage *snap* was followed by the sound of shattering glass.

I was hit before I knew it, grabbed and turned, hardness pressed against me until my back slammed into the wall.

"You think I hate you?" Russell groaned, pressing his body against mine as he searched my eyes. All I could smell was him, musty and raw, filling me with every breath.

More tears slipped free, blurring his hand as it rose.

"No, you *fucking don't!*" Justice roared.

The towering Vampire was beside me in an instant, his massive fingers lashing around Russell's wrist in a vise-like grip. "You don't fucking touch her."

"Get *your fucking hand off me, Vampire. Before I remove it...at your goddamn neck!*"

There was too much male. Too much aggression. Too much *beast.* Russell's fingers darkened, turning black in an instant. The black raced along his hands, and spilled through the veins in his arms. Black that somehow reached his eyes, bleeding that perfect shimmering blue into the darkest depths of the sea.

In an instant, he wasn't the bodyguard I knew, he was something else entirely.

Immortal my mind whispered, but I couldn't understand...*what he was...*

Male fought male.

Force against force,

Elithien and Hurrow were right beside him, Hurrow on the other side, leaving the Alpha Vampire at his back.

"I just want to touch her," Russell growled. "I just want to touch her cheek."

Black veins popped along the muscles of his arms as he strained against Justice's hold.

They battled. They raged, but not an inch was given...nor was it taken by force.

I couldn't move, couldn't breathe, stuck between two walls. Only, one of them was made with steel and concrete, the other a rippling, powerful chest.

Until in an instant, Russell started to sag. He stepped backwards, jerking his hand from Justice's hold. "I get it." Pain twisted his face, deepening the furrows along his brow as he jerked his gaze to mine. "I never wanted to hurt you, but I can see if I'm around...there's no other way this will work out."

"No," I whispered as the air rushed to fill my lungs. *Don't...*the word resounded in my head.

But they never made it to my lips as my bodyguard was gone in an instant, leaving nothing but the ache of an almost-touch in his wake.

21

RUTH

"Let him go."

I shook my head and shoved away from them, from their coldness and their cruelty. "No. I can't do that."

But Elithien was in front of me in an instant, moving so fast my hair fluttered then settled around my shoulders.

"Let *him go, Ruth.*"

I couldn't...couldn't fight the memories of my past, not when they were so *visceral*.

*Run...Ruth, run...*Russell whispered inside my head as I pushed past Elithien and stumbled toward the open front door. The night was there, blackness...empty, unforgiving blackness that wrapped itself around me tight.

"Russell!" I screamed his name as I hurried past the Explorer and stopped in the middle of the driveway. "Russell, come back! *Russell, come back to me!*"

In the echoes of my screams, I found the pain I'd been afraid of. Choking pain. *Heart pain.* Pain that left me empty like a receding tide, and I was abandoned once more.

"Don't go," I cried. "I don't want you to go."

I stood there, staring into the night as the owls hooted and settled. Footsteps echoed all round me, hanging back…not game to come close.

"He has somewhere safe to go. Somewhere he can learn to control what he is now."

The words didn't comfort me. I spun, glaring up at the man I loved. "Where? In a cell?"

Elithien took a step closer, but I couldn't look at him. Not now. I turned, giving him my back once more.

"Don't touch me," I warned as the air shifted around me. "Don't you dare fucking touch me."

I stood like that, hating how my protectors stood with me, hurting just like I hurt for the same fucking reason. *For love.*

"He's safe. He has somewhere to go if he needs it. You think this is cruel, but he's not the same man you once knew," Elithien spoke behind me. "He needs to find himself again. He needs to learn how to control what he is, and he can't do that here with you."

I turned on him, teeth bared, eyes wild. "So *you* get to decide that, do you?"

But he didn't flinch…didn't move, just looked at me with those perfect eyes and answered. "When it comes to you, I do. I don't expect you to agree with me. I don't even expect you to understand me. But know this…I will be *unmerciful* in my judgement when your safety is involved. That is why I want your promise you won't go anywhere without a damn escort. If it can't be one of us…then let it be the Wolf."

I sucked in a breath, the fire in my words dwindling. "You mean, Arran?"

The muscles in his jaw bulged as he clenched his teeth. "You think I don't see you. You think I want to change who you are. You were a powerful woman when I met you, Ruth Costello, and you'll be even more powerful when you're done. I know that and I accept that. So if you need to go out…in the daylight, the Wolf—"

"Arran."

Dark eyes glinted like steel. "Arran," he repeated, "will escort you."

"Good." I straightened my spine and lifted my chin. "Then I want to go out...*across the river.*" I pointed out. "Tomorrow, after I sleep."

A tilt of his head. "Done."

"And Elithien," I added, my voice softer as I shifted from one foot to another. "There's something else." *God, I hated this...hated to...ask.* "I need some money."

There was a twitch at the corners of his lips. The bastard was enjoying this. "Money?"

"You heard me correctly the first time." My cheeks burned. "I can't very well go to the bank, can I?"

"No, you can't. How much are we talking exactly? Fifty thousand? Five million? *Fifty million?* Whatever you want...it's yours."

I swallowed hard. I'd grown up with money all my life. The kind of money that made others sick with envy. *But never that kind of money...never...Vampire wealth.* "How about we start with five hundred dollars and go from there?"

"Five hundred." He said it with a shrug and raised one perfect brow. "You sure you don't want more?"

It was hard to stay pissed at him. Hard not to fall for the goddamn suave perfection he was. I felt my lips trembling, felt that shiver through my body, even as the loss of Russell gripped me tight. "I'm sure."

"Then five hundred it is." He searched my eyes, and stepped closer, lifting a hand to brush aside my hair "Your pain is my greatest torture. I can't stand to see you cry, it does something to me, makes me feel...more inhuman than I've ever felt before. It makes me long for you...and when I feel like this, *I don't want to share.*"

Hurrow moved closer, reaching out to trail his fingers along my arm. The mere touch made Elithien stiffen, his eyes growing colder and more savage until, with a possessive snarl, he spoke. "Not tonight…tonight she's all mine."

In a second, I was lifted. My chest smashed against his side as Elithien grasped the back of my neck and pulled me close, taking my mouth with a savage hunger before he broke away. His lips found that throb in my neck, fangs pressing against the skin, stinging…*waiting.*

"Do it," I whispered, and closed my eyes. "Take what you need."

A growl slipped from his lips and raced along my skin, the sound unforgiving and wild. There was a second where I braced myself for the strike, where my heart didn't just stutter…it stopped.

And I floated in the silence.

Until with a moan of desire, he picked me up, swinging my feet into the air until he grasped my legs behind my knees. We were striding, leaving the emptiness of the night behind, along with Hurrow, Justice, and Rule.

Elithien's beast was riding too close to the surface tonight, he was too *wired…too strained.* I lifted my hand and cupped his cheek, finding the man I'd met in that alley months before. The house was a blur as he strode to his bedroom, gripped me against him with one hand, and punched in the code, never once taking his eyes from mine.

Darkness swallowed us but the air still smelled faintly of deep, musky cologne. He placed me down on the bed and straightened. "Stay right where you are. *Do not move.*"

My breaths deepened as I nodded. He was gone in an instant, leaving me sitting on the bed. "Um, what's going—"

The steel doors hissed as they closed behind him. The *click* of the bathroom light filled the bedroom with a perfect glow. I stared at the soft leather flogger, and the red rope from the other night draped in his hands. "Now," he murmured and stepped closer. "Are you ready for lesson two?"

I swallowed hard, unable to take my gaze off his hands. My heart was pounding and my head started to swim. But a heat bloomed inside me as the memory of their hands on my body... and their fangs between my thighs returned.

Jesus, I wanted him there. I wanted this...*Alpha* on his knees. I wanted him to do things to me that made my skin quiver and my knees go weak. "Yes," I whispered and lifted my gaze to his. "I'm ready."

"Hands," he commanded, dropping the flogger to the bed. "But first your clothes, take them off...*take them all off.*"

I froze at the words, my heart pounding as my head tried to catch up. I hadn't done this before. Sure, I'd *seen* it...who hadn't seen *those* movies. I was the one who sniggered and checked out Mr. Grey's helicopter and his car instead of putting myself into the shoes of Anastasia Steele.

It had just never occurred to me that something like that would ever touch my life...except it had...*now.*

"Clothes," Elithien demanded, one brow rising. "Are still on your body."

I lifted my shaking hand, grabbed the oversized sweater, and lifted it over my head. I wasn't wearing a bra, and for some strange reason, I wished I had. Maybe it'd be sexier that way...*more seductive.*

The slow reveal...the tease between soft lace.

But as a low, inhuman snarl rippled from Elithien, I knew bra or no bra...he wasn't in a waiting mood. I tossed the sweater aside and shoved to the end of the bed.

"No. Stand right where you are."

"In the middle of the bed?" *What am I...five?*

"Yes, in the middle of the bed."

I held his gaze for a second, then pushed upwards, standing on the mattress like I was ready to jump and hurl a pillow at his face. The idea occurred to me...for just a second, until he leveled me with *'that look'.*

I worked the button and the zipper, pushing my jeans down before I stepped free with one leg and flung them toward the wall with the other.

"Your panties..."

I slid my thumb under the waistband at my hip and drew them down.

"Good, now hold out your hands, exactly like we practiced the other night."

I balanced on the mattress and moved forward, holding out my hands, wrist side up. He took one end of the rope, hooked it over my thumb, and wound it around my wrist and my hand, just like he had before. In a heartbeat, he'd slipped the loop from my thumb and tightened loosely, leaving the remaining length of the rope to dangle toward the bed before he moved to the other.

He worked fast, tying and checking before he met my gaze. "Kneel."

Kneel? I did as he commanded, sinking until my knees dug into the soft mattress, keeping my knees together for some degree of decorum as he moved to the side. "I'm going to tie this around your ankle. You won't be able to stand, but it won't be tight, okay?"

He waited until I gave a slow nod, then caught the end of the rope and tied it around my ankle. He was right. There was no room to move, no way I could stand, let alone walk. I was immobile...and naked, while he stood there in his midnight blue pants and crisp white shirt. There was nothing vulnerable about him, nothing bare, while I was *completely at his mercy.*

He moved to the other side. "Talk to me. Do you like this? Like being bound...like being all alone...*with me?*"

In a heartbeat, I was back in that alley once more, back when we first met, his hand on my breast, swiping aside my blouse to stroke my nipple in the dark. I ached now, just as I ached then. "Yes."

He tied the other ankle, then moved around to the foot of the bed and looked at me. "Spread them."

"What?"

He didn't answer...didn't command, just waited. My thighs trembled...shifting a little as I watched his gaze. He can't mean for me to be splayed open like this, could he? *Jesus.*

I shifted my knees open, just a little.

"Wider."

I flinched, my heart thudding. Desire raged in his eyes. I held them, clutching hold of his stare as I inched my knees further apart...until the cold air licked between my thighs.

Electricity hummed through me, spilling between my thighs. He wanted me weak, vulnerable. But this wasn't about him... was it? It was about me.

It was about giving my body over to another...it was about saying...*see me.*

And he did.

He slowly lowered his gaze to my lips and my neck, which made my heart flutter.

"Easy," he whispered, which only made me tremble more.

My nipples tightened with the slide of his gaze. I swallowed and tried to slow my breaths, but the longer he stared at me, the faster they came...until finally he glanced lower.

Heat raced through me as he stared at my splayed legs. Jesus, I already knew I was wet...

"I want you like this all the time when you're with me."

"And how often will that be...*just the two of us?*"

He took a step closer and reached out, caressing my cheek as he stared into my eyes. "As often as I can."

Confusion crowded my mind. "Then why share me...with the others?"

He smiled for a second, and in that heartbeat, it wasn't the man I spoke to. His gaze hardened, his words had a bite as he answered. "Because to keep you to myself would be to condemn you to a life without me...*if* I die. This way...you'll be protected. You'll be loved and cherished, and most of all...you'll be sated. Every hunger, every thirst taken care of down to the...very... last...drop," his finger traced down the swell of my breast. "It'll be as it was always meant to be...*always about you.*"

The soft leather strands of the flogger brushed along my thigh, making me shiver.

"I won't ever hurt you. Do you trust that?"

Trust that...but not trust me? I stared into his eyes as he dragged them up from between my legs. Did I trust that he'd protect me, that he'd never intentionally hurt me? "Yes."

The *crack* of the flogger was so fast I didn't realize he'd moved. I flinched, heart hammering with the sound before I tried to move. But my hands were tied to my ankles. The red rope bit as I yanked and twisted. "Wait...*I...*"

"Did it hurt?"

I sucked in a deep breath and stilled. Warmth radiated from the sting...warmth and that rush of the strike. But it didn't hurt exactly. It felt...*like a hunger,* and that desire moved through my body to lick between my thighs.

Elithien moved, leaning down, his lips moving to mine. I tilted my head, desperate to taste him. But instead, he slipped a finger along my crease and into my slick. His fangs extended as a carnal look of desire moved over his face.

I never tried to control him. I let him do what he wanted to do, let him take what he wanted to take. I let him...*touch*...what he wanted to touch.

My breath caught, my pulse fluttering like a bird in the top of my chest.

"Fuck me, Ruth," Elithien moaned, and pulled away.

Leather and flesh. Black straps over pale, blushing skin. "Harder," I whispered. "Please, *do it harder.*"

He rose, in an instant turning into that ravenous Alpha once more. Dark eyes glinting, his wrist moved, and the *crack* of the strands slapped against my thigh once more.

Panic moved in, driving to the surface like I'd done escaping from the river.

But I wasn't in the river. I was here…with him.

The *slap* came again, this time on my other thigh. He bent, sliding that hard leather handle between my thighs. I shivered with the sensation, feeling the *burn,* and the rush.

"Fuck, you're so wet," he murmured, drawing my gaze.

I lifted my head. Hunger raged between us.

A primal hunger. A *desperate* hunger. "Again," I whispered.

I closed my eyes, my body anticipating the strike.

When it came, the thrash didn't disappoint, letting the heat travel through my body, pushing my thoughts aside.

In that moment, I wasn't the daughter, I wasn't even the survivor. In this pure second of perfection, I was just a woman…allowing herself to *feel.*

His fingers slid along my crease, making me whimper and drive my body upwards until the strands around my wrists pulled taut. I trembled under his touch, *ached* as the *slap* came once more.

I sank into the feeling and drifted away, turning into that primal need to be wanted…

And he wanted me.

The flogger hit the bed beside me. I opened my eyes finding him standing in front of me with a predatory look of longing.

He undressed, his fingers glistening with my own desire as he worked the buttons of his shirt. No words were needed. With an uncontrolled shiver, I knew what I was in for. I trembled, watching the light bounce off his perfect skin. He looked like a god standing there, peeling his shirt free before he moved to the leather belt.

"We might not always see eye to eye out there." He jerked his head toward the doorway. "But know this, in here…when we are together, there is only you. Only perfection. Only love."

I burned hotter, holding his gaze as he stepped from his shoes and let his pants drop to the floor. Muscles rippled as he moved…sleek and powerful. A predator. That's what he was. *A pure…unrivaled hunter of the night.*

A moan slipped my lips at the thought of him…and me, naked, splayed…*vulnerable.*

"It's always a rush when you become aware of your own fragility, isn't it? Like, you think yourself Immortal…until something or someone shifts that perspective." He moved in silence, sliding those fingers that smelled like my own sex along my jaw. "You are that shift."

I realized then he wasn't talking about *my* fragile existence, that he was talking about his own. He sank to the floor in front of me and lowered his head.

Soft lips found the peak of my breast. I clamped my lips closed and swallowed a whimper, shaking instead as he drew me deeper, dragging the points of those fangs across my tender skin.

"Fuck me, you are exquisite," He groaned, and grasped me under my arms.

I was lifted, hands tied to my ankles, as he laid me gently on my back. My knees splayed open, my pussy bare for his gaze. He took his time, his fingers finding every delicious part of me as he slipped inside.

"Oh." I closed my eyes, holding on…fighting that ravening need to drive my hips forward, to fuck any part of him he was willing to give.

He sank lower, kissing my stomach, then my thighs, before he sank further, licking along my core. "Jesus…"

He chuckled and licked again, taking his time before he ran his fangs upwards to gently nip at my clit.

I ground my teeth, forcing that wave back, and whimpered, "I'm going to come if you do that again."

He did it again. Making sure that time to draw that throbbing nub into his mouth. I drove my hips forward. "Please, Elithien...*please.*"

He lifted his head, those dark eyes glinting with desire, or was it madness? Pure unadulterated *madness.* My knees pressed wider as he rose, his hips flushed with mine. I looked down to find his cock hard and ready, pressing against me.

This moment had been building between us, like a tug of war, ever since that moment in the alley...ever since he made me his. "Take me," I pleaded. "Take me now."

He pulled his hips away from me and held my gaze. One hard surge, and he drove his cock deep inside me. That *kick* of shock claimed me, tearing me from my body for a second before I slammed back into my skin.

"Fuck...*me,*" I whispered as he thrust hard and slow, driving his hips against mine until the join was all I could feel.

There was only him and me.

Only *this.*

Only...*us.*

Only the surge and the crash in my body. His hand moved to the inside of my knee, pushing me wider. But not once did he tear his gaze from mine.

He fucked me alright.

Claimed me with his body...and his stare.

I'd thought I knew sex...thought I knew pleasure. But this... this was an *Immortal* stealing me from my skin and sending me into the stratosphere.

His stratosphere.

That wave was rising inside me, and there was no pushing it aside...no denying that out-of-body experience...for...a... second...longer.

He pulled away at the last instant, his cock still hard and

unspent as he moved lower, watching my sex clench and quiver.

It was lips that found me as I arched my spine from the bed and cried out. I pumped my hips against him, letting his tongue find every spill. "Bite me," I whimpered. "Elithien, *bite me.*"

He struck, hard and fast. Pain shot through the juncture of my thighs, and heat followed. Red against pale skin as he captured the tiny spill of blood with his fingers and slipped them inside me.

A moan tore free with the sight. He sucked against my thigh, holding me in the silver glint of his eyes as his fingers worked me. That shudder came again, bucking and colliding until, with a slow draw, he pulled his fangs free, leaving two deep puncture wounds behind.

His tongue darted outwards, licking the wounds before he kissed me.

My heart raced as the wounds closed up in front of my eyes.

He grasped my hand, moving fast to tear those wicked fangs through the strands until the rope broke. My other hand came away just as fast before he spun me, turning me over. My hands went to my sides and slid upwards until I fisted the sheets above my head.

He pulled my hips upwards, lifting them from the bed before he pushed inside, returning to those slow, hard thrusts once more.

"You are mine, Ruth Costello. Never forget that."

How could I…when he drove the point home with the brutal strength of his passion, until he came with a deadly growl. The sound slipped along my skin and sank into my body, sheathing itself deep into my senses.

Until he was all I knew.

And in the spill of his body, I knew he was right.

There was no one else but them now.

I could never go back…even if I wanted to.

I was utterly addicted to them.

22

RUTH

H e left me, sliding from the warm sheets sodden with our desire. I closed my eyes, listening to him move around in the bedroom before the mattress dipped beside me.

"Rule will be outside if you need anything. I'll be back before sunrise...although I doubt you'll be up for anything other than sleeping."

There was a sound of pride in his voice, making his tone husky and very...very sexy. I smiled at the sound and dragged my knee higher. He moved, fingers trailing over the curve of my ass, then down my thigh, until he moved to my ankle. He worked the bindings, peeling away the frayed rope from one ankle then the other before moving to my wrists.

"Where are you going?" The question sounded needy and very unlike me.

But the betrayal I'd experienced with Alex pushed to the surface.

"Meetings with the Wolves and the Fae. Don't worry, I'll remember to organize your escort for the morning. If the furry bastard had his way, he'd be hanging off your damn arm like a purse. Come to think of it...I could turn him into a damn satchel...fur and all."

I sniggered at the flare of jealousy and tilted my head, knowing instantly what he wanted. He kissed me deep, fingers spearing through my hair before he pulled away.

"Sleep," he murmured. "I'll be back before you wake."

There was a flare of panic as he rose. My heart thundered and an ache tore free. I was so used to them now, so used to being around them. I listened to the thud of his steps, and the rush of the stainless steel bedroom door. I tried to close my eyes, tried to let sleep move in. God knows I was exhausted enough, my body and my emotions spent. But the darkness wasn't my friend, leaving me feeling lonely...and desperate.

I groaned and pushed my feet from the bed, slipping to the side and let momentum take me, forcing my head from the pillow. I gathered the comforter around me, draping it over my shoulders, and stepped from the bed.

My fingers danced over the keypad before the door opened and I was greeted with the silence of the house once more.

"Can't sleep?" Rule asked from the living room.

The crackle of a fire drew my gaze. Rule sat on the sofa, legs crossed, his face glowing from the amber blaze. "No. For some reason—"

"You crave company?" He lifted his arm, the invitation all I wanted.

I gripped the comforter and headed for the living room. He watched me, eyes drifting to where the comforter exposed the top of my breast. He was different from Elithien, quieter, more controlled. I sank onto the sofa and his arm slipped around my shoulders.

"I never did thank you for the clothes." I lifted my gaze to his. "You sized me up to perfection."

"Yeah, I have..." he answered, and turned his head, looking into my eyes.

Heat moved through me with the stare. But Rule just pulled me closer, letting me slide my arms around him. God, he smelled good. Deep, faint desire.

"Close your eyes, Ruth," he murmured. "You're safe here. Sleep, beautiful."

Exhaustion hit me as I laid my head against his chest. The crackling of the fire lulled me, drawing me into that heaviness. I could feel the warmth in his body, warmth that enveloped me... and in the perfection of Rule's arms, I finally let go...and slept.

I woke sometime later, feeling movement, and cracked open my eyes, finding Elithien. He carried me, the comforter still wrapped around me. A small smile broke free as I closed my eyes once more. "I was having the most delicious dream about you."

"Were you?" he said, giving me a seductive smile of his own.

I let that feeling sweep over me, cradled in his arms as I fell back into the darkness once more...and woke sometime later with his body curled around mine, his hand resting protectively on my thigh. I tried to get back to sleep, still feeling that pull of exhaustion, but the moment I started to think about my family, I knew there was no hope of more rest.

I rose and looked behind me at the bed. He'd not only carried me to bed, but he'd set beside the bed a mountain of designer bags which I expected were filled with clothes. I walked to the bathroom and switched on the light, wincing as the glare filled the room.

I guess there was one advantage to sleeping with the undead. It didn't matter how much noise I made, they wouldn't even notice. I strode to the mountain of bags and carried them into the bathroom. Inside one was a brand-new cell phone. I pressed the button, and it was charged and ready. Contacts saved...the only ones that were important, at least.

A glance at the bed, and my heart swelled. He'd saved all their numbers for me, as well as Arran's. There was a message already. One Elithien had sent from his own phone. It seemed I had an escort arranged at noon. I checked the time and it was almost eleven. I had to hurry.

I yanked clothes from the other bags. They were exquisite, as I expected, high-end dresses and power suits with plunging necklines. He wanted me to look good, to find that fire in me once more.

But then my gaze settled on a matte black paper bag with gold etching of the company name on the front. *Dirty Needs.*

"What the hell?" My heart gave a stutter.

All of a sudden, I didn't care about Arran, or anything else, for that matter. A tiny *clink* rattled inside as I lifted the bag closer. It was heavier than the others. I opened the top, to find black wrapping paper. Excitement took a flogger to my nerves as I slipped my hand inside the mouth of the bag and touched leather.

My stomach tightened. Something fluttered in my chest.

I gripped whatever it was and lifted.

Chains...leather. It looked like a jumble of leashes and lace as they hit the counter. Brass caught my eye. I lifted the mess of chains and held it up. It almost looked like a...*harness?*

My pulse thundered in my ears as I put it down. The black leather was next. I lifted, finding the back and the front, in my mind, putting the straps into place just under my breasts. Heat flared through me and, as I turned to the last accessory, that thunder turning deafening in my ears.

It was lace...black and *exposing.* I lifted the garment up and knew this was the one he'd spent time choosing. I could imagine his fingers running down the fabric, remembering what we did...and what he wanted to do with me in this.

High neckline...made from lace that wrapped around my throat.

Three straps ran down from the lace, joining to a metal ring at my chest.

The middle was exposed, just one strap running all the way down, enough to separate bare breasts. I wanted to wear it... wanted it more than any Gucci dress or Jimmy Choo heels.

I wanted to look sexy for him...*for all of them.*

I wanted to find power in the submission.

I sucked in a deep breath and placed the garment down, laying it out. I'd be wearing this...sometime very soon, and I couldn't wait to see their reaction.

The thought made me feel powerful. More powerful than I'd felt in a long time. I smiled and hurried to the shower, turning it on and letting the steam fill the room before I stepped under the spray. I stood under the hot water, tilting my head to let the water run through my hair before I reached for the body wash.

But there were more bottles sitting next to his on the shelf. I blinked through the water and grabbed the midnight blue bottle, popped the lid, and lifted it to my nose.

Deep, sultry, and seductive drifted out. The scent was faint, and sensual, so very different from the wash Justice had for me. This one was all predatory, all...*Alpha.*

I squeezed the liquid onto the washcloth. That's how Elithien saw me, not as someone to be dominated, *but as an equal.* I smiled as I washed, feeling the ache between my thighs from last night.

My fingers traveled to the juncture, feeling that pang. But there were no wounds, not even a bruise. Just two tiny red marks...which I knew would fade. My body might be unblemished, but the Vampire was doing some serious damage to my heart.

I washed and conditioned my hair, and just stood under the spray. I was falling for these Vampires, falling hard and fast. The thought terrified me, like I was toppling into a void of darkness...one where there was no bottom...there was just the fall—and them.

I hit the lever and ended the spray before I grabbed the towel neatly placed for me. I hadn't noticed a cleaner come and go. But this place was far too immaculate for someone not to come every day. I made a mental note to ask Elithien about them and hurried to dry and dress.

Tailored midnight blue wide-leg slacks and a simple pinstripe blouse were perfection. I slid them on and brushed my hair, taking the time to look at myself in the mirror.

I looked like me. Moved like me.

But I wasn't me...I was inherently changed under this skin.

My senses were different, emotions too deep to be anything other than dangerous.

And I had *them.* My protectors. My *Vampires.*

I slid my hair back over my shoulders, grabbed the last bags on the counter, and reached inside, pulling out black Valentinos and Louboutins. But I grabbed a set of lower heels and slipped them on. They were perfect, matching the outfit without betraying that newfound sense of strength.

I grabbed the phone and a small midnight blue clutch. There was a wallet inside, one filled with hundred-dollar bills.

Any other woman might be giddy at the thought of any man dropping twenty thousand dollars in clothes, shoes, and cash on her. But I wasn't one of those women. I lifted my head and met my gaze in the mirror, feeling that tremble of hunger ripple outwards.

I wanted my own empire, my own money...my own *justice.*

That's what I wanted. I wanted Alexander to *see me...and fear me.*

I wanted *everyone* to know who I was...and what I came from. "You mess with Ruth Costello, don't expect to survive."

I turned away, heels clacking on the tiled floor before they sank into the carpet. I moved to the side of the bed, knelt, and kissed his cool cheek. "Sleep well, my love. I'll be back when I've figured out my way forward."

He didn't move, didn't breathe. But I knew, that somehow he heard me. He wouldn't have bought me an entire wardrobe without knowing this was where I was heading. I rose and went to the door, punching in the code before I stepped out.

I checked the phone. Arran should be here any minute. My stomach grumbled, reminding me that, unlike my companions, I was very much mortal. I stepped into the kitchen and yanked open the refrigerator door.

It seemed clothes, shoes, and perfume weren't the only things they'd anticipated. The shelves were full to overflowing, fruit, vegetables, and meat still sealed. But a plate of blueberry muffins sat neatly on the second shelf with a small handwritten note from...I was betting Justice.

For you.

My heart gave a flutter. "Okay, settle down," I told it, fighting a smile as I lifted the plastic wrapping and grabbed one from the plate.

The Vampire had baked for me.

Who knows when...my cheeks flushed with heat. I knew exactly when...

I took a bite and closed the refrigerator door before I slowly made my way to the front of the house. There was no Kern this time, no cruel remarks that made me feel like shit. *Fuck him.*

Fuck everyone who had an opinion.

Including my family.

I unlocked the front door and pulled it open, closing my eyes at the rush of heat as the sun hit my skin. I stood there, waiting...until I finished the muffin, then checked my phone. Elithien had said noon...and noon had come and gone thirty minutes ago. I stepped out onto the drive and glanced around the simple gardens.

Waiting had never been my strong suit. I paced the drive, checking my phone every couple of minutes, and with every minute that slipped away, my impatience grew. I grabbed the phone and pressed an icon, mentally running through my head what I wanted to say. But I never got there. The voicemail picked up with a seductive growl.

"...you've reached Arran. Leave your number if you're hot. Fuck off if you're not. I don't give a shit either way."

"Nice," I snarled and left a message, keeping it calm and controlled.

It was after one now, heading to two...I paced again for a bit, then strode back into the house, sinking into the shadows and quiet once more. Leather creaked as I sank against the sofa cushions. My foot swung agitatedly, my legs crossed and uncrossed as I checked my phone for the tenth time. When it neared two fifteen, I stood up, crossed the room, and headed for the study.

The door was closed but unlocked. I knew exactly where the Explorer's keys waited and grabbed them from the desk before striding out. The Wolf forgot...or something came up. That was okay. I'd meet him at the Hunting Ground.

I unlocked the front door as footsteps echoed from Kern's side of the house. I knew he was there, knew as soon as I left, he'd be locking the damn door behind me, hoping I'd crash into a ditch somewhere and die. But he was shit out of luck. Elithien wanted me escorted, so I'd play chase with Arran.

That was Elithien's hard line...

One I respected.

I'd not put myself into danger like that ever again.

I climbed into the four-wheel drive, started the engine, backed out of the drive, and shot forward. The drive to the Wolves' club was beginning to feel a little too comfortable. Even as I gripped the wheel, I saw the dancer in my mind, and the woman with her hands tied.

I knew how that felt now. How powerful it was to allow another to control your very existence. Elithien had shown me that night...I shivered with the memory.

The streets were busy for this time of the day. Cars were parked outside the nightclub. But none were a red Jeep Wrangler. "Damnit." I swung the Explorer into a vacant space further down and climbed out, locking it with the press of a button.

A slow, throbbing beat echoed from behind the closed doors. It seemed sex sold every second of the night and day. I steeled myself for the onslaught and stepped up, pushing open the door.

There was no bouncer today, no frisky pat down or grumble of how much he wanted to grab my ass. The entrance was empty. But there were a few men sitting on darkened plush velvet lounges watching the dancers as they ground and bent over. I made my way down the stairs and headed for the bar, drawing the eye of a male bartender. "I'm looking for Arran."

He just gave a shrug and gave me the onceover.

"I'm supposed to meet with him."

He flipped a dish towel over his shoulder, gave me the once-over again and jerked his gaze toward the rear of the building. "Newcomers are to go into the back, dress, and wait."

A twitch of a smile found my lips. "I'm not a dancer."

"She's with the Vamps," a voice came from behind me.

I turned and froze, finding myself face to face with her. My gaze sank to her hands and her long, elegant fingers, remembering how the rope wound around and around her arms and her throat before delving between her thighs.

"He's in a meeting with the Alpha, Phantom. You said he was to meet you?" She was concerned.

"Yes, at my home...I mean at the Vampires'."

"I know what you meant, honey. You don't have to explain

anything, especially to me." She reached out and placed her hand on mine.

She was nice, like *really fucking nice*. Deep brown hair tied up in a high pony-tail, a simple white button top and black and white stripped shorts that showed her long legs off perfectly.

"I'm supposed to meet Phantom there. I can give you a ride over if you want?"

"Blaisey," the bartender warned, placing his hands on the bar. "You're not supposed to give out the locations of their dens to strangers."

Her smile turned cold. "She's not a stranger, Rudy. How about you just mind your own business and I'll mind mine?"

He didn't like that, shoving away from the bar and growling over his shoulder as he turned away. "Phantom gets wind of this, and it's on you."

"If Phantom gets wind of anything, it'll be you feeling up the dancers on your damn break," she muttered, and gripped my hand. "Come on, I can drive. I know exactly where they are."

I glanced back at the bartender before following her as she made her way toward the back corner of the club, shoved through another door, and out into a hallway. This one didn't lead into a black painted hallway, but instead to perfect white, with the sound of chatter coming from the back.

"Come on, I'll introduce you to the others." She tugged me with her, and strode through the open door into a dressing room that seemed to stretch for miles.

Chatter stopped and heads turned. These women were fucking stunning. I'd seen more than one gracing the covers of modeling magazines.

"Girls, this is…" She turned to me.

"Ruth," I supplied, smiling at the perfect faces, my gaze stopping at the stunning blonde in front of me. She was the dancer from the main floor, the one who had made my pulse race and made me question my own sexuality. Dusty pink lips the same color as her shirt and dark blue jeans made her look spectacular.

"She's with the Vamps," Blaisey clarified.

"So you're the one they're infatuated with. Well done." The blonde rose. "This side of the river can get...pretty intimidating at the best of times, so feel free to come to us when you need some girl-time." She thrust out her hand. "Your phone. I'm Stevie, by the way." She nodded at the others, "that's Asher, Jamie, and Romeo."

They all lifted their hands, one by one. But it was Stevie who punched her number into my phone before she handed it back with a smile. "Call me anytime, gorgeous."

I shook my head as Blaisey backed away. "Come on, let's get out of here."

I followed her to the back of the dressing room before she punched a code into the keypad and pushed open the door.

"They seem nice," I commented, totally out of my depth here.

"We stick together, it can be..." she looked around before finishing. "Dangerous out here."

My gut clenched at the words as she headed for a sleek little dark blue Alfa Romeo parked beside a monstrous white Ford Raptor that gleamed in the sunlight.

She unlocked the door and climbed in, leaving me to follow as I slipped into the passenger's side. "I'm happy to drive myself," I started.

"It's totally fine," she smiled, before glancing over her shoulder and hitting the central locks that gave a *clunk*.

"Ah, everything okay?"

"Yes, of course. Can't be too careful, right?" she said, and gave me a wink.

But I had that sinking feeling that everything wasn't okay as she shoved the car into reverse and backed out. My pulse sped as I gripped the seatbelt across my body and held my breath. We hit the driveway hard before the tires caught, spearing us out onto the street. I caught a glimpse of the Explorer before we turned left, raced along the street under the gunned engine, and left the Hunting Ground behind. There were more strip bars, all of them open and turning a dollar. The Wolves ran a tough line of businesses, so Rule said. He'd also said this was nothing compared to the clubs they owned, most of them on the mortal side of the city. There were clubs over there that catered to men who wanted the pleasure of a woman who was a Wolf. I'd shivered as he spoke about it and pulled the comforter closer around me...they put Costello Corporation to shame.

But the moment I asked about the Fae, the conversation with Rule had stalled, and ended with a warning. *You don't want to know about them, Ruth. They aren't the kind of creatures you want to mess with.*

They were the kind of Mafia Monsters that sent a shiver of warning along my spine.

Blaisey lifted her gaze to the rear-view mirror again. It was the third time she'd scanned the cars parked along the streets as we drove past, but as I shifted my gaze ahead, I felt the saliva dry up in my mouth. The gigantic warehouse rose up like a mountain. A mountain that held Russell like a prisoner.

Pain flared through my chest. My hand clenched around the armrest, nails digging into the stitching of the leather. Desperation made me want to wrench the wheel and demand to stop. But we were by in an instant, tearing past and headed for a part of the west side of the river I'd never been to before.

The screech of tires behind us wrenched Blaisey's gaze to the mirror. "Oh, shit," she whimpered, her skin turning ashen.

"What is it?" I turned, glancing over my shoulder at the red Ferrari riding our ass like a second layer of paint. "You know this asshole?"

"Fucking psychopath client." Blaisey worked the gears and the wheel as fast as she could.

But she was heavy on the clutch and the wheel, jerking it

hard enough to slam me against the door as we turned. But the racing engine behind us kept pace, and instead sideswiped us as we turned.

The hard jolt sent us spinning. Tires howled as the wheel was jerked from Blaisey's hands. We hit something with a *crash*. I was thrown sideways hard, my head smashing against the window. Pain plunged across my head as we came to a stop.

The engine hissed, ticking like a bomb as Blaisey let out a low moan. I winced, and lifted my hand to my head. Warmth slick against my fingers and the smell of blood returned. Terror tried to push to the surface as Blaisey blinked and opened her eyes.

"You okay?" she moaned.

Shadow spilled across the inside of the car as the driver's door was yanked open.

"Thought you could get away from me, huh bitch?"

I winced with a stab of pain and turned my head. The shadows shifted as he leaned forward. I tried to breathe, tried to stop the uncontrollable fear from claiming me...as Alexander leaned through the open door and reached for me.

23

RUTH

"**N**o...*no!*"
My scream ripped through the car as the shadows shifted across his face. One blink and his features changed, and I realized he wasn't Alexander at all. But someone with the same dirty blond hair and animalistic, savage gaze.

"Damien, *get the fuck off me!*" Blaisey roared as he fisted her hair, stabbed the seatbelt release, and yanked her from the car.

"Fucking *bitch!*" he dragged her upright, then shoved her so hard she stumbled, flinging herself toward the car door to keep from falling.

That's when I saw the gun. Stainless steel glinted in the sun, freezing me with terror.

You're stronger than you think, Elithien's voice found me as I sat in the car. Blood slipped into my eye. I blinked, trying to figure out what to do. *You can find freedom in being confined.* His strength seeped through. My thoughts were slow...*achingly slow,* until my hand dropped to the seatbelt clasp.

I took strength from Elithien's words in my mind. Took strength from him, for it was all I had. The seatbelt was gone before I knew it. I pulled the door handle and shoved it open. I stumbled from the car and lifted my hand.

"I fucking *told you not to lie to me,*" the guy roared, lifting the gun in his hand. "I fucking warned you. But you go running back to that fucking *dog!*"

Blaisey cowered, lifting her hands in front of her defensively. The look of terror on her face pinned me to the ground. I stood there, heart hammering, unable to find the right words to say. I just said anything, the first words that came to mind. "You know who she works for, right?"

Only then did he even register I was there, lifting that unhinged gaze to meet mine. "You think I give a fuck about the Wolves? I *own* them. They'd be *nothing* without me. I know about the Fae, too...about what they do. How about that?"

He was high on adrenaline, and power... a deadly combination.

"Damien, please. I'll do whatever you want." Blaisey pleaded as she cried.

Tears glistened, sliding down her cheeks as she held onto the car door, desperate to keep standing. But the guy was unhinged, waving the gun in her face as he loomed over her.

There was something about seeing her cowering that triggered that uncontrollable sense of fragility in me. I took a step on trembling legs and clutched hold of the memory of my Vampires. Cold, steely hunger flared deep. I used that hunger, driving it into my words as I fixed my gaze on the piece of shit and spoke. "What did you think was going to happen here? You think you can walk away from this? Drop the gun and leave...at least you'll have a head start to run for your life." The bitch in me rose to the surface. "They'll kill you, you know that, don't you? You hurt her...and you're a *dead man.*"

I took a step, my ankle buckling as I straightened, grabbing the door to stay upright. The pounding in my head was all-consuming, like my head was being crunched between two massive jaws. *Crunch, bang. Crunch, bang.* Blood ran thick into my eye, blurring the asshole as he stepped away from her and pointed the gun at me.

"Shut the fuck up, *slut.* I'm not going to warn you again."

"She's not going to love you, no matter what you do to her." I shook my head and was rewarded with a pain like a sledgehammer blow. "She's *never* going to be anything other than afraid of you. So I ask again, *what did you think you were going to get out of this?*"

He swiveled to me then, just as I knew he would. He shoved her, and she sank against the front of the Alfa Romeo as the engine hissed and spewed steam from under the hood.

"You *bitches* think you can fucking take whatever you want, don't you?" he snarled, eyes wild as he came toward me. "You like the money, you like the *thrill.* But the moment you have to hold up your end of the bargain, you back away like the *cunt* you are."

"No, Damien. It's business. It's just business," Blaisey whimpered.

"*Business?*" He never once took his eyes from mine.

I fought the need to fall to the ground, fought that weakness in me to survive, to make no sound, to just close my eyes and disappear...and *sink.* I could keep sinking, slipping deeper into that midnight water once more until I ceased to exist.

As the gun rose in the air, I knew I'd finally get my wish...*I'd cease to exist forever.*

"I tried to stop this," he muttered, and that *disconnected* look filled his eyes. "Tried to make the bitch see reason. I paid for her. I paid for her, so she belongs to me."

He was no longer a man, no longer human. He was nothing but *injustice.* Nothing but his own pathetic pride. I froze as he slowly lifted the gun, the muzzle trailing up my body until it stopped at the center of my chest.

"I'm going to finish this, and I'm going to take *her.* She needs to learn her place. She needs to know I paid for her. I..." there was a flicker of hesitation in his eyes. "I own her."

Finish this...he means finish me.

His finger curled around the trigger as his gaze sharpened and he came back to reality in a rush.

There was no stopping this. No amount of screaming would change what was coming.

I'd screamed and begged for my life before...*and look what'd happened.*

My hands trembled, slipping against the smooth metal of the car door as I fought to stay upright, closed my eyes, and braced for the end.

It came in thunder.

It came in the deafening *boom...boom...boom* in my ears.

It came in an inhuman roar that made the world around me tremble.

And the ground beneath me quaked.

Darkness swallowed me, like the sun was snatched away in the afternoon of the day. Tires howled as the car was shoved sideways, and Blaisey screamed. I wrenched open my eyes, to find Russell, towering and terrifying, one massive fist wrapped around the fucking psycho's neck.

I *knew* it was him, knew it by the sandy blond hair. Knew it by the way he moved. Knew it by his smell. But the beast inside I didn't know...and it was the beast that rose in front of me now, terrifying, with hard muscles rippling under a torn, grimy shirt as he drove our attacker into the air.

The asshole jerked and grunted, his long legs kicking wildly

"Russell?" His name was a whisper on my lips.

But he jerked his head toward me. His hard, bestial gaze traveled over my body before meeting mine once more. This wasn't the Russell I knew. This man...*this creature* was inhuman, darkness and death. *Fae,* my mind whispered.

He was Fae.

I was drawn back to the dock…to the night Arran had made me relive the terror. To that creature that had slipped from the shadows. That darkness. That terrifying *thing*.

The same endless dark eyes.

The same shadows that swirled and danced all around him—even in the middle of the day. Shadows that clung to his body in ways my mind couldn't understand. Darkness that slashed like whips. Like *he* commanded the night.

His fingers…*dear Jesus, his fingers.* They were nothing more than claws, long, black, tapered, the tips sinking into the asshole's neck.

"Fuck you!" the piece of shit gurgled. *"Fuck you, you Unseelie motherfucker! I OWN HER!"*

There was a *bang* that made me jump, then another…*bang…bang…bang…* The sounds kept coming, and the hot, biting stench of gunpowder stung my nose. The gun trembled in the psycho's hand, the muzzle aimed straight for Russell's chest until there was only the *click* of an empty chamber left, and Russell turned those savage, dark eyes to him, and *smiled*.

"Wait, WAIT—" the asshole started.

But he never got to finish.

A *crunch* ended his plea, followed by a sickening *slop*. Russell released his hold…and the psycho slid to the ground. His neck was crushed, the indents of Russell's fingers still embedded into his flesh. But it was Russell's eyes that gripped me as blood continued to run down my cheek.

"Ruth," Russell whispered, drawing my gaze.

There were bullet holes in my bodyguard's chest. Bullet holes and a blackened mess as he turned toward me.

"Did he hurt you?" His growl tried to sound gentle…his claws carved through the air, *aching* to touch. But he was too much beast in that moment. Too much Unseelie. Too much *predator*.

Those midnight eyes glinted as his hand fell to his side. His massive chest expanded as he inhaled, nostrils flaring as he breathed deep once more. I realized he wasn't just breathing...*he was scenting me.*

Drawing me deeper inside him, down to where the darkness lay.

"I heard...I heard you," he mumbled. "You were like an explosion in my chest."

I flinched at the words as movement came in the corner of my eye.

"*Ah...hello?*" Blaisey called. "What about me?"

Sirens wailed, sharp and piercing. I flinched and whimpered as the sound thundered through my head. In a heartbeat, my feet left the ground as Russell swept me into his arms and lifted me close. Then there were hard steps, savage steps. Jolting and shuddering as he carried me, stumbling away.

"Keep you safe...*keep you safe*," he moaned, and jerked those inhuman midnight eyes to mine. "I'll keep you safe this time."

Darkness closed in, slipping from the cracks in the walls to shroud the building as we walked. It was the darkness I saw in him as the veins along his arms darkened, and spread upwards. But it wasn't just inky veins and his savage hunger...*something else slipped into the air.*

Something cold and inhuman.

Something that made the pounding in my head press in like a knife in my skull.

I whimpered as shudders tore up my spine.

"Keep you safe...*keep you safe. Keep...you...safe...*" Russell's voice shifted to a growl, one that made the darkness creep closer. Darkness that reached out as we passed the corner of a building. Darkness that stung my leg as it touched me.

"Stop...*Russell.*"

"*Keep...you...keep...you.*"

Agony cut deeper, like claws that raked my calf and scratched down my shin. I lifted my head, finding the bottom of my pants torn in a long savage gash. A gash that hadn't been there a second before.

Shadows slipped away as we stepped off the curb and crossed the narrow alley, heading once more into the murky shadows. The pain was searing, pulsing all the way down to my ankle, and still the darkness was rising, calling the shadows to arms. Those midnight fingers reached outwards, reaching for me once more. "Russel, *please. Russell...STOP!*"

Hard breaths crushed his chest against me as he froze and turned his head. Dark eyes shone like endless pools. This wasn't Russell...this wasn't the man I knew. This was...*Unseelie.*

"*Look at me!*" he roared, his eyes wide with fear and making me cower away from him. "*Look at what I am! I'm a beast...a... monster. If I had a shred of humanity left, I'd walk away. But I can't... I can't...*"

Elithien's warning consumed me. *He's dangerous, Ruth. He's not the man you once knew.*

"I can't stop," he whispered. "*Can't stop wanting you. Can't stop this fucking need to have you.*"

The smell of blood wafted into the air as he sank to his knees in the middle of the pavement. A car drove past, slowing to a crawl until Russell wrenched his head upwards, his lips curled as a guttural, possessive warning slipped free.

I shoved my hand against the concrete and kicked out my foot, scurrying out from under him.

"I can smell your blood." Russell shifted that threatening hunger to me. "...I can feel your pain. Your screams were deafening over and over *and over.* I need to touch you. I need to feel...you. *But I can't...I can't do that. Not to you.*"

He rose from the pavement to tower over me and for a second, fear plunged deep. He wasn't the man I once knew, not the bodyguard who'd fought to save me. This was something else. Something primal...*something terrifying.* But as I looked in his eyes, I saw a glimmer of that man...that man who had been murdered...that man brought back from the darkness. Still it clung to him, infected him like a virus.

Kapre. The beast rose in my mind like a nightmare. It was *his* blood in Russell's veins. His blood that called the shadows to life. *His blood that pumped through my bodyguard's heart.*

"You won't hurt me."

He lowered his head, that inhuman stare seizing mine. "Won't I?"

The way he said it made my blood run cold.

"No," I assured. "You won't. You'd tear apart anyone and anything else before you'd let that happen. Look at how you suffer. Look at how you *fight.*" I licked my lips and fought the tremble in my words. "It's okay...it's all going to be okay. You can come to me."

Horror filled his face, turning his skin ashen as he looked at the gash on my leg. "You don't understand. You don't know what I am now. You have *no idea what I can do.*" He stumbled backwards before he spun and slammed his hands against the brickwork of the building...and in one long, inhuman howl of rage, he emptied that blinding rage into concrete and bricks.

His roar was deafening, making me cower against the pavement. Darkness plunged down, stealing the sunlight from my day. But this was no twilight sky waiting...this was an *absence,* a hole...a *void* of *everything.*

Gone was the building. Gone was the street.

Gone was the world.

There was nothing but his screams.

Nothing but his fury.

Nothing but him...*him all around me. Him moving through my soul.*

Until slowly, the sound tapered and the wounded whimpers of pain took hold.

Light bled into the emptiness once more, like the passing of an eclipse. But something had changed in that eclipse, some *irrevocable change* that resounded in me. I shoved upwards as Russell sank to his knees, dragging his hands down the building's wall once more.

He wasn't just a bodyguard in this moment...he was...*more.*

He knelt there, head bowed, shoulders curled in an attempt to protect his heart.

"Russell." The pain pounded in the base of my skull as I moved. Still I pushed myself upwards, driving to my knees. The sting of my leg made me catch my breath, but I reached out to him and gently placed my hand on his shoulder.

He sank into that touch, his muscles quivering, rippling down his spine.

"I...can't control myself with you. I don't know how to fight this *hunger.*"

"Then don't."

He froze, tiny shudders of his body all that remained.

"Don't fight this...whatever it is."

"You don't mean that." His tone was stone cold. "I have no choice here. I *have* to protect you, even if it's from myself."

He pulled away from me, shoved against the ground, and stood.

He didn't meet my gaze, only stared at the claw marks on my leg. "I need to take you to them...the Vampires will protect you." *From me.*

He didn't have to say the words...they rang in the air, a remnant of those tortured whimpers.

"The nightclub...the Wolves' nightclub. The car is there," I directed.

He nodded and clenched his jaw, his steps stuttering as though his body and his head fought for control. In silence, he bent, slid his arms underneath me, and lifted me once more.

He carried me, his long strides eating up the ground, but he did not look at me.

Not once did he meet my gaze. Instead he kept his focus in the distance.

Warm, slick tears fell, and as I shuddered, they hit my arm. The *boom...boom...boom* in my head was savage, forcing me to close my eyes until he finally slowed.

"Keys," he explained. "I'm just finding the keys."

There was a brush against my thigh. Hard, callused fingers skimmed my hips and delved into my pocket.

The *beep* of the locks sounded. The car door was opened and I was lifted inside, to the leather seats of the Explorer.

"Keep your eyes closed until I can check your head, okay?" he urged.

I whimpered and lifted my hands, cradling the back of my head as the muscles knotted and bombs detonated inside my skull. Something snapped tight across me and the *click* of a seatbelt followed before the gentle *thud* of my door closing boomed through my head.

He was so gentle, so utterly gentle. His hand grazed my thigh, and this time there were no claws. This time, there was no darkness out for blood.

I cracked open my eyes to meet his gaze. Behind the inky darkness of his eyes he was still in there, that guy who'd made me laugh on the day of my father's funeral. That guardian who'd stood behind me bare-assed and bruised as I walked across the hospital room to give a doctor a piece of my mind.

The bodyguard who'd given his life to protect me.

And came back from the cold embrace of death to do it again.

The Explorer started with a roar, making me wince at the sound.

"Sorry," he murmured as I sank back into the seat. The gears *clunked* and the four-wheel drive surged forward. Tires skidded and the car lurched and braked, throwing me forward, until it slowly rolled.

"I can't fucking do this," he growled.

I reached out blindly, finding the bulging muscles of his arm, and whispered, "You will...*for me.*"

He was bred for protection. It was in his DNA. But now, with the Unseelie creature's blood in his veins, he needed to learn how to contain all that strength once more. He was a lighthouse weathering a storm. Only this storm was unrelenting, this storm was for life.

The car crept forward little by little. I opened my eyes as something shot past us like a rocket. "That was a scooter...that went past us like we were standing still." I gently turned my head and looked at the speedometer...*ten miles an hour.*

Massive hands swallowed the wheel as Russell stared at the road with deadly concentration and finally, the car moved forward.

It was like a toddler behind the wheel of a Lamborghini, all power...*all grunt.* Only, his body had all the horsepower under the hood, it was just his senses that needed to catch up. I closed my eyes as we picked up speed, moving forward. I tried to keep the pain away, but it gnawed and crunched, consuming my head with every savage thud of my pulse. We seemed to drive forever, until the car slowed...and pulled into the Vampires' drive.

"Hold still, I'll come for you," he ordered as the engine died.

The pain was growing now...stabbing an unseen blade through the base of my skull to rearrange my brain. The driver's door opened and closed. He was around to my side in a heartbeat, yanking open the door to gently lift me free.

"I don't know where else to take you," he spoke as he carried me, stopping as the front door was yanked open.

"You're not welcome—*oh, it's you.*" Kern's biting tone made the agony rise another notch.

"Fuck you," I whispered, and winced at the flare of pain.

"Where?" Russell growled.

"The living room. It'll be sundown soon, anyway. They can deal with her then...*again.*"

"That's it." I forced my eyes open and shoved against Russell's arm. "Imma beat your *fucking* ass."

Russell whipped his head toward that nerdy motherfucker and snarled.

"Fine, suit yourself." The tattooed groupie backed away. I had just enough strength to lift my middle finger in a perfect salute.

Russell laid me on a sofa and hurried to the kitchen, the rush of water sounded before the heavy thud of steps returned. Cold pressed against my skin...and the cruel sting followed. I whimpered, wincing.

"Easy, easy now," he murmured, and gently pressed his fingers to my hairline. "It's deep...it might need some stitches."

A growl filled me, pressing against my head like thunder. But this time it wasn't Russell...*it was my Vampires.*

I could feel them, restless...feel them opening their eyes... desperate for the day to be over, and for night to come, feel them fighting that natural instinct to sleep...for just a little longer. But more than that, they smelled me...smelled my blood...and my fear. Smelled death's touch against my skin... and they were coming.

I let out a low moan, and the sound burned through my chest.

"Ruth?" Russell held my stare as he rose. Shadows spilled around him once more. Something was triggering him. *No, not something...someone...*

Four someones.

"I'm trying to fight this," Russell forced through clenched teeth.

Leather squeaked under me, and my head hit the armrest. I ground my teeth and swallowed a scream, then inhaled deeply before I whispered. "Step back..." The air around me trembled as darkness slowly moved in. "Step back from me."

That dominating sound spilled out from the rooms along the

hall. Vampires in the throes of rage was one thing...but mated ones when their mates were hurt...*was another level of rage altogether.*

The sun retreated slowly, inching away from us. But it was still too early as the steel door opened and that rumble of rage spilled out into the hall.

Along the hallway, another door opened, and Justice's anger quaked through the darkening house.

"Step away, Russell," I pleaded, and slowly lifted my gaze to Russell's. "They'll hurt you."

He dropped his hand and rose as shadows spilled through the house. Doors opened again and again with a hiss, and the sounds sent chills along my spine. I felt them hovering at the doorway, the heavy rushes as they breathed the scent of my blood deep.

"What the fuck happened?" Elithien yelled as he strode through the darkened doorway, yanking down a t-shirt over untied sweat pants.

His skin hissed as he reached for me, pale skin turning black and cracking under the caress of the dimming sun. But he didn't care about that now. His long fangs punched from between his lips. His dark eyes glittered with rage as he bent over me and lifted a hand to the cut along my hairline, searching my head for wounds.

"Elithien!" Justice roared. His voice boomed through my head, making me whimper.

The house was filled with the thud of heavy steps...and the stench of a Vampire's rage. I winced, lifting my gaze to them as Russell stepped back. They were all around me in an instant. Justice lifted me from the leather sofa and into his arms as Elithien rose from the floor.

Fingers pressed on me as they reached out to touch me to reassure themselves. Pain flooded me, taking me further away from them...making me desperate and weak.

"Explain" he forced through his teeth, those dark eyes chilling as they settled on me.

"She was—" Russell started...and stopped as Elithien whipped that unmerciful stare toward him.

"You?" the Alpha turned on him. "You did this?"

"No!" I shoved their hands away. "No, Elithien!"

"You *motherfucker,*" the Vampire turned on my bodyguard in an instant. "I told you to *stay away from her!*"

Desperation took over, battling the flames in my chest with thunderous wings as I fought against the agony and forced the words, "He...*he saved me.*"

"Stop it! You're hurting her!" Russell roared, his eyes shell-shocked wide, skin almost gray. Hard breaths consumed him... savage breaths as the air around him danced with black tendrils of Unseelie power. The same shadows that'd reached from the cracks of the buildings to claw my leg.

The room fell silent. Hard breaths filled the space as every hair on the nape of my neck stood on end. Russell was outnumbered, four deadly Vampires to one. Still, he took a step forward, meeting Elithien's gaze head-on and demanded, "Look at her."

Darkness descended and it wasn't just the sun that slipped away. It was Elithien...that beast in him...that part of him that saw only betrayal and rage, that part shattered.

"Jesus fucking Christ," he groaned as he stepped forward. His hands trembled as he touched me, sliding along my cheek to brush my hair from my shoulders. "Talk to me. Tell me what the fuck happened?"

I closed my eyes as the terror rose. The screech of the tires, the shattering of the glass. That moment where I was sure that Alexander had returned to end me once and for all.

Through the deafening booming of agony in my head, I started talking. The words were only whispers...but in the quiet of the house, they rang out. "I waited...like I promised, but Arran never came."

"Sonova—" Hurrow snarled, and turned his menacing look away.

"Go on," Elithien urged. But that chill was back in his tone and when I looked into his eyes, I saw only vengeance.

"I waited until almost two, then drove to the club to find him. But he wasn't there, and Blaisey..."

The sharp intake of breath that came from Rule made me stutter.

"B-Blaisey offered to drive me to where she was supposed to meet him and Phantom."

"I told you we can't trust them." Hurrow turned his head to Elithien. "I warned you they only look out for themselves."

There was a twitch at the corner of Elithien's eye, but he didn't answer his second, only held my gaze and gave a slow nod for me to continue.

"There was some kind of psycho...some crazy fucking guy with a gun. He drove us off the road and we crashed. I thought...I thought—" panic consumed me, dragging me back to that moment in the car as he reached for me. I closed my eyes and continued. "I thought it was Alex...for a second, as he opened the door and reached for us, I thought it was Alex all over again."

"Fuck..." Elithien spat. "I can assume you disposed of that piece of shit?"

But there was no answer...nothing but silence. Silence that made me open my eyes.

Russell was gone...gone in the midst of anger...gone in the tsunami of rage.

And as the engine of the Explorer roared to life and the howl of tires burning on the asphalt tore through the open door, I answered for him. "Yes, he protected me with his life, as always."

24

ELITHIEN

"He protected me with his life..." She winced as she answered.

...because you weren't there...again.

She didn't need to say it. I knew it anyway. I saw it in her flinch, in the way she caught her breath, in that wide-eyed frozen look that had returned to her gaze.

I wasn't there...I wasn't *there*. I clenched my jaw, shifted my gaze to Hurrow, and saw that vengeful fucking slap in my face. He'd been right about the Wolves, right when he said they had their own agenda, one that didn't involve us.

But I'd thought I could trust Arran...thought the Wolf would keep her safe.

I was wrong.

Justice shook his head. "Elithien, no," the towering Vampire stepped toward me as I glanced at the front of the house.

There was no way out of this...no way we could protect her during the day...no way we could allow anything like this to happen ever again, and no way we could change her. I knew that now. She was Ruth Costello, head of the Costello Corporation, and powerful in her own right. I would not shackle her to a lifetime of living in fear. I would not have her used as a pawn in my fucking existence, either. "If you have another option, then I'm all fucking ears."

I met each gaze, first Justice, then Hurrow...and lastly Rule, as he probed the back of her head. I was desperate, my mind racing, tearing through every face and every name I had in my arsenal, and it all came down to one simple thing.

He loved her.

Enough that he'd take a bullet for her...enough he'd forfeit his goddamn life. He'd done it once...*and he'd do it again.*

"*Elithien,*" Hurrow called as I turned.

"Take care of her...*I'll be back,*" I barked, and headed for the door. The sting was brutal as I stepped out the doorway. I lifted my arm, shielding my eyes as the last of the sunlight slipped over the mountains and disappeared. The sound of the racing engine of the Explorer drew me as the need to protect her consumed me.

I lunged, driving bare feet against the asphalt, and hunted. Out here, only beasts raced through the night, this side of the river, at least. I cut across the tree line and plunged across the turnoff rather than the highway as the red brake lights flared once and then the Explorer accelerated.

Powerful strides ignited the beast inside. I lowered my head and charged, driving my body faster and faster until the ground was nothing more than a blur...and my four-wheel drive drew closer.

One more plunge, and I charged through the grass at the turn in the road then, with one savage roar, I surged ahead, cutting through the grass and stopped in the middle of the road.

The headlights from the Explorer were blinding, but I didn't look away as the brakes locked on the four wheel drive and the vehicle skidded sideways, coming to a stop a hairsbreadth in front of me.

Shadows inside the cabin shifted. But he didn't climb out...

he just sat there, hands clenched around the wheel…staring at me with that midnight Unseelie gaze.

He was more creature than I'd anticipated.

And more trouble than he was worth.

"You were not supposed to live," I started, knowing damn well he could hear every word I said, even over the growl of the engine. "And now that you have, you're a…*complication.*"

Through the piercing glare, I caught the curl of his lips as he bared his teeth.

But I wasn't here to fight with him.

I was here for one reason, and one reason alone.

Her.

"Stay."

Silence.

"Stay with her at the house. We…*she needs you.*"

The engine revved and the Explorer moved forward…barely an inch. But it spoke fucking volumes. *No,* it said. *Get out of my way.*

"If you don't, then she will die," I challenged, the words tasting like bile in my mouth. "Is that what you want? Maybe next time, you won't make it in time to save her. Maybe next time, the bullet will be one second too fast. Maybe next time, Alexander will be back to finish the job." I forced the last through clenched teeth. "If you don't care for her, then I'll let you go. You can take the car…take it and run like the weak and insignificant male I think you truly are. But if you stay, if you stay, then you ensure her survival, and you might be one step forward in changing my fucking mind."

The bastard was fast for his size, shoving the door open and charging for me, just like I knew he would. I didn't fight him, didn't even lift a hand to protect myself as his massive hand clenched around my throat and lifted.

My feet dangled as they left the ground, and sweet darkness claimed my sight.

"You piece of fucking shit." His fingers clenched tighter around my throat. "I ought to kill you right fucking here."

"I can't...can't let you leave," I forced out, but I didn't battle... I didn't rage.

I hated him, hated the way she looked at him...hated his fucking name on her lips. I hated that he was her first desperate fight when we pulled her from that river...and the last as she sank into unconsciousness.

But right now, that didn't matter. "She...*needs you.*"

He let me fall with a savage snarl and turned away, pacing in front of the Explorer, his massive thighs eating the road as he stopped at the shoulder, then charged toward me once more. His Unseelie eyes glinted with unhinged malice. "*You* know what *I'm* fighting here."

"I know." That icy blade of jealousy cut deep. "You think I don't know you want her? You think I can't smell your desperation a thousand fucking miles away? The stench of it reeks and I'd rather *anyone* fucking else...Hell, I'd rather the goddamn Wolf touching her. But today has proven that hope is fucking dead now. So *you,* Unseelie...are my *only* goddamn choice."

Stunned silence followed. He stared at me for a long fucking time.

"Give me one fucking reason I'd come back with you right now."

I swallowed hard and met that savage Fae stare with my own. "Your name is her safe word."

He froze, his chest sank and there it sat, until I was sure he was dead. "What did you say?"

"Her safe word." My voice turned cold. "Your name is her safe word. *You are her fucking safe word.*"

He rocked back on his heels for a second, then lifted that soulless gaze to mine. The beast moved faster than I expected, charging forward, grabbing me as though I was nothing more than a fucking mortal. But I was past not fighting, past not being involved in her survival.

I grabbed him as he came for me, swung him harder than even he could control. It was my turn to grip the Unseelie around *his* goddamn neck until I was the driving force here, slamming him back on the hood of the four-wheel drive with a brutal *bang*!

"She *fucking needs you!*" I raged, fangs punched out as terror and cold cutting anger collided. I took in hard breaths and eased my grip a bit. "And she wants you. She fucking wants you, okay?"

I let the bastard go, releasing my hold around his throat, and stepped away.

He reached for his neck, massaging his throat.

He wanted me dead in that moment. I saw it all in his eyes. I winced and straightened my spine. I was fucking Elithien Venadi…and more than one had fucking tried—and failed.

"I don't like you." He straightened and tugged the ruins of his shirt. "Can't fucking stand you, actually. *Any* of you, especially those assholes back there."

The twitch came at the corners of my lips as I answered. "I think the feeling is mutual."

He stilled at that, his gaze boring into mine as the line was drawn. He seemed to think for a second, like the need inside him weighed a ton, until he swallowed hard.

I tried to brace myself for what was coming, tried to drag her face to the forefront of my mind. I tried to remember the way she loved me, how she opened up the darkest parts of herself for me. I held her there…held her while the sonofabitch took a stake to my heart.

"I won't be just a bodyguard."

I lifted my gaze to his, letting my emotions slip away.

"If she wants me like I want her, then you have to let it happen."

I tried to stop the snarl from vibrating out of that empty pit in my chest, but the warning spilled out.

But the bastard didn't stop, clenching his jaw before he continued. "I'll never push her. I'll never force anything to happen she doesn't want to happen. But if she makes a move... you can be damn sure I'll follow it up."

Mine! That savage hunger consumed me. I'd take his fucking throat out right now, spill his Unseelie blood across the asphalt and leave his body on the side of the road.

I closed my eyes. I'd tear his beating heart from his chest and drink the last of his miserable life. I'd undo all I'd done just to please her... then claim her body once more...with the blood of this Unseelie still on my lips.

I'd do it all...and I did, in my mind. I played out what would happen if I let the beast roam.

I'd explain him away, give her comfort while she grieved. I'd watch while Justice tended to her wounds, and Hurrow stole her grief with an insatiable need.

I'd do it all...and in the end...in the daylight, I'd still lose her.

One day, it could be today, I'd lose her, and there wouldn't be a damn thing I could do to stop it.

But he could.

This...Unseelie. Maybe he'd die before she wanted him in her bed. Maybe I didn't have to bloody my hands at all. I settled my gaze on the fucking mountain of a male and saw that Unseelie blood in his veins. He'd be hard to kill. But mistakes can always happen.

"Fine," I answered, meeting his gaze. "*If* she makes a move, then I won't stop it." His eyes widened. I'd taken him by surprise. Good.

"And the others?"

"Are under *my* command."

He smiled then, curling one side of that fucking mouth higher. "It's cute you think that."

The curl of *my* lip was instant. "Are you saying my men have been corrupted?"

My thoughts raced, sifting through every one of them. I'd known them for hundreds of years, killed for them. Sacrificed for them. I'd die for them…and they for—

"Ruth has a way of corrupting a fucking saint," he finished, and took a step forward. "I want your word they'll stand aside on this. I want your *fucking word I won't have to watch my damn back every second I'm with her.*"

"Watch your back?" I repeated. "If you're smart, you'll never stop watching it. You want her…then *prove to them you fucking deserve her.* I said I'd stand aside, but I never said they would."

"You're a piece of fucking work," he started.

"Welcome to the life of an Immortal. Now use that to protect her." I took a step closer, standing so close I could taste his fear. "You guard her…you never leave her fucking side, and when the darkness comes for her, and it *will* come…then you shield her with your pathetic Unseelie life. Because I promise you, if we lose her…I won't have to kill you…*you'll destroy your own fucking self.*"

A rumble sounded from the male's chest as I turned and walked away, giving the bastard my back as I strode toward the passenger's side, yanked open the door, and climbed in.

He stood there, bathed in the blinding glow of the Explorer's headlights, until finally the sullen bastard turned and strode to the open driver's door. Just like I knew he would.

We didn't speak, didn't utter a single fucking word as he climbed in and closed the door. Gears shifted and tires spun, kicking rocks against the undercarriage of the four-wheel drive as he spun the wheel and drove back home once more.

"I'll need a room," he announced.

"It can be arranged," I answered, remembering the antagonism Kern had unleashed about Ruth.

The mortal pissed me off.

"And clothes," Russell added.

"An account will be set up under your name. Whatever funds you need will be at your disposal."

"And my own car."

I felt a twitch and growled, "*Whatever* you need."

What if it's her? What if the thing he needs is the one thing I can't ever give?

He turned the Explorer, nosing it into the drive of my house and pulled to a stop in the front. The engine ticked softly in the quiet. Still, both of us sat there, silent...unable to move.

Until the front door opened and Hurrow strode out, his face a stony mask of rage. Times slowed for me as he lifted the phone in his hand. I yanked the door handle and shoved the door open.

"It's Villain." My second's eyes were wide and that unhinged, bestial look closed in. "They found him...they found Alexander."

The sharp inhale from the Unseelie was followed with a snarl so deadly it stood the hairs on my arms. I took the phone, lifting it to my ear. "Speak."

"We have him." The Wolf growled. "Hunted the sonofabitch until he made a mistake. We were waiting."

Relief swept through me, the surge so cold, I closed my eyes and hissed with the sting. "Alive?"

"And fucking breathing. But we can always change that."

"No." I opened my eyes and stared at the house...*my house... where the love of my life waited.* "I want him brought here, charter a flight. Under no circumstances are you to kill him, Villain. *Do I make myself clear?*"

"Crystal."

He *had* to understand...he needed to know. My hand shook as I lowered the cell and ended the call. I needed to end that motherfucker myself. I'd feast on his blood...I'd tear him limb from fucking limb and then I'd turn him. I'd rip that mortal sheath wide open and make him part of my line...

Just so I could do it all over again.

I lifted my gaze to Hurrow as the Vampire smiled.

We'd end him, we'd burn him. We'd render his existence null and fucking void.

And in the wake of his silence, the memory of him would disappear.

Ruth would be safe.

"You have him?" the Unseelie growled. For a second, I'd forgotten he was there...I knew nothing but vengeance...*nothing but rage.*

"Yes." I met the bodyguard's gaze. "We have him...we have the sonofabitch who murdered you."

He was once a mortal. But the male that now held my gaze was mortal no longer. Darkness shifted around him, pulling closer as that whisper of what he was becoming crawled to the surface. He was all beast now, all savage night...and limitless rage, until that shimmering violence died in his eyes and he whispered, "What are we going to tell Ruth?"

25

RUTH

"How's that?" Rule pressed the cold compress more firmly against the back of my neck and stared into my eyes.

I could feel his touch against my mind, feel the whisper of his power sweeping through me, and the aching throb inside my head dulled. "Better," I murmured and managed a weak smile. "Much better."

"Good. I can try to tape this," he said, glancing at the gash on the top of my forehead. "Or we can call in the good doctor to put in a stitch or two. Either way, your hairline will cover the scar, so you'll still be devastatingly beautiful," he added with a smile.

But I wasn't the one devastatingly beautiful. I lifted my hand and touched his cheek, sliding my thumb across his perfect lips. They parted under my touch. Stars sparkled in his perfect eyes as a cell phone rang somewhere behind me and was answered with the cold bark of a commander.

Hurrow's growl rang out. "You want to repeat that?" he demanded, drawing Rule's gaze from mine.

Confusion flared for a second, until not even my touch

could keep Rule close to me. He lifted his hand and captured mine before he kissed my palm and whispered "Hold this, I'll be right back."

I grabbed the compress, holding it to my neck as he strode from the bar to the living room.

"I understand," Hurrow growled as the headlights of a four-wheel drive flared across the house. "He'll want to hear this himself."

I lowered my hand as Hurrow turned away from Rule and headed to the door.

"What's going on?" I asked Justice as he watched his commander stride from the house.

Justice pushed up from the sofa, his voice trailing into a murmur. "I don't know."

But it was something. I *knew* it.

The engine died outside. Car doors opened and closed...*two of them.* I turned my head as Elithien's deep baritone voice drifted faintly through the open front door. Cold seeped into my fingers from the ice pack wrapped in the towel. But I could barely feel that now. I could barely feel anything as that bitter disconnected feeling filled my mind, making me float.

Something was happening.

Something *profound.*

The deep snarl from outside grew in degrees before silence returned. Stony silence...leaving the thud of my heart beating in my ears until the thud of steps followed. *Thud...thud...thud.* I stared at the corner of the hallway, stared until I felt the air on my eyeballs, and blinked.

A warning slipped from Russell, making him take a step forward, making him meet the movement as Elithien stepped into the room. But Justice's gaze didn't track him, it didn't even move from the entrance.

Elithien's eyes were wide when they met mine. He looked...*shocked.* I'd never seen him like this. Not barefoot, not with a crumpled shirt and sweat pants. Not *haunted,* and that's how he looked as he headed toward me and pulled me up into his arms.

"What's wrong?" I insisted, winding my arms around him, pressing the ice pack against his back. "Talk to me..."

"Everything's okay now. Everything's okay."

Hurrow stepped around the corner, shadows spilling against the cream-colored walls behind him. The darkness spilled upwards and outwards as Russell stepped into view. My heart stuttered and my body froze. I pulled away from Elithien as Hurrow went to stand beside Justice.

"What's going on?" I demanded, meeting Elithien's gaze as Justice unleashed a roar.

"Fuck, no, he isn't!"

But Elithien didn't answer, just stared into my eyes.

"E?" Justice barked and that savagery returned in my warrior as he turned on his own. "E, wanna fill me in on this?"

Elithien lowered his hands and stepped away from me before he turned to face the pissed-off male. "Russell will be staying. He's her bodyguard. He travels with her during the day, whatever she needs, he's there. Nothing changes here."

"Bullshit, nothing changes..."

Elithien swallowed hard and lowered his voice. "I gave him my word, Justice...and that's an *order.* He stays, he protects her when we're not able to. He is her..." Elithien stopped for a heartbeat.

He's my...he's my what?

"Protector," the Alpha finished. "He's her damn protector when we can't be. I *will not* have her life at risk...not anymore, and *you* shouldn't want that either."

"No...*no fucking way!*" Justice roared again, clenching his fists. He cracked his gaze toward my bodyguard, hate raging in his eyes.

But Russell didn't back down. He just met the Vampire's

stare with his own threat of violence and in a low voice murmured, "I gave my life to protect her once...you can be damn sure I'll do it again."

Tears filled my eyes as Justice took one gigantic stride forward. My heart hammered, punching into the back of my throat as Russell turned toward the attack. They were ready to fight...they were ready to kill...*and it was because of me.*

"No!" I left Elithien's arms behind and stepped forward. "No, I won't allow this to happen. I care for you...*both of you.* To hurt each other is to hurt *me.*" I moved to Justice, lifting my gaze to his.

He shifted his gaze toward me...like I knew he would. My hand trembled as I reached for his cheek. He was my wall, my cocoon...my *lover.* He washed my body, and kissed my skin. When I'd told him he could do whatever he wanted with me... he took care of me instead. Because that was the kind of man he was...the kind of man who'd give anything for my happiness...

I was asking him to do that again.

"Please, Justice. For me."

Pain flickered, tightening around his eyes as those perfect lips parted. I lowered my touch, taking his hand in mine. "I won't stand here and see you hate, not each other...not because of me."

Russell said nothing, just stood there, watching every flicker of emotion.

"You don't want me to end his life..." Justice started. "I won't. But I also won't stand by and watch while he...*while he...courts you.*"

My thumb stilled, gliding across his knuckles. "Court me?"

A sad smile touched his lips. "You really are perfect, Ruth. Too perfect for a fucking Unseelie. E, I'll be outside. I need the air."

He slipped his hand from mine and stepped away. Pain slashed across my chest as he backed away from me and turned, giving Russell a cold stare. I waited for words, for rage. But there was nothing but the heavy thud of his steps as he barged past Russell with a bump of his shoulder.

My bodyguard took the hit, wincing as he stumbled with the impact.

Court me? I couldn't swallow the words.

"Ruth, I'm going to need you to help Russell." Elithien forced the words. "Hurrow's clothes should fit him. You can use my amenities while I arrange a room."

I forgot about my head...forgot about the accident and the psycho, forgot about everything as I watched Elithien go after Justice.

"I think he's a bit too big for my shirts...but the pants should fit," Hurrow muttered, and stepped away. "I'll grab some of Justice's things."

"I'll, umm...I'll see what I can do about a room," Rule mumbled, and left quietly.

Then it was just the two of us.

Standing on opposite sides of the room.

I stared at him as he looked at the floor, then slowly lifted his gaze.

I hadn't looked at him before...*really looked at him.* I hadn't seen him as anything other than this awkward powerhouse of a male. A friend. That's how I saw him. Maybe there had been a moment after my dad's funeral when I'd thought I wanted something more...but as our gazes connected, the beat of my heart grew deeper. "Court me, huh?"

The color of his cheeks deepened as he gave a small smile. "Yeah, about that. I can explain."

"Don't even worry about it." I met his smile with my own, desperate to break the tension. "Let's just see about a shower, shall we?"

He reeked, his shirt stained and filthy. His black pants were ripped and worn in patches. The longer I looked at them, the more I was sure they were the ones he'd worn on that night.

They hadn't bathed him, hadn't really helped him, only made him alive. I took a step toward him and lifted my hand.

He flinched, his eyes wide with panic. "It's okay," I murmured. "I won't hurt you."

But that panic didn't seem to go away.

"I'm more worried I'll hurt you," he answered.

"That's *never* going to happen." I shook my head. "You could balance me on the end of a knife and I'd still feel as safe and secure with you as I've always felt." *Including that night.*

Surprise engulfed him as I reached out, grabbed his hand, and pulled him with me. "Let's get that shower going, and I'll see about those clothes...and, Russell." I stopped walking and turned to face him. "It's really good to have you here."

It felt *good* to have him here. It felt solid, and safe. I enjoyed Arran's company—panic pressed in around me—but I couldn't go through that again. I couldn't be stranded in the middle of nowhere. I couldn't put myself in harm's way, even accidentally. Not again...not when I was finally finding my way out of the dark.

His eyes dimmed a bit, and the panic slowly faded. "I'm glad to be here, too."

I gave a nod, tugged his hand, and led him to the steel door to Elithien's bedroom. Four numbers later, and the door hissed and slid open.

"Vamps, huh?" he muttered.

I'd forgotten for a second that this was his first time here, forgotten that he didn't know them like I knew them. "They aren't always so...*volatile*." I walked through the door. "Not when you really get to know them."

I walked across the bedroom and hit the lights for the bathroom. Brightness assaulted me, leaving me to blink until my eyes focused.

"I'm pretty sure you see a very different side to the one I'll see," he responded as I turned and faced him.

A quick scan of the bathroom, and he smiled at the shower stall. But for a second I saw pain...*and suffering*. I saw a man broken, a man *not healed*. He didn't have someone to protect him, someone to wash the blood from his skin, someone to bathe him, to touch him, and remind him he'd *survived*.

"I...I won't hurt you," I whispered, drawing his gaze. The white bathroom blurred as I stepped closer. "I can take care of you...if you'll let me."

His harsh breaths filled the space.

"If you don't want me here, it's fine." I tried to reassure him.

"No...*I do want you.*"

I moved slower, feeling that heavy thud of my heart return. This wasn't how it was meant to be with us. This wasn't what I'd envisioned before that night. He was my bodyguard...my protector, my ride. But now, as I lifted my hands to the ruins of his shirt and worked the buttons, I felt something more.

Elithien...

Justice...

Hurrow...

Rule.

I loved them, loved them more than I loved any other. The battle raged inside me as the wreckage of his shirt slid free. He was beautiful, so very beautiful. I reached out and placed my hand against his chest...*so warm*...the thud of his heart pulsed under my palm.

"You make me nervous." He forced a smile. "No one's ever done that."

Desire surged inside me and desperation followed. It crashed against my control and devastated my morals. I dropped my hand and took a step away, watching him as he took a step toward me.

"I'll, ahh, get that shower going," I mumbled, heat rushing to my cheeks.

What the hell are you doing?

I reached to the shower and turned on the spray, set the temperature on the water, and gestured to the bottles. "You can use anything here, the washcloths are under the basin, towels are over there. I'll bet you're hungry...*yeah, of course you're hungry.* Clothes, food...okay, coming right up."

"Ruth," he called.

I gave him a smile over my shoulder and hurried for the door, closing it behind me.

"Fuck." I pressed my spine against the door and leaned my head back. "You're *such an idiot.*"

I *was* an idiot, my damn heart was an idiot. My own body betrayed me. "Fucking school girl, that's what you are. Just get it together, you're a goddamn Costello, for Christ's sake."

I shoved away from the wall, pressed the code in once more, and waited for the door to open before I walked out of the bedroom.

The bedroom I shared with my lover...

And walked to the *other* bedroom I shared with my lover...

Past the *other* bedroom I shared with my *other* lover.

"I mean, this is fucking ridiculous," I muttered as I strode to Hurrow's door and punched in his code. The bedroom light was still on, the bedsheets messed. I smelled my scent in here...in every room, for that matter. Sex and something deeper, something *hopeful.* Now my fucking heart wanted one more...I had to be out of my fucking mind

I hurried to Hurrow's closet and rifled through his clothes, grabbing some track pants, a pair of black cargos, a new pair of socks, and boxers still in the package before I hurried out again.

Hurrow was right. Justice's shirts would fit better. He and Russell were almost the same size, and the same height, for that matter. A pang of regret cut through me as I hurried back to

Elithien's room. In the turmoil, I'd found the only path I knew was right.

I'd tell him no, let him down easy. I wasn't someone who betrayed…even in this fucked-up turn of events. I couldn't hurt Justice like that. I couldn't hurt *any* of them.

I'd tell him no. I'd help him find clothes, and another place to stay.

I'd help him find a new life, no matter the cost.

Even if that meant I'd live my life in the darkness.

With every step, I grew surer. I lifted my head and caught the bark of Kern's voice drifting to this side of the house before I flinched at the *slam* of a door. "What the hell's going on now?"

Concern moved deeper, even as I tore my focus from the sounds of an argument and made my way back inside Elithien's bedroom. The shower was still going, steam seeping out from around the closed door, and for that I was thankful. I gripped the clothes, gave a small knock, and cracked it open. "It's just me," I called. "I'm putting some clothes on the counter."

I lowered my gaze and focused on the white marble tiles and white mist as I stepped inside and hurried to the counter. "Russell…I've been thinking. This whole *courting* thing is just too much for me right now."

The hiss of the shower deepened, like the needle-point spray hit something harder, something bigger.

"It's just that…" I hesitated, fighting the desperate urge to lift my gaze. "I love them and I'd never do anything…"

My body froze as my head rose, and in the misted mirror I saw him, saw the outline of his body…saw his hand as he pressed his palm to the shower's glass.

"It's okay," he sighed.

Sadness filled the bathroom, the feeling so cruel, it was an ice pick to my heart.

I tried to stop myself from turning, tried to stop myself from falling as my breath caught and my heart trembled. But the movement was undeniable. *He* was undeniable. I was turning before I knew it, lifting my gaze to that massive hand, perfect fingers outstretched against the glass before he lifted his gaze to mine.

Cold eyes...dark eyes, filled with longing and pain. And with desperation. Pink flushed skin, hard muscles flexed. I jerked my gaze to perfect lips as they parted and his own breath stilled. A ravenous hunger raged between us, one so powerful it shook me where I stood. I wanted him...wanted him as much as I wanted my Vampires.

*Mine...*Russell's voice spilled through my mind, even though those perfect lips never moved. *You are mine.*

He straightened, reached behind him, and turned off the spray. Mist wafted and swirled in the air as he stepped out of the open stall.

"I..." the simple word spilled from my lips. He was stunning, big, smooth muscles rippling as he reached for a towel. I couldn't stop myself...I couldn't turn away as my gaze drifted lower to the hard ridges of his stomach and that hard V at the top of his hips.

His cock was soft, flaccid, smacking the inside of his thigh as he moved.

*Sweet Jesus...*he was huge.

"You were saying?" he questioned. "You love the Vampires, and this isn't going to work..."

I crossed the floor as he toweled his hair and pulled him hard against me...then kissed him.

His hands were on me in an instant, one sliding around my hip to press against my lower back, driving me harder against him as he speared his fingers through my hair.

God, his lips, taking, driving, mashing mine against my teeth until they throbbed.

Still, I couldn't get enough of him. I gripped the hard muscles of his arms, warmth spilling through me. I pressed against the hard throb of his chest, one that seemed to echo in mine…and inhaled the scent of soap.

He was the one who broke away, his eyes glinting with desire. "You…are *breathtaking.*"

I wanted to keep going, to pull him with me. I wanted him inside me, riding me…*hungry for me.* I wanted him stretching me until he was the one who couldn't stop. "I want you…I want you to fuck me."

"Jesus Christ." He raked those perfect fingers through his wet hair. His lips curled, trembling into an awkward smile. "You like to torture me, don't you?"

I shook my head. "I'm sorry. I…"

"Don't…don't be sorry."

Stars shone in his eyes as he reached for my hand and pressed it against his chest. "I'm *always* tortured around you, Ruth. I guess that's a little telling on my emotions, but I think I'm too far gone to either stop this…or care. If we're going to do this, I *want* to do it right. I want to be part of…*this, with you.* I won't…share, but I understand my place here and I'm prepared to wait my turn. Besides," his voice grew deeper, more dangerous. "I'll have you all day, every day…*all to myself.*"

A chuckle spilled free.

"Oh, you think that's funny, do you?" he teased as that mating instinct raged inside me. Heat pooled between my thighs, making me wet.

"I have *other new skills*, it seems," he commented. "Skills I plan on honing." His gaze drifted down my body, until it rose once more and let me see how much he wanted me.

"You never did tell me what you were doing today…" he asked.

I sucked in a breath as the memory crashed into my mind. I thought of my hunger, of that tiny flickering flame I'd felt as I lay beside Elithien. Was that flame gone for good? I searched the darkness, sank under the ache of my head…and the terror of the day, and answered. "I wanted to go across the river...I wanted to take back my life."

Surprise filled him, widening those midnight eyes...*Unseelie eyes.* "You did?"

"Yeah," I nodded. "I did."

"I'm here now." He stepped back and wrapped the towel around his waist. God, he was gorgeous. "I'll help you any way I can."

And he would...they all would.

The hiss of the bedroom door sounded behind us. I turned, watching as Elithien strode through. His cold, controlled stare finding Russell in only a towel, before he shifted his gaze to me. "The opposite side of the house is now yours to do with as you wish. I have a room being set up for you to rest...Ruth, you're more than welcome to stay here...or with him."

The pain-choked words made my pulse race. "I'm fine right here," I answered.

There was a gleam of happiness as he nodded. "I'll be busy tonight. But Rule...Rule will be here if you need anything."

One more glance at Russell, and my Vampire turned to leave.

"Elithien, wait." I hurried after him as the steel doors opened once more.

There was too much left unsaid between us. The ground I stood on was shifting under my feet. I couldn't catch my breath. He stopped outside the doorway, his back to me, shoulders straight.

"I love you." I slid my hand along his arm.

He turned toward me, that same love shining in his eyes. "And I you. You are safe here. You will *always* be safe here. I have things to take care of, but I'll be home as fast as I can."

He brushed a length of hair behind my ear and moved, kissing me gently before he pulled away to whisper, "I can smell him all over you. I can feel him moving in, slipping under your skin...piercing your veins to travel to your heart. Just remember, you are first and foremost...*mine.*"

That dark possessive hunger raged in his stare.

Before he took a step away from me...

And left.

261

26

RUTH

I slept that night, tossing and turning, waking still in the dark, my eyes burning and my head throbbing and finally climbed from the bed. The sweet smell of hot chocolate wafted through as the steel doors opened and I stepped into the hallway. "Oh, that smells heavenly."

"I've been listening to you moan and sigh for the past three hours and figured you'd give in soon," Rule reported, coming from the kitchen with a steaming mug of hot chocolate in his hand.

"I've got the fire on," he said, nodding toward the living room.

I took the cup, lifted it to my lips, and blew gently. "You know me too well."

The corners of his lips curled as he turned. I was starting to understand them, starting to see all their little quirks and hang-ups. I was starting to fall in love with every tiny facet of their Immortal beings. I lowered the cup, stepped forward, and cupped the back of his neck before I kissed him.

His hands went to my waist and the top of my silky, red boxers, his fangs pressed against my lip as he moved against me.

The cup was gone from my hand in a heartbeat. I walked, moving with him, as he pulled me back into the kitchen and tilted his head so our brows touched, breaking the kiss.

"They've all touched you," he sighed, sliding the cup to the counter before he grabbed me by the waist. "They all tasted you, and I've been *so* damn patient. But Christ, all I can think about is you."

One boost and my ass was on the cold stone counter. He gripped my hips, splayed fingers softly digging into my flesh as he pulled me against him. "I can feel your exhaustion, feel it in the tenseness of your body. You're so stressed," he murmured, and lifted his hand to the back of my neck, massaging the ache there.

I closed my eyes, sinking into the feel of his fingers. A brush across my mind followed...and like his touch, I let him do what he wanted.

Desire flooded my veins and slipped between my thighs. He sensed it, moving harder against me, pushing my thighs wider apart. His other hand moved to the bottom of my shirt and worked it over my head.

I opened my eyes as he pulled his hand from my neck to let the shirt fall. "But my hot chocolate," I teased, glancing at the cup.

"Who said I made it for you?" Rule protested, and lifted that steely gaze to me.

I smiled, knowing damn well he had. There just something about Rule, some *ease* inside me when I was around him.

"You are wound up tight, aren't you?" he observed, dropping his head to my breast. One flick of his tongue, and I felt that tension coil like a serpent.

His hands went to my waist and eased the elastic over my hips. I lowered my hands to his shoulders and rocked from one side to the other...until the red boxers slid free.

"No, the chocolate wasn't for you," he clarified, pushing the boxers aside on the counter. "It was for me."

He gripped my hips and lifted, sliding me back along the counter to the middle. His fingers grazed along my leg, cupping the back of my knee and lifting. The sting of the gash from the shadows was still there, making me catch my breath, until Rule brushed across my mind.

Let me take your pain...

I closed my eyes and opened myself to him. There was no motive with Rule, no lesson, no exploration of my fears. There was just...lips pressed to my calf as the pain faded away. Then warm breath caressed me as he parted my thighs and dropped his head there. "Oh."

His tongue found me, found that heat...that desperation snaking in my belly. The scrape of the cup on the counter made me open my eyes. He lifted the cup and dragged it over to hover above my parted thighs.

"Made it warm," he whispered, those perfect eyes glinting with desire. "And you know what I love more than chocolate?"

It wasn't a question he needed an answer for as he held my gaze and tilted the cup.

Warm chocolate dribbled between my thighs. I shuddered with the sensation, gripping the edge of the counter as he placed the cup down and lowered his head again.

Warmth met cool, finding the center of me. This wasn't about heartache, or about control...this was just pure unadulterated pleasure. Pleasure that grew deeper as the tip of his tongue danced around my clit.

"Oh my God." I splayed my thighs wider, my fingers tangling in his hair as I bit my lip. The press of his fangs on the most sensitive part of me made me whimper. I left the terror of the day behind as he gripped my ass, lifted my body to meet his mouth, and drew me in.

"Come for me," he commanded, pushing my body until I laid

back along the counter, one leg hooked over his shoulder. "Let me taste your release."

I opened my eyes and looked down at his darting tongue, glistening lips, and desperate eyes. He was ravenous, predatory...with a look of savage hunger. I pressed against the back of his head as that rush roared to the surface. I wanted to spill and release. One more lick, and I teetered on the edge of nothing.

Right where I wanted to be.

Nothing. Fucking. All primal...all *theirs.*

Fingers slid inside me and my body clenched down, driving spasms that pulsed...and pulsed...and *pulsed* as he slowly slid his fingers from me.

I couldn't move...couldn't feel...couldn't even think.

"I think you might be able to sleep now," he murmured, picking me up once more.

I wrapped my body around him, legs at his waist, bare breasts pressed against his shoulders.

We were moving before I knew it, the door to Elithien's bedroom sliding open, and the moment it did, the words came tumbling out, "Will you lie with me, just for a little while?"

"I thought you'd never ask." He kicked off his shoes and lay down beside me, arms sliding around me, drawing me close. "Sleep is becoming your nemesis, isn't it?"

I nodded as the demons came closer in the dark. "I don't know what I'm doing. I thought I did once...but not anymore."

"Here, you mean?"

"Anywhere." The truth spilled free and tears followed. My own demons were unleashed. But somehow, I felt at ease with Rule, like I could tell him anything and, as my tears spilled down my cheeks, I started talking. "I hurt Justice tonight. Hell, I hurt everyone. I guess my father called me Ruthless for a reason."

"I don't think that's the reason."

"No?" I tilted my head.

"I think that love is never easy and none of us understand it. We just do our best. Justice will come around. It might not be tomorrow...*no, definitely not tomorrow.*" He hooked some hair behind my ear. "But he will. Russell has a claim on you, he had to have to survive. Justice knows that. We *all* know that, and he will come to respect that. *We all will.* But you have your own hopes and dreams to conquer. Our job now is to stand by your side every step of the way forward. Your father left you a legacy."

"That's now in ruins."

"Aren't some of the greatest castles rebuilt that way? The foundation will be stronger. The walls like bonds, unbreakable through blood, sweat, and tears, and you, my Queen, have cried enough."

A brush against my cheek, and he captured my tears, then slipped his thumb into his mouth.

"My tears, too, huh?"

"There's not a part of you I wouldn't kill to taste."

"I feel like I can talk to you. The others are always so..."

"Driven."

I smiled, "Yeah, driven."

"You can always talk to me, about anything." He drew me closer and curled his powerful body around me. "Everything is going to work out, just you wait and see."

I closed my eyes. "I hope so."

"I *know* so."

I smiled at his faith in me, and as the smile faltered, darkness rose up...and this time it didn't let go.

27

RUTH

"You ready to do this?"

I stopped pacing across the living room and turned to find Russell striding toward me from the other side of the house.

For a second, I couldn't speak. He looked good...*better than good*. Freshly showered, shaved, his hair trimmed at the sides. He was dressed in black, from thick-soled boots, and cargo pants that hugged his powerful thighs, to a shoulder harness strapped over a black t-shirt that showed every rippling muscle in his chest and back.

"What is it?" he asked, stopping in mid stride.

"Nothing."

"Is it the guns?" he glanced down and reached for them, his arms flexing.

"No, it's not the guns." I slowly lifted my gaze, meeting that Unseelie stare. "It's not the guns at all."

Jesus, he was stunning.

"Are you sick?" He came toward me, long strides consuming the space as concern moved in. "You look flushed."

He really was oblivious when he pressed his hand to my forehead. "No, I'm not sick. I was just looking at you."

Confusion flared for a second before it dawned. His eyes widened for a heartbeat before the ghost of a smile flitted by. "Oh," he murmured, and lowered his hand. "Okay then."

I smiled and shook my head as reality dawned. We were really doing this…really going to see my uncle. "Oh God, what the fuck am I doing?"

"You are beginning to take back what's rightfully yours, and it starts today, with your identity."

I nodded slowly as fear moved back in. He was there for me, reaching out to grasp my hand and lift it to his lips. "I'm going to be with you every step of the way. You're safe with me."

I was safe with him…even without the guns. "Yeah, I think I am ready to do this."

"Good," he said, lowering my hand. "Then let's rip the band-aid off, shall we?"

He turned then, scanning the house and its deathly silence before he went to the front door. Keys jangled in his hand as I followed. It seemed clothes and weapons weren't the only things he had now, and for some strange reason, this moment felt like destiny—but not my destiny—*his.*

He moved with purpose, throwing his jacket across his arm and opening the door for me. I stopped in the middle of the entrance, turned, and stepped closer. Desire came alive, mingling with the panicked racing of my heart as I gently kissed him. "Thank you." I whispered. "Thank you for being here."

"There's nowhere else I'd rather be, guns, cars, and black AmEx or not. But hey," he joked. "They sure add to the excitement."

That was the second time this morning he'd made me smile I thought as I strode to Elithien's Explorer and climbed in. Seconds later, the driver's door opened and my bodyguard got in, started the engine, glanced my way, and drove.

He was made for this, with such kindness and strength. Those big hands held the wheel firmly as he backed out of the driveway, then shifted, taking me toward the bridge and the other side of the city. I stared out the window as we drove in silence. In my head, I replayed Rule's words from last night.

Aren't some of the greatest castles rebuilt that way? The foundation will be stronger. The walls like bonds, unbreakable through blood, sweat, and tears, and you, my Queen, have cried enough.

I *had* cried enough. I'd worried, and feared, and hidden enough. I reached out and grasped Russell's hand as the bridge came into sight. I'd hated enough, and now I was desperate to put all that behind me.

We made our way back to the familiar streets to where towering mansions were the backdrop of manicured lawns, and perfect gardens, where the address where you lived spoke louder than your voice. We drove until my heart thundered, and I lifted my gaze to my uncle's house.

"You sure you want to do this?"

I nodded, not trusting myself to speak. The house seemed bigger, the porch mammoth, as Russell nosed into the drive and pulled up at the same stairs where my cousins had been arrested. I winced as the engine died. Judah and Blane were assholes, there was no denying that. They were cruel and disgusting, and I hated the thought that we shared a bloodline, never mind those dark secrets of what they'd done to me. But I was wrong when I'd accused them of trying to kill me, and I was here to say just that.

The front door opened and my aunt stepped out. For a second, she didn't register who I was and annoyance moved across her face. She opened her mouth, that forked fucking tongue at the ready to snap and snarl, until I rounded the front of the Explorer and stepped to the stairs.

Her eyes widened...her face paled.

"Who the hell is it?" My uncle growled from inside the house.

"Ruth?" my aunt whispered as I climbed the stairs, Russell close behind me.

"Gloria?" My uncle yanked the door open wide and stepped out onto the porch. There was a savage grunt in the back of his throat as he saw me. "Ruth?"

"It's me," I answered quietly. "It's me, alive."

"What? How?" he stuttered.

"None of that's important now. What matters is that I'm here."

"I..." tears shone in his eyes as he stumbled toward me and yanked me against him. "I thought you were dead, thought I'd never see you again."

I didn't hug him back, but I didn't fight him, either.

I remembered that night when I'd watched him standing at the edge of the pier, looking over the shimmering midnight water. A pang of guilt turned my voice husky and raw. "For a while there, I thought the same."

His eyes shone as he gripped my shoulders and held me away, staring into my eyes. "Where have you been?"

"Safe. I've been safe."

"And you couldn't come to us before?" There was a bite of anger in his words.

"No, I couldn't."

He stilled with the words, and stared into my eyes. In an instant, that spark of annoyance was gone. Only then did he shift his gaze to Russell behind me, and then to the four-wheel drive. All the fight went out of him, and in that moment, he wasn't powerful and controlling. He was just a man...humbled by the loss of an empire, and a family he once took for granted. "It's all gone, Ruthy. Everything...*all...gone.*"

"It is." That spark of rage flickered in my belly, turning my voice cold. "That's why I'm here. We've both said things and done things that hurt each other. I'm ready to put the past behind me and move on. I want to forgive you for everything that's happened."

Relief filled his eyes as he swallowed hard. There was no gushing sentiment from my uncle, no tears of joy, just a hard swallow and a small nod.

"Which is why I'm taking back my company and removing you, your sons, and anyone else from ownership. You will not sit on the board, you will not receive any funds. You'll share the name, and that will be as close as you'll ever come to Costello Corporation again."

Red moved into his cheeks and a burning spark raged in his eyes.

"I will rebuild my father's company. I will run it how I want it to run. I will find investors with deep pockets and I'll take what was always mine to begin with, and you, uncle…you can disappear from my life for good."

I shifted my gaze to my aunt, who stood there, mouth agape.

Forgiveness was a balm for the soul…and a path to my future. I turned away from him then, and slowly made my way down the stairs.

"Who will you find to back you now? All the investors are gone. They followed your father, but they'll never follow you."

I stopped on the last stair and turned my head. "Old, rich white men filled with greed? How will I ever compete with that," I taunted, and kept on walking.

"You have no one, Ruthy!" he called out as I rounded the four-wheel drive.

"Oh? You'll be surprised who my friends are, uncle. You'll be *very surprised.*"

I climbed into the Explorer and sank back into the seat as Russell started the engine and got us the hell out of there. I had one more stop…one more ghost I wanted to confront…

I curled my fists, trying to stop the shaking, as we drove out the driveway and headed into the city. My heart waited in the shimmering building in the middle, and as we worked our way closer, merging with the rows of traffic, I felt a surge of hope.

I was doing this. *I was really doing this.*

I was taking my father's company for my own.

Russell pulled up outside my building. The doors were still chained, the white notice flapping wildly just as it'd done before.

"Don't get out," I said. "I'll only be a second."

I shoved open the car door and hurried across the pavement at the front of the grand foyer. As I reached for the page, tearing the tape from the window, that warm, golden sunlight seemed to darken…and a chill settled into the air.

"Ruth?" Russell called through the open passenger's door.

I grabbed the notice, turned, and hurried back to the Explorer. But that chill stayed with me, even as I yanked the door closed.

"Everything okay?"

I nodded, pulled the seatbelt across, and snapped it into place. Everything I wanted was at the tips of my fingers…so why did I feel like this wasn't just the beginning…*why did it feel like it was the end?*

"I'm fine," I sighed, and lifted my gaze to the crowded city street. "I'm perfectly fine."

28

ELITHIEN

"Rule is going to stay with you." I stared into her eyes. "He enjoys spending time alone with you."

"Why?" That haunted look darkened her eyes.

"Why does he like spending time with you?" I forced a smile...*one just for her.*

"Why is he staying? Why are you all going out..." she glanced behind me to the Unseelie before she shifted that piercing gaze to me once more. "What aren't you telling me?"

She knows.

She fucking knows.

She'd been distracted and jumpy, flinching every time someone moved quickly, and every time I gently prodded her about today, she repeated she was fine. Even the bodyguard had no news. The meeting with the uncle had gone to plan, and she now had the connections to call about the company building.

Her life was starting over, only this time she had us standing with her. But was that enough?

Was my reach far enough...was my power terrifying enough?

Was I enough?

I pushed that panic down and gave a small shake of my head. "We didn't want to upset you, that's all."

"Spill." She crossed her arms over her chest. Fierce. Loyal. *Fuck, she was magnificent.*

"Russell is going back to the Fae," I started as fear filled her eyes. "Just for a few hours. They're going to train him...going to teach him how to control what he is."

"It's for your safety," the bodyguard murmured behind me, taking a step toward her. "I promise I'll be back before you even know it."

"And you?" She turned that terrified stare to me. "Where are *you* going?"

She'd been jumpy ever since I'd awoken. A look of desperation filled her eyes. "I've got a few errands to run, nothing big. I'll be back in an hour or two."

"You promise?" She tried to hide the tremble in her voice.

Still, I caught it. "You sure nothing happened today?

"I'm sure."

I lifted my hand and brushed her cheek before stepping close and leaning down close to her ear. "I don't believe you, not for one second. But I'm going to trust you...besides, I have better ways of extracting the truth from someone...and for you, leather seems to be involved. The gloves are beside the bed...but whatever you do...*don't let Rule start without me.*"

Her cheeks bloomed red. The desired outcome. I closed my eyes and kissed her softly before pulling away. It fucking stung, turning from her, but I swallowed that down, driving it all the way into the burning pit in my belly, and headed for the door.

She'd be safe here. Safe with Rule.

And after tonight, she'd be safe forever.

Only nightmares would plague her then...only a memory of what once was.

My cell phone vibrated in my breast pocket as I opened the

passenger's door and nodded to Hurrow. I snatched it free, swiped the screen, and answered. "What's the status?"

"He's here...and alive, just like you asked."

"You know the address?"

"We know. We'll meet you there."

The line went dead...

Death waited patiently this night. Death in all its faded glory...and he *would* fade, until he was nothing more than a name...nothing more than *insignificant.*

"They're meeting us there," I said, and the four-wheel drive surged forward, the motor roaring under the hood.

We drove in silence, tearing through the night until the bright city lights grew closer. But we didn't look at the Wolves' clubs as we passed, only the road ahead...only the light that waited. The light for her.

Anger was what I held onto as we slowed at the gate of the Fae compound.

Anger was better than grief.

It was better than disgust.

It was even better than satisfaction...*just.*

The steel barrier rolled open slowly. I lifted my gaze to the warehouse doors. *Where were they? They should be here by now.*

"Pull up around back," I ordered, and the Explorer nosed around the building.

Headlights splashed against the ruined buildings further back from the Fae compound. But as the light bounced back from graffitied and ruined walls, I caught the shimmer of something else...something *otherworldly.* A portal, one into the darkness. A darkness that called to the Unseelie like blood called to me.

The bodyguard would feel that calling now, he'd be drawn to it like a magnet. If he was to protect her, I needed to know he could control that desire. But I was asking a male barely

Immortal to do what came naturally to the Unseelie. That was an impossibility.

The car pulled up hard. I climbed out and lifted my gaze to the door at the top of the stairs as it opened.

Car doors opened and closed behind me as Shrike made his way down the stairs...and from the savagery in the bodyguard behind me, I heard a deep, throaty snarl of rage spill out.

"Leash it," I commanded. "This is not the time."

In an instant, the sound ended as the Unseelie warrior stepped away from the building and headed toward me. "He's inside."

"Already?" Surprise stained my tone.

One jerk of his head and I turned my attention to the darkness, deeper than the empty lot next to the compound. You could hardly see the black steel, just a tiny glimmer...but it was there...*fucking Breeds.*

"Vicious?" Even as I uttered his name, I felt the hairs rising on my arms.

"Right here."

He leaned at the corner of the building, legs crossed at the ankles, watching me with that feral stare. The fucking Breeds were someone you didn't mess around with, and that included me. Vicious pushed away from the building, head down, long black trench coat flapping behind him as he headed toward me.

He was bigger than most Wolves, thicker across the shoulders. Much *hungrier.* Pure purpose. Immortal with a side dish of genetic enhancement. But he wasn't the only one of his kind...there were others, *a lot of others.* Every Immortal you could think of, squads of them ran in this Immortal line by a secret government organization. One created to hunt...*one created to destroy.*

Only, the bad guys they hunted had once been one of their own.

They had their own problems...but fangs for hire was what

they did best. In this case...I'd bought exactly what I wanted. Five hundred thousand dollars of a pathetic excuse for a male, and one delicious opportunity to send his soul back to the blackest hell where it came from.

"He's inside...unharmed, as requested." His growl clawed the air as he lifted his gaze, scanned my men, and froze. "What the fuck?" he grunted.

"He's with me," I declared, and stepped forward.

Nostrils flared from the Alpha, the permanent scowl on his face grew deeper. "That's not possible."

"I'm right fucking here," Russell barked, and took a step forward.

"No," Hurrow snarled. "Not here, and not now."

I felt the Vampire move behind me, stepping in front of the bodyguard.

"You'll want to put that one down before he gets too powerful." Vicious nodded toward the Unseelie and turned that warning to me. "Or mark my words, he'll be trouble."

"You want to have a crack at it, *Wolf?*" the bodyguard offered, sneering. "I think you'll be disappointed with the outcome."

I clenched my jaw as anger flared, but still, my fangs carved along the inside of my lip until I tasted blood. "Thanks for the warning. But he stays."

"Your own fucking funeral, Vampire." A shrug of his massive shoulders, and the mercenary Wolf turned away, heading for the exterior stairs to the upper floor of the warehouse.

I followed, cutting a glare at Russell as I went. The bastard had the gall to glare back, driving me that much closer to the killing edge. But he wasn't the one I wanted dead— Alexander's time had come. For Ruth, I'd be judge, jury, and executioner. Nothing would stop me...*not now.*

We followed Vicious as he headed up to the warehouse's side door. Powerful Unseelie energy sent sparks of blue across his hand as he grasped the handle. One snarl of "Fucking Unseelie," and he twisted, shoving the door wide.

This place was more than a warehouse...it was a branch from the portal the Dark Fae used, and their power ran through every brick and every room. No one would get in or out without their permission...and that wasn't given freely.

"I can fucking hear you!" Came a male's scream from further inside the warehouse. *"I know you're here!"*

That savage sound rumbled in the throat of the bodyguard and spilled out again.

"Easy," I cautioned. "You'll have your turn."

That seemed to calm the beast. But still, as we stepped inside the warehouse and closed the door, I felt that menacing Unseelie darkness rise. Vicious was right. The bodyguard was going to be a problem...if not now...then one day it'd happen. I'd take care of that problem, swiftly and *savagely*.

And make sure Ruth would never know it was me.

"I *demand* you let me go! *Do you hear me?*"

We strode toward the sound. One wave of my hand in the complete darkness, and a spotlight came on, directed at a lone figure strapped to a chair in the middle of the huge room with a black hood over his head. I winced at the sight.

"Jesus," Hurrow snarled.

The mortal *stank.*

Fetid and foul. He smelled like he'd soiled himself...about two days ago.

"You said unharmed...you never said anything about comfortable," Vicious muttered.

"That I didn't." I stopped in front of him, glancing from his feet, one with a missing sneaker, to the filthy khakis and blood-splattered grimy shirt.

"About that," the Wolf started.

I lifted my hand...I didn't care...all I cared about was that he was alive…and able to see. I raised my gaze to the hood covering his head.

"I have money," the piece of shit whimpered, jerking his head from right to left, desperate for a sound. "I have lots of money."

Money you stole from her…

My tongue danced over the sharpened points in my mouth. Harsh breaths echoed in the space behind me, loud enough for the spineless lawyer to flinch and whimper. Justice had said nothing, no demands…no threats, but I could feel that hunger rising in him.

The same way it rose in me.

"Who the fuck are you people?" Alexander screamed.

"Hurrow," I murmured.

My second strode forward, stepping out of the darkness and into the spotlight. He grasped the hood and yanked it free, making the worm cry out and lift his cuffed hands in front of his face. "Get that fucking light out of my eyes!"

I smiled with the sound of his pain. But it wasn't enough. It wasn't anywhere near enough.

My hunger was rising, cutting through me like sharpened claws.

We'd feast on his blood…and later, when I fucked Ruth in my bed, I'd kiss her…and let her taste his death on my tongue.

"Did you think we'd never find you?" I hissed, and took a step closer. "Did you think we wouldn't hunt you to the ends of this world and beyond?"

He froze, hands shielding his face from me.

"Did you think you would live to see one more fucking birthday after what you did to her?"

He slowly lowered his hands, widened eyes blinking, panicked breaths panting.

"I want you to look at me." I demanded, and stepped out of the darkness. My hunters moved with me, flanking me on all sides.

Justice, Hurrow...Russell. "We plan on killing you slowly...and then I'll force my blood into your mouth, and tomorrow the pain will start, and you will be reborn Immortal. So I can kill you over...and over...and over again. And when I'm done killing you... then Hurrow, here, will start. Your existence will be an endless cycle of death and pain, and when we're done with you, when this *untapped rage* inside us has finally eased, then we will drag you out into the middle of an empty paddock and wait for the sun to rise."

"No," he whispered, shaking his head. "No...*no...not you.*"

"Yes, us." Hurrow growled. "You will never know a second of peace for the rest of your miserable life."

"I want my turn." The bodyguard stepped forward. He lifted his powerful hands and clenched his fists.

"Y-you?" Alexander shrieked. "I k-killed you...I fucking *killed* you."

"You did," Russell agreed. "And now I'm about to repay the favor." Shadows swirled around him, drawing from the power of this place.

Until, in an instant, the lawyer stilled. His breaths deepened, and there was a look of total satisfaction on his face before his lips curled. "Well...well...well. Aren't you the dark horse, then? But you made a mistake, *Vampire.*" He turned that manic stare to me. "You made *one very big fucking mistake.*"

"Did he?" Justice sneered. "You want to let us in on the joke?"

"You." Alexander lifted his gaze. There wasn't a hint of terror in those blue eyes now. Not a trace of anything but *pure fucking enjoyment. "You're the fucking joke."*

I turned my head, finding Vicious in the dark. The Wolf caught my gaze, confusion making him shake his head.

"You think I planned this on my own? You really are fucking stupid, aren't you? The USB drive...the Prince, the money? Did you think they didn't have a hand in all this?" He leaned forward, staring through the glaring light to me. "Caedes knows what you've done, Elithien, and the Inner Circle is *pissed.*"

Caedes? The name was a blade against the back of my neck. The cold, savage Immortal was the head of the Vampire army and our representative in the Inner Circle. He was the one Alliard had gone to about change. He was the one who'd listened while the prince had pleaded for a reform, for a better society. He was the one who supposedly pleaded for the mortals.

Deep down, I'd known Caedes was behind the prince's assassination. I just didn't have the proof...*until now.*

"What the fuck did you just say to me?" I snarled, my blood turning to ice.

"You *stupid bloodsucking cunts!* You think the Inner Circle isn't ready to clean house?" He threw his head back and laughed.

"They're coming?" I muttered as panic started to rise.

"They're not *coming!*" Alexander met my gaze, his eyes sparkling with mania. *"They're already here!"*

"No," I denied, and took a step backwards.

My thoughts turned to Ruth...alone in the house with Rule. *NO!*

Ruth! I screamed in my head.

RUTH, RUN!

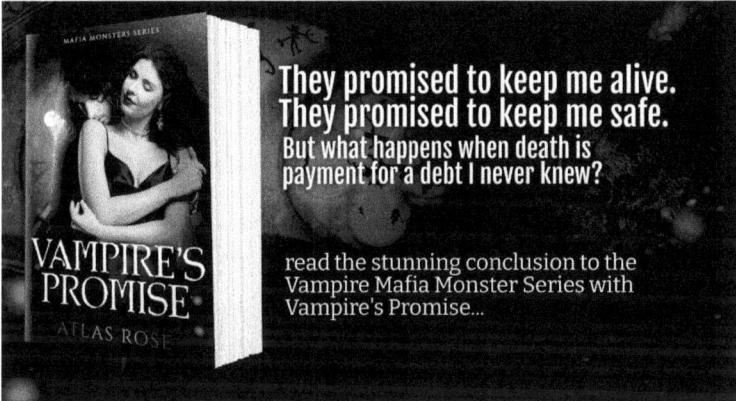
Click here for Vampire's Promise

WHO IS ATLAS?

Gothic Paranormal Romance Author
- Chosen by the Vampire Series
- Loves black cats
- Eats all the black jellybeans
- Book hoarder

Connect with me on Facebook and Instagram

Milton Keynes UK
Ingram Content Group UK Ltd.
UKHW022245270923
429475UK00015B/444